The King of
Terrors

Books by John D. Spooner ("Brutus")

The King of Terrors

JOHN D. SPOONER

Little, Brown and Company
Boston   Toronto

FIRST EDITION

T 03/75

LIBRARY OF CONGRESS CATALOGING IN PUBLICATION DATA

Spooner, John D
     The king of terrors.

     I. Title.
PZ4.S759Ki3   [PS3569.P6]   813'.5'4   74-23290
ISBN 0-316-80754-0

Designed by Susan Windheim

Published simultaneously in Canada
by Little, Brown & Company (Canada) Limited

PRINTED IN THE UNITED STATES OF AMERICA

For Alan R. Trustman and David M. Wolf —
whose inspiration and friendship made
everything possible.

He is torn from the tent in which he trusted
and is brought to the king of terrors.
— Job 18:14

The author is grateful for various technical
assistance and advice to the following contributors:

Alan C. Fagan
David H. Fairburn
Howard J. Fine
James R. Hammond, Jr.
Weld S. Henshaw
Stanford Janger
Michael Pantaleoni
John Quick
C. Scott Sykes, Jr.
Lawrence Walsh

Book
1

April 15

Record temp for April in New York. People
say it's because of the bomb. No more springs;
winter turns right into summer. Went to
Atlantic Beach with Glory. One of the town
beaches, a narrow strip separating the West-
bury Beach Club from the Inwood Beach Club.
Glory told me that her parents had belonged to
Inwood and that they allowed her to charge
cheeseburgers and ginger ale when she was only
six.
We saw a handsome faced young man with a
muscular torso. His legs were withered,
deformed from birth. Why do these things happen? Why do people look away from the young
man? There are fences between our beach and
the private clubs. If I am right, and I must
be right, all the crap, all the fences will be
swept away. Glory wanted to take off her
bathing suit and gross out the club members.
I told her that she would only be a curiosity
to the people on the other sides of the fence.

They'd call the police and watch. It would
serve nothing.

"It would make me feel good, to see them
disapprove," Glory said.

"They disapprove anyway," I told her. "Better to do it the way Alex says. Much better
that way."

Got the '69 T-Bird from Mass. The '67 Continental from D.C. The dynamite has been
no problem. Construction workers carry big
rolls of cash, easy to move them. One supervisor at a shopping mall going up in Hempstead
will sell us what we need for ninety dollars
a case. He wants small denominations in
old bills. Everybody has the TV words down
pat. We have the pickup and tarp to cover the
cases. Dynamite always comes in 50 pound
crates and the sticks are always 1 1/4 inches
in diameter by 8 inches in length. Different
strengths weigh different amounts, so cases
have cartridge counts -- the number of sticks
per 50 lb. case. Sometimes there are 110
sticks to the case.

Most of the smaller situations will require
plastique, easier to get off with blasting
caps. Have found two national guardsmen from
Richmond Hill in Queens who used to get kicks
fighting with chains at Smokey Park (95th
Avenue and 127th St.). They'll supply all
C-3, C-4 (military jargon for plastique) we
need. They don't care what it's for. They
don't ask. I am assured we will only destroy
property; no lives. The plastique is curious
stuff, almost like Silly Putty. Actually

```
RDX is the explosive.  Smells like shoo polish.
Not unpleasant at all.
Have been amazed at the ease of supply.
In America, no one questions what you want or
why you want it.  One of the best reasons
for my understanding of why our time has come.
```

Extract from the journal of Michael Cagnina

The reporters crushed around the elegant woman with the cameo pin at her breast.

"Mrs. Cagnina, you got something to say?" the reporters asked.

"Whatever my son did, he did out of honest conviction."

"What about the terror? What about his journal?"

"I've said all I can. My son had a dream."

"Wouldn't you say, Mrs. Cagnina, it was more like a nightmare?"

She stared beyond the reporter and walked without expression into her hotel.

It was springtime in New York, just enough green to make people forget for a few moments that life was hard. Kirk Abbott, now the president of United Stores, had just finished taping the Susskind show. He walked down the corridors of NBC with Neil Bloom, the real estate entrepreneur who had appeared with him, discussing "Cowboy capitalism! Is it dead?" Bloom was expansive, big, the kind of man who calls every other man "kid."

"Kid," Bloom said to Abbott. "The secret is all in what you owe. Let me tell you a story, kid, while we go in the john and wash this shit off our faces." Kirk listened to him.

"Remember, kid," he said, "if you owe five hundred dollars to the bank and you can't pay it back, you're in trouble. If you owe five million to the banks and you can't pay it back, *they're* in trouble. You've gotta be in a position to dump on 'em big." They washed off the pancake base, toweled themselves and continued to the exit. A tough-looking, expensively dressed young woman was passing them with three men in tow, all chattering at her and fixing their ties. She was one of New York's most lavish call girls and had just written a best-selling memoir, naming names. Bloom stopped. "Juanita," he said to her.

"You know me?" she said.

"How about a blow job after the show?"

She flushed. "May you get cancer of the prostate, fat man," she said, and hurried away. Her three companions glared back at Bloom, still fingering their ties.

"Old friend of yours?" Abbott asked him as they went out the door.

"I must know every credit card pussy in the East," Bloom said. "It's part of being a developer." He entered a limousine parked at the curb. "Remember what I told you," he said to Abbott. "You gotta go into hock in this country to make it big. What do you owe, kid? A hundred-grand mortgage on your house? Your company got a few convertible bonds?"

Kirk leaned down and got close to Bloom's face. He blew a thin stream of cigarette smoke into the limousine.

"What would you say if I told you I owed fifty million? Personally!"

"I'd say that a lot of people got trouble with you. Who'da believed it about a good-looking blond kid. That Susskind don't let no shitheels on his show."

The window hummed closed and the car pulled away. Abbott flicked his cigarette into the gutter. Grace Abbott emerged from a taxi a minute later, looking serene. "Sorry I'm late, darling. Bendel's was making holes in my good intentions."

"Bendel's is always making holes in your good intentions,"
Kirk said. "Bonwit's, Bergdorf's, Sakowitz's, are always making holes in your good intentions. If we hadn't gotten married, think where I'd be."

"Yes, darling, think where you'd be. Let's have a drink."

They walked to P. J. Clarke's and had Polish vodka martinis with slices of orange peel. Civilized screwdrivers, Kirk
Abbott called the drinks. There was a silence between them
for a while, and they avoided each other's eyes. The bar was
crowded and the self-conscious conversations of the advertising and magazine people floated around them: mixtures
of laughter and tinkling ice in glasses. "What are we going
to do, Kirk?" his wife finally asked him.

"About what?"

"About us. It's easy to get divorced when there are problems. I was raised to find answers and stick with things."

"One thing about New Englanders," Kirk said. "They always know their way is right."

"Well, I'm sick of being a cliché for the great American
success story," Grace said. "We've got money, paintings,
beautiful children, very good acquaintances. We're also in
debt. You hardly ever see the beautiful children. You never
look at the paintings. When I see you, which is seldom, your
eyes and mind are a million miles away. We never screw
anymore. And you won't see a psychiatrist."

"What you're trying to say about me, Grace, is that deep
down I'm really very shallow."

"I'm trying to say that it's becoming impossible to hold
things together."

"Perhaps we'd screw a little more if you didn't sound like
a *Cosmopolitan* article."

Grace looked at her husband as if she pitied him. "That's
a laugh. You know how funny that is? When we first met,
you were so full of fantasies. You always wanted to live near

the sea. Would you call that the *Saturday Evening Post?* Christ, the dreamer calling the kettle black."

"The bastards have a way of knocking dreams out of you."

She put a hand on his hands across the table. "Let's go away, Kirk. United Stores can run itself. You've got flunkies for the flunkies. Let's take the QE2 to Europe. Let's go places without phones and planes and flunkies."

"Being a romantic doesn't really suit practical Grace, you know," Kirk said. "You always loved my ambition more than my fantasies. Now you've got it in spades."

"Everybody's got a laughing place," Grace said.

"What?"

"A laughing place," she said. "From some Walt Disney movie. Br'er Rabbit sang it and it was the first movie I ever saw. I guess everybody's got to have a secret place, a laughing place, to keep from going mad."

"This conversation is telling me we should go to a party," said Kirk. "Somewhere we don't have to talk to anybody."

"No dinner?"

"I can't tonight. Call Teddy or the Wheelocks. Christ, call Margo. You haven't bitched at her in ages. I've got a meeting uptown."

"We are uptown."

"I mean up, uptown. We're thinking of opening a store on 130th Street."

"I like it. Brotherhood before business?"

"Let's go, I'll be late."

"Let's go. I'll be late," she mocked. "When am I going to see you again?"

"I'll be crawling into your wee bed around two."

"I'll try not to disturb you."

"You know something?" Kirk said to her, as they went out into the street and he put her into a cab, "you'd really be a piece of ass if you'd let yourself go."

"I'll leave some aspirin on your night table." The cab pulled away.

Kirk Abbott walked quickly up Third Avenue, slapping his attaché case against his thigh. He walked across town to the Plaza, which he entered by the Fifty-ninth Street doors. He immediately took the stairway leading down to Trader Vic's, went into the men's room, and deposited a dime in the pay toilet booth. Sitting down, he snapped open his attaché case from which he took a circular travel mirror and a black stretch wig that had been made for him by George Masters in Hollywood. It was cut long and fully covered his blond head, including his sideburns. Kirk combed it into place, looking critically at himself. Then, satisfied, he put the mirror away, flushed the toilet and came out. The attendant took a quarter and noticed nothing. Kirk walked to the Bloomingdale's entrance of the IRT, hurried downstairs, and checking his watch, waited for two uptown cars to pass. He boarded the third. He hung onto a metal strap looking at advertisements, aware that someone was watching him from the other end of the car. A dark man eased from strap to strap toward him.

"Hello, Boaz," Kirk said, as the man became his neighbor.

"I picked you up at the bank on the corner," Boaz said.

"I saw you. That's why I let two cars go by. To see if it would irritate you."

"One thing I got, Alex," he said, "is patience."

"A virtue in hungry men."

They bumped along until there were few white faces left. Day help from midtown cooperatives chattered and laughed, relaxing finally above the Eighties; sad old women with battered shopping bags sat with their faces looking at the floor; punks with gang jackets cockily dared people to look them in the eyes; dudes who owned the world clicked their platform heels as the wheels squealed and rambled on.

Kirk Abbott and Boaz got off at 125th Street. "Any questions about anyone?" Abbott asked. "They seem all right to you?"

"Most of them can't believe it. But none of them thinks things are real anyway. I think it's going to be the best game in town. If you're as good as you seem, Alex."

The two dark-haired men waited at the bottom of the platform for three minutes until an automobile slid to a stop beside them. Kirk Abbott and Boaz got into the back seat and the driver headed toward the Hudson River.

2

WANTED

THE ENTERPRISING RIGHT PERSON TO MAKE IT
BEYOND HIS WILDEST DREAMS. BOX 4821.
Advertisement in *Hump* magazine

*E*nrico Boaz was the illegitimate son of a Nuevo Laredo whore and an Italian medical corpsman stationed at Fort Sam Houston, San Antonio. Enrico Boaz grew up a handsome, gutter-shrewd sadist. Practically from the time he was old enough to walk, he became the towel boy at his mother's work, a stucco motel complex employing twenty-five girls and run by a single-minded ex–U.S. Army sergeant who grew fat on poker and Carta Blanca beer. When Enrico was fifteen, he caught the sergeant beating hell out of his mother and he tore a large crucifix from over her bed and smashed it across the back of the sergeant's neck. With his mother screaming curses, the sergeant kicked Enrico across the room, then came after him with a belt wrapped around his fist. Enrico smashed a Carta Blanca bottle, and holding the neck, jammed the jagged end into the sergeant's face, twisting out one of his eyes and making the other a useless joke. Still holding the bottle, Enrico stuck the bloody piece as deep as he could into the man's fat gut. "You beat no one anymore but the goats," Enrico panted. That night he waded across the Rio Grande and never again saw his mother. He sent her a card at Christmas from wherever he happened to be. She soon ceased caring, drifting from whorehouse to whorehouse and finally to Boy's Town, the section in every border town reserved for the hopeless, where she would simulate exhibitions for drunken tourists. She died of septicemia at age forty-eight on a dirty mattress on a dirt floor.

Enrico cruised, never caring what he did. But whatever he did, he managed to impress people with his efficiency and intelligence. He attributed this to a burning belief that his father was rich and famous somewhere. All he knew about his father was that his first name had been Enrico also, and that he had come from New York.

Boaz drifted. He picked lettuce in the San Fernando Valley; he drove semi's across the desert; he roughnecked in Tulsa; he shrimped in the Gulf; he was a cabana boy in Miami Beach. Boaz drifted, but he always worked. Until the late 1960s, when he discovered he needed to work no longer. That was when he discovered that there was a middle class in America who would admire and support him. By this time he was a man, with wild eyes. Large black eyes that burned in his head. People who knew him remembered his eyes for years afterwards. He could play the guitar, with rippling chords that backed up a throaty baritone, rich with overtones of the inhumanity that he had seen, rich with his travels. Boaz sang about the land and railroads and lost loves. And he talked with girls about charms, spells, and witchcraft.

He walked into a commune outside of Charlottesville, Virginia, one day in 1969 and, within a week, it was his: Chevy pickup truck, vegetable garden, two men, four women, two babies: one named Pope and the other, Violation. A girl. There Boaz played songs, chanted, cast spells, and screwed everything in the commune. One of the women gave Boaz her father's American Express card. He bought a secondhand Volkswagen bus for three hundred dollars, painted it orange Day-glo, and skipped with the four women and half the contents of the vegetable garden. He discovered, from that moment on, that if he carried his guitar, and enough drugs to supply others, he would never have to lift a finger. For a few years he never did lift a finger and he was able to develop changing circles of women who would lie, steal, and prostitute themselves to satisfy the dark bastard from Nuevo Laredo.

But Boaz realized what millions of Americans have come to realize: that although he had it made, he could not seem to keep anything. He was living in a house on the beach in Rehoboth, New Jersey, a summer place belonging to a doting father who was in insurance and would do anything for his daughter as long as she agreed not to marry a black man or a Jew. She was a slave to Boaz.

"I'm sick of giving everything away," he said to her one day. "I'm fed up with spending everything I take in. I'm sick of trading it or giving it away. What about this land of opportunity? What about real money? Fuck the credit cards. Fuck the secondhand automobiles. Am I going to rip off department stores all my life?"

"What do you want me to do, Rico?" she asked him. "Daddy will send me a check. Just play 'Stew Ball' for me. One time."

Boaz cracked two of her teeth throwing her across the room. He brooded on his future and sat in a full bathtub in the beachhouse in Rehoboth, drinking eight-star Metaxa from her daddy's liquor cabinet, and reading the personals in *Hump* magazine.

You can play with yourself when you're sixty-three but it doesn't do much good, thought the watchman. "Nothing does much good," he muttered to himself, waiting for his coffee to boil. The night watchman's shack squatted like a corrugated frog amid the giant oil tanks. The man had nothing to do but wait until six A.M. for his relief. He thumbed through his paperback, *Special Duty Nurses,* and felt a slight twinge below his belt. A Lawrence Welk rerun sang at him from his portable television but it didn't bother the watchman that he was able to do both things at once. He was beyond caring about anything except staying awake until his relief.

There was a splatter of gravel against the shack's tin sides. The watchman turned the book over, and listened. The truck sounds along the New Jersey Turnpike rattled by. They were familiar sounds. The automobiles whined their engine noises in the distance. They were familiar sounds. He went back to his book.

Scrape. The sound of footsteps outside the shack and the watchman grabbed his shotgun and electric torch, turned the TV up a notch louder and eased his way outside. He released the safety on his Winchester 1400 in 12 gauge, and shone his light all around in frenzied arcs. The oil tanks he guarded mocked him like the silence of a modern Stonehenge. As if they needed protection. He turned to go back to the comfort of his chair when the length of pipe he never saw cracked him across the side of his head.

"Rang him like a goddam bell," Boaz said, leaning over the watchman's body and clubbing him a second time on the other side of the head, and again across his neck. Two others pulled him away, one of them quickly checking the throbbing vein in the watchman's neck with his fingers.

"He'll live," Boaz said.

"Fucking animal," said Alex, the man who had checked the jugular. He shoved the others away and kneeled to strip the body of its watch, wallet and Masonic ring. He piled these in a plastic bag and hissed at the others, "Okay. Move, move, move." They moved, racing away in the darkness, bundles under their arms, toward the dark oil towers lying silent and half-buried in the earth.

There were no more words, just the sounds of running feet and the whir of wire being strung out rapidly along the ground. The silent figures worked swiftly, splitting into teams of two, each with spools of wire, explosives, electronic detonators that sounded off softly and regularly like the beepers that doctors carry to cocktail parties. The frequencies on the detonators were set, and affixed to the explosives. The teams covered the wires with dirt and then ran toward the breaks they had previously cut in the steel mesh fence. There was nothing frantic in their efforts. They threw the plastic bags with TV set, radio, ID cards, and jewelry over the fence and moved swiftly through, scrambling up an embankment to an access road where two automobiles waited. One was a 1969 Thunderbird stolen from the parking space marked Company Doctor in the lot of Manda Fabrics Corporation, Great Barrington, Massachusetts.

Three of the scrambling figures piled into the Thunderbird. The driver snapped on the ignition. He was a black man in his late twenties, sweating mightily from his forehead. He rubbed a sleeve across his brow. "I love the shit outta these T-Birds," he said.

"Scratch gravel, White Wind," said a voice from the back seat, and they took off, following the lead car, a 1967 navy blue Lincoln Continental lifted that morning from in front of Clyde's in Georgetown, Washington, D.C.

A driver had waited in the Lincoln while the others had raided the oil farm. She wore soft kid gloves and held her hands in the two o'clock–ten o'clock position. "Cale Yarborough, as I live and breathe," Alex said as he slid into the seat beside the girl. Two other men jumped into the back and slammed the doors. The Continental leaped up the access road, leaving rubber, with the Thunderbird right on its tail. "Go all right, Alex?" said the girl.

"Piece of sponge cake," he said. "You think so, Rico?" He spun around to look at Boaz, who slouched in the back seat.

"I don't like to be called animal," Boaz muttered. "I don't let family call me names. Why do you think I'm going to take it from you?"

"Because I'm going to make you rich. And all you ever got from your family was a boot in the ass."

The girl laughed and her eyes flashed to the rearview mirror, staring briefly at the handsome Mexican who refused to smile but who looked back at her eyes until she flicked her gaze away, back to the road.

The two cars roared along the New Jersey Turnpike, mingling with the trucks, the other cars, the buses from the South, the shuttles from Fort Dix, loaded with Basic trainees off for their first weekend in New York.

"Glory," Alex said to the girl. "The first rest area. Pull over."

"What's the matter?"

"Nothing's the matter. Just pull over when you hit one." She shrugged and looked into the mirror, into the eyes in the back seat. At the first rest stop, the Continental pulled off and lurched to a halt. The T-Bird passed them, roaring toward New York without a hesitation. Glory reached over to Alex and they slid toward one another, meeting halfway on the front seat. They kissed, while Glory ran her hands over Alex's face. Then she dropped one hand between his legs.

"When can we celebrate?" she asked him, when they broke the kiss.

"We celebrate, baby," he said, "when it's over."

"And when is it over?" she asked, as Boaz, the Mexican, stared at them sullenly from the back seat.

"Child," Alex said. "We haven't even begun."

He slid out of the Continental and shut the door. Slapping his hand on the trunk, he waved the car off. It soon became lost in the tangle of steel and fiberglass bodies all hurrying on their way. Alex had already forgotten about the receding taillights and he began to walk toward the edge of the highway as light began to appear in the sky, far away, like the glow from screens of drive-in movies.

Alex walked with a slight swagger, the way high school football players used to walk down lunchroom corridors, knowing people watched them. Trucks roared past him and Alex stuck out his thumb.

Gordon's Gin
Gouda
Clamato juice
London Broil
No Lead gas
Rm. 27

From Grace Abbott's
shopping list

3

*T*he Westchester County Airport is a clubby place. Businessmen who are friends see each other coming and
going into the small terminal, driven by taxis and wives from
Rye, Greenwich, Purchase and Armonk. A Lear jet, with
the orange sun logo of the Peerless Oil Corporation on its
tail assembly, taxied into the private plane sector and shut
off its engines. The Gulfstream jet, painted robin's-egg blue
with a white cash register on its sides, sat quietly next to the
Lear. The cash register was the familiar symbol of United
Stores, known nationwide as the first retail chain to hire
minorities, the first retail chain to open in ghetto areas. A
Mercedes 600 limousine, also painted robin's-egg blue, pulled
onto the tarmac. Kirk Abbott jumped out of the back seat,
not waiting for his chauffeur to open his door. The chauffeur shrugged an apology. "My contract says I open all doors,
Mr. Abbott."

"A contract provides its own excuse to break it," said
Abbott, and he walked quickly toward the waiting stairs of
the Gulfstream, swaggering slightly in his characteristic
manner. The chauffeur leaned against the limousine, knowing he would have time to watch the takeoff before he had
to return to New York.

Abbott waved to the passengers of the Lear as they came

down their own ramp. Louis Carlson, president of Peerless
Oil and a renowned son-of-a-bitch, waved back. Two of his
vice presidents, who never stopped talking to one another,
paid no attention. Carlson looked around for his limousine.
Abbott hesitated at the top of his stairs. "You being met?"
he called to Carlson.

"I'm late. And still he's late," said Carlson, annoyed.

"Traffic was murder coming up here. Although chances
are he was leasing it out while you were away."

"Very funny when you're on a tight schedule."

"Take mine," said Abbott. "I won't need it until late
tonight. Skelton has to go into the city anyway."

"Well, that's goddam nice of you. You sure? Well, thanks
very much. Let's go, boys," Carlson said to his vice presidents, who continued to chatter to one another. They didn't
even look up as they moved toward the robin's-egg blue
Mercedes. "How are Grace and the kids?" Carlson called
to Abbott as an afterthought.

"It's their America," said Abbott, smiling. "See you tonight at the University Club."

"Oh, that Warren Center thing. You're going?"

"Have to go," said Abbott. "My community responsibility."

Carlson chuckled and got into the limousine. The chauffeur slammed the door and slid behind the wheel.

"I didn't know you knew Mr. Abbott," said one of the
vice presidents, settling into the cushions and pressing an
array of buttons beside him, surprised when bar tables and
glasses hummed out in front of him.

"I don't," said Carlson. "I don't really know either of
them. Not many people do. But you've got to play the game,
boys. That's why I'm the president and you're the boys."

Skelton, the chauffeur, glanced into the rearview mirror
and headed the Mercedes into traffic.

Kirk Abbott settled himself into his seat on the plane and buckled his seat belt. "Anything to drink?" asked his steward. "Anything you want me to take on in Chicago? You brought back those steaks last time."

"Nothing today, thanks."

"Mrs. Abbott, is she fine?"

Abbott smiled at the steward and turned his attention to reports in his briefcase as the pilot's voice cracked over the plane's intercom, "We'll be flying at 24,000 feet, Mr. Abbott. Weather's choppy, not too bad. Should arrive O'Hare in one hour six minutes."

Good enough, Abbott said to himself. Good enough.

The plane accelerated, took off, and banked out over Westchester. Kirk Abbott, who, at thirty-eight, ran a company ten places out of the *Fortune* 500, concentrated on the figures on the papers in his lap. He had long since lost interest in the comforts and conveniences of private aircraft. He was one of those maddening people who looked fit with no exercise, healthy with no attention to health, blond through heredity. No fault of his own; he was one of those maddening people. Making games with the numbers on his lap was his exercise, his sport, his amour propre. The Gulfstream bumped in the chop above Buffalo, but Kirk's eyes never strayed from the figures.

Round Hill Road in Greenwich, Connecticut, is one of the great streets in the country.

Grace Abbott, who always thought of herself as Grace Kelly without the breaks, drove her yellow Country Squire out of her Round Hill Road driveway. *Honk, honkety, honk-honk,* she punched the horn in farewell to her two children, Scott and Nancy, who shoved each other on the front lawn, each eager to be the most vigorous waver after Mummy. They waved after Mummy, and Mummy's Country Squire, and Daddy's dog Sandy, who perched in the front seat and bit at the upholstery the way cocker spaniels in Connecticut bite at upholstery.

Grace Abbott was the former Grace Mason of Chestnut Hill, Boston, Beaver Country Day School (in the days when Beaver was not a disgrace) and Wellesley College. Growing up, she thought only about the good things: summer vacations, shetland sweaters, boys. At Wellesley, she belonged to that group of young women who used the college as an ivied backdrop for finding a husband. She never won the hoop race, but she was chosen for Tau Beta and majored in the modern novel and dated boys she begged to walk her around the lake. She never questioned the thought that she deserved a happy life. Winter vacations. Jewels. Children. In no special order.

Grace drove down Round Hill Road, along Greenwich Avenue, through the town and into the train station where she parked the wagon; she walked the cocker spaniel for one block south where she got into a cab, gave directions and settled back into the seat to flip through *Women's Wear Daily*. The cab pulled up to a shopping center where Grace Abbott got out in front of a Home Sewing store. She paid the driver, watched him leave, and crossed underneath the highway by a pedestrian tunnel, surfacing outside a motel-restaurant complex. Hurrying with the dog to an upper level of the motel, she came to number 27, took a key from her Hermes shoulder bag and, fitting the lock, opened the door and entered. "If there's anything I like, it's intrigue and romance," she said to the man in the three-piece suit who talked into the telephone. He blew a kiss and waved her in.

"That's right," the man was saying into the phone. "The cash flow projections for the next six months, every division separately and all of them consolidated line by line."

Grace shut the door and bolted it. Sandy went to a spot

of sunshine glowing on the carpet horizontally as it filtered through the venetian blinds, and lay down.

"I want them keyed to the same numbered accounts we use with the computer," the man said, "and I want them on my desk by noon and I want the meeting with divisional comptrollers for my office at two o'clock. Please order my lunch for 12:45 — clear consommé, celery stuffed with cottage cheese, black coffee. See you later." Ted Bronson hung up the phone. "You're a little late . . ."

"I couldn't help it. I always seem to run a little behind. If you can screw to a schedule, you've got a big future."

Bronson laughed. "I thought for a minute you weren't going to show up. I was afraid Kirk was back. Where is he anyway, the West Coast?"

"Chicago. Home this afternoon. Then off again somewhere else. What would he have done in the age of the horse?" Grace sat in a straight-backed chair and lit a cigarette.

"Did you have to bring the dog? I suppose the kids are waiting in the wagon outside."

"You've got schedules; I've got schedules."

"I love you, Grace."

"Oh balls, Teddy. You were put in by the creditors to watch my husband and his company and keep an eye on the financial planning. You were put in to chop heads and cut corners and report to the board and the executive committee. You'd love to get Kirk tossed out on his wheeling-dealing ear and you'd love to take over United Stores yourself, but I doubt if you love me. Now come on over here and let me taste that greedy mouth."

He didn't even glance at his watch as he went to her.

Ted Bronson's father had been a pharmacist in Evanston, Illinois, and Ted Bronson had forced himself to become the best cross-country runner at Evanston Township High School, a place that fostered excellence. When he came east to college he was surprised at first that cross country didn't matter to anyone except the coach. Nor did Evanston Township. At first surprised, he became bitter, and forced himself to become a student of the movements of money. He was trying to understand the casual indifference of the people who had grown up in the East and been sent away for training to perpetuate inherited wealth.

"Be lean and mean and dedicated, son," his father, the pharmacist, had told him, wanting his son to be like Gary Cooper. And lean and mean was what Ted Bronson had become.

He kissed Grace Abbott and touched her as they kissed, moving his hands over her breasts, between her legs, his kisses straying to her neck.

"Take off my things, darling," Grace said. "My shoes, my stockings, my pants. Leave everything else."

Ted did as she asked and she lay on the bed looking at him, her legs spread wide apart, her eyes dull with concentration.

The cocker spaniel ran over beside the bed and pushed one of Grace's shoes around with his nose.

Bronson looked at Grace and started to unbutton his vest.

"Oh no, my financial wizard," she said. "Just the pants. Leave your shirt and vest on. If it's going to be a quickie, let it be a quickie. When we've got time for each other, we'll do it right."

"It won't be long," Bronson said, taking off his trousers. "Kirk can't run a business. He's in Chicago because he's hocked to the eyeballs. And he's trying to come out with his skin." He slipped out of his shorts which he ordered by the dozen from Chipp in New Haven.

"My, my," said Grace, drawing her knees up to her chest, with her legs still apart. "My parents would be amazed if they knew how tales of money turned me on. Now I'm tired of stories."

Bronson walked to the bed and knelt above Kirk Abbott's wife. She shut her eyes and held her arms up to him and she pulled him down.

The cocker spaniel pulled the white handkerchief out of Bronson's pants pocket and slowly, quietly, began to chew it up.

IBM 411   UNS 1200 8 9   X 200 8 42⅛

New York Stock Exchange opening prices
(United Stores — UNS)

4

The robin's-egg blue limousine disgorged Louis Carlson, president of Peerless Oil, in front of his own towering glass and steel headquarters on Park Avenue. He was home, and he relaxed in the comfort of his power base, the feeling of safety surrounding him in silent waves. The two vice presidents, chatting away behind Carlson, never felt this safety, never could allow themselves the luxury of thinking about Peerless Oil as their home. They followed Carlson across the tiled lobby into one of the elevators. Each elevator in the bank of twelve had a mural painted around the inside. These murals depicted the progress of the oil industry from its beginnings in Pennsylvania to the offshore rigs of today. They had been done by a brilliant young Mexican of Communist persuasion who needed the exposure and the money. Swoosh — up to the forty-fifth floor went Carlson and his vice presidents. Out they went as the doors slid open on the executive floor.

"What is this, the company picnic? You waiting for a speech?" Carlson said, looking into the faces of all his regional sales managers. Their faces were eager and expectant. They were geared to remembering speeches and moving the goods.

Dick Donnelly, assistant to the president, stood nervously

with a letter in his hands. Dick Donnelly believed that being assistant to the president of a corporation meant that he was an executive, not an errand boy.

"What's the matter, Dick?" Carlson asked impatiently. "You're all standing around sniffing as if somebody farted."

"Burglary at the Newark Oil Farm."

"So? Report it to the insurance company. Is that why operations have ground to a halt?"

Donnelly held out a message. Two secretaries looked the other way. On a plain sheet of Eaton bond paper, typed on an Olivetti elite typewriter in the office supply department of Bloomingdale's, was a letter to Mr. Louis Carlson, President — Peerless Oil Co.

Dear Mr. Carlson:
This letter cordially invites your corporation to a month of peace at your expense. In return for your subscription of $100,000, you will be guaranteed something that others will not have; and that only money can buy. You will be contacted by telephone at nine-thirty A.M., Tuesday, April 9th. And you'll be sorry to learn this is no joke.

Cordially,
The People's Revolutionary Army

"People's Revolutionary Army, my ass." Carlson crumpled up the note and tossed it at a secretary.

"But they said they'd call at nine-thirty."

"Don't try my patience, Dick," said Carlson. "We've got a sales meeting and I don't want to be disturbed. We're losing enough time with these people in from all over the country. Let's get cracking."

Carlson joined his sales managers, who smiled at him, hovered near him, looking for that blink or twitch of approval that could be carried back to a wife in Des Moines or Indianapolis and savored over cocktails.

Another secretary shut the door to Carlson's inner office as his voice boomed to the salespeople: "Are you cranked up for spring, boys? Is Peerless cranked up for spring?"

"Call, Mr. Donnelly," one of the outer receptionists said to the assistant to the president. "It's for Mr. Carlson but he doesn't want to be disturbed."

"Switch it to me," said Donnelly, resting his back against the girl's desk.

"The man is terribly rude," she whispered to him.

He picked up the phone. "Dick Donnelly," he said.

"Who the Christ are you? I asked for Carlson."

"I'm Mr. Carlson's assistant. Who is this speaking?"

"I wrote him a letter. Kind of an invitation. I said I'd call at nine-thirty."

"What letter? Who is this speaking?"

"Tell Carlson don't play games with us. Next time tell him to take the call himself. I'll ring again at ten-thirty."

"Next time you get through to nobody."

"I'll get through, errand boy," said the voice. "I'll get through."

The receiver at the other end was crashed into its cradle.

Donnelly tried to look composed; he tried to look as if he could make a decision. "Get me a coffee, will you, Judy?" he snapped at the girl in back of him.

"You want a danish?"

"Make it a jelly donut. I need something sweet."

It's difficult to believe that there is a busier airport in the world than Chicago's O'Hare. Kirk Abbott let himself be carried along with the hurrying hundreds, slapping his brief-case against his thigh as he walked. Before he came into the main terminal, still moving, he slipped a pair of tinted horn-rimmed eyeglasses from his breast pocket and put them on. They had the effect of softening his face, making him look slightly older, somehow vulnerable. He knew from experience that the simplest disguises were the best. People would remember only the thick horn-rimmed glasses. When he appeared as Alex, he was sure he would be described as having thick black hair. No one would think it was a wig, so well was it made, so well did it fit, so well did he look.

Kirk paused at American Airlines Information Center and set his briefcase down.

"Mr. Anastos?" came a voice beside him. Kirk looked up and nodded. "Ahh. I must say people are not usually on time at O'Hare. So many people. I don't like to fly myself, being one of the last of the great train buffs. Don Sperling is my name. Sperling and Sperling."

"Which of the Sperlings is the headhunter?"

"We dislike that term, Mr. Anastos. As we dislike words like input and parameters and interface. Graduate school clichés, don't you know? I am, in fact, an attorney. My aged father is an attorney as well. We specialize in bringing people with specific needs together."

"What have you done about my needs?"

"The young lady is in the coffee shop." He handed Kirk a résumé. "Gena Reynolds. Age twenty-four. Honor graduate of Stanford Business School. Just what you specified. And look at the test results. I'm sure you will agree that she is extraordinary."

"Why don't we let the young lady tell me herself? Does she have a car here?"

"Yes, Mr. Anastos. She didn't wish to come with me."

"I want you to leave after you introduce us."

"As you wish, Mr. Anastos. But . . . in the event that you do hire her? And she is extraordinary, even to her shape, which I'm sure you will agree . . ."

"I'll give her the money. You bill the young lady."

"Whatever you prefer. Whatever."

They went to the coffee shop and walked over to an auburn-haired woman. She was well tailored, well groomed, looking as if she were sitting in the Connaught Grille and not Chicago's O'Hare. She was indeed extraordinary. The young woman wore a rust-colored tweed suit over a yellow cashmere sweater that grabbed at her front like a newlywed. She was reading the *Journal of Commerce* and smoking a cigarette without a filter tip. Gena Reynolds stood when the two men arrived.

"Gena Reynolds," Sperling said to her. "This is Mr. Anastos. Costas Anastos."

"You should have heard it before it was changed," said Kirk Abbott, motioning Gena to her seat. He sat down opposite her.

"If there's nothing else?" said Sperling.

"Based on what you've done so far," said Kirk, "you and your aged parent have done a remarkable job."

"We bring people together."

"Now, take one person away," said Kirk.

Sperling waved and walked from the coffee shop. He looked back once at them, once, and he was gone.

The waitress was sleepy and bored, her apron spattered with the leavings of others. "Have you seen a menu?" she said.

"The lady has coffee," said Kirk. "Nothing for me."

"We've got a fifty-cent minimum to take up the seat, mister," the waitress said.

"How much is coffee?" Abbott asked.

"Fifteen cents."

Abbott peeled a five-dollar bill out of a roll held together by a silver clip monogrammed with an Old English A. He handed the five to the waitress. "Buy yourself thirty-three cups and bring me a nickel change."

She barely thanked him. There was little in life she had not seen before.

"Can I ask you something?" said Gena Reynolds. "What do you leave at '21'?"

"You tell me first," Kirk said. "What did you learn at business school?"

"I learned things I suppose you're going to make me forget."

"Are you in love?"

"Are you, Mr. Anastos?" She smiled at him, showing even white teeth in a mouth that looked like an invitation to leave a dance early.

"Do you appreciate money?" Kirk asked her.

"My father was a gardener in Bel Air," Gena said. "He spent his life making things beautiful for others. 'You make it beautiful for yourself, Gena,' he told me. And I'm going to. I not only appreciate money; I know how it's made."

"You don't mind travel outside the United States?"

"My suitcase is in the trunk of my car; my passport is in my pocket."

"You're not asking me any questions about the job," Kirk Abbott said to her. "Or about me."

"I can't resist rich men who wear glasses," Gena said. "And I've never known a blond Greek. I imagine you'll tell me when you want me to know."

"All right. Let me see what kind of car you drive." They walked from the terminal to Gena's red Fiat convertible.

"A little rough on your legs," she laughed. "When it rains, the damn thing never starts. And I think it's really meant only to go between Venice and Milano. But every once in a while I stuff a pepperoni pizza in the gas tank, and it's great for another three thousand miles."

Gena drove confidently in the heavy Chicago morning traffic, moving from one lane to another impatiently, not content to drift with the herd.

"You'll be going to Costa Rica first," Kirk told her. "A little banking assignment. I see you were with the Chase Manhattan last summer."

"Banking interests me."

"Good. I hope bankers interest you also. You'll be getting very well acquainted with a few."

They approached the new Regency Hyatt House, twenty stories in the round, rooms on the outside, four elevator tubes inside.

"Let me off at the main entrance," Abbott told her. "Park. Then come in and wait for me in the lobby."

When Gena pulled over, she turned off the ignition and smiled. "Is the interview over? Do I have the job?"

Abbott reached into the breast pocket of his jacket and handed her an envelope. Slitting it open with a long red fingernail, she whistled. It contained a great many bills, all new crisp United States hundreds. "Number one," Kirk said. "I've always admired Ben Franklin. Number two: you've got the job. Number three: the interview is not yet over." He got out of the Fiat and shut the door gently.

After checking with the front desk, Abbott took one of the cylindrical elevators to the eleventh floor, walked down a hallway and knocked. He had placed his eyeglasses in his inside jacket pocket, where the money envelope had been. Seconds later the chain lock was opened and the door clicked and swung in. "Hello, Franco," said Abbott. "Sorry to bring you out of town. I know you hate the sound of airports."

"I like big cities. I trust the cities. You know what I mean? That's where I do business."

"So how's business?"

"You worry about your business, Mr. Abbott. I worry about mine."

Franco Bertelli was a smooth man who never raised his voice, because he never had to. He wore seven hundred dollars' worth of clothes on his back and a gold signet ring with a phony crest.

"My business is usually exciting. You know that, Franco."

"It's going to get more exciting, I have that feeling. Thirty days, that's all. Cost you six percent."

"That interest sounds low. Is this Christmas?"

"No, it's not Christmas. A flat six percent for thirty days."

"A flat six? On fifty million? That's three million dollars. Three million interest for thirty days? Seventy-two percent a year? Extortion and bullshit."

"Extortion? Call the banks, Mr. Abbott. Don't complain to Franco. The banks hold your paper. It ain't bullshit, I can tell you that."

Franco Bertelli walked to the bathroom, took the complimentary felt shoeshine cloth and came back to the living room. He spit on the cloth and rubbed it back and forth over the tips of his black shoes, which needed no polishing in the first place.

Kirk stared hard at him. "The banks hold my notes as straws for you."

"In a pig's ass they do. We deny it. I hate to remind you, Mister Abbott, but United Stores opened at nine today. Your cost is fifteen if I remember correctly. You want the banks to sell the collateral? I don't have to tell you that in Singapore and Geneva, banks charge what the traffic will bear. All bankers care about is that you owe them money and you can't pay. You're in the big leagues, you know, Mr. Abbott."

"You're pushing me, Franco. I'm a bad man to push. I do funny things when the pressure is on."

Franco spit on the shine cloth and rubbed one of his black shoe tips. "Tell your psychiatrist about that, Abbott, not me. Anything else you want to talk about?"

Kirk nodded slowly as if thinking about matters far away. He said nothing.

Franco got up from his chair and walked to the door. "Enjoy the room. It's yours for the day. Don't bother to call me anymore. The loan is due in thirty days. If you want conversation, call the banks. They have all the certificates. If you don't pay, they'll be happy to close you out." Franco bunched the shine cloth into a ball and tossed it at Abbott. "Good luck," he said. "I hope you make it."

Kirk went immediately to the phone and called Teddy Bronson in New York. He stared out at the Chicago skyline as he waited, thinking about the good times he had had there in the past: The Palmer House, the Playboy mansion with Hefner, dinners with Bobby Hull, lunches with Ernie Banks. Good times. Oil tanks bearing the Peerless Oil logo loomed out of the smoky haze he looked upon. "Teddy," Kirk said when his call was connected. "I'm in Chicago and I want to be met at three o'clock, Westchester. No, I didn't go to the store. I don't like the merchandise."

"I'll tell the Board of Directors," Bronson said, laughing.

"Yes, you do that."

"You sound preoccupied."

"I'm just looking at the skyline."

"Anything I can do on this end?"

"Just have Skelton meet me at three."

"Will do. Best to Grace. She been all right?"

"She's the same."

"You mean ill? Or like all wives?"

"As far as I know, she's never looked healthier. See you tonight."

The oil farm shimmered suddenly as the morning sunshine broke through the haze. The golden reflections bounced off the surface of the tanks. Kirk hung up, took his glasses from his inside pocket, put them on, and left the hotel room. Moving through the hallway and into the elevator, he got off at 2, walked to the rail and stared down into the lobby. From his pants pocket he took a Kennedy half dollar and flipped it, end over end, into the air. It landed with a thud on the cushion beside Gena Reynolds, who sat on a couch looking at people walk by. She jumped with surprise, then looked up. Seeing Mr. Anastos, she grinned and tucked the half dollar into the top of her sweater. He stayed at the railing and watched her as she got up, still grinning at him, and headed for the bank of elevators.

The watchman's shack at Peerless Oil's farm in New Jersey looked pitiful in the daylight, a tin woodman amid the towers of the Emerald City of Oz.

Glory, her black hair held back by a beaded headband, drove a Pinto wagon at close to the speed limit by the Peerless tanks on the New Jersey Turnpike. Enrico Boaz sat next to her, uncomfortable in a middle-class car of the suburbs. He preferred big, fast automobiles. Next to those he preferred subways. He had never been in a Pinto and he was not in a good mood.

The black man called Silver Wheels Edwards sat in the back seat fingering the button on a detonator.

"Ten nineteen, Silver Wheels," Boaz said to him, pronouncing every syllable. "Give it to the fuckers."

Edwards pressed the button and the oil farm blew up suddenly, as if John D. Rockefeller had signaled judgment day. The night watchman's shack splintered in a thousand directions and balls of flame shot hundreds of feet into the air. Traffic accidents on the Turnpike multiplied in an accordianlike sequence, and other motorists pulled onto soft shoulders to watch the smoke and flames. Everyone turned on their radios, including Glory, whose thighs filled with the warmth of destruction. She turned the Pinto easily in and out amid the halted traffic. After a minute, she fiddled with the radio to get a rock station and put her hand onto Boaz's thigh. Her nails dug in. "It was beautiful, wasn't it? Just beautiful." She ran her tongue over her lips.

"I didn't hear nothing," said Silver Wheels Edwards. "Why is everybody pulling over?"

"It was beautiful," Glory said, still squeezing Boaz's thigh.

"It's going to be that way all the time," he said.

.0 0 T

2 5 0, 0 0 0.0 0
2 5 0, 0 0 0.0 0 T

**Torn from the calculator
of Kirk Abbott**

5

Ten of the richest men in New York were having cocktails and clam chowder. They had assembled in a private
dining room at the University Club as members of a committee of the wealthy and famous appointed by the mayor
to lend support to Warren Center. The center would house
a historical museum, a zoo, and a new refuge for the State
Supreme Court. It would also overshadow Lincoln Center
as a home for the arts the way that Central Park over-
shadows that narrow patch of grass donated by Bill Paley.

Most men dislike business meetings and will discuss anything for any length of time to postpone the inevitable. "The
sons of bitches blew up my Jersey oil farm," Louis Carlson
was telling the others. "Another Jack Daniels," he called to
a waitress. "Can you believe that I've been chasing around
all afternoon playing tag, helping the police track the sons
of bitches down? I've put dogs on all our domestic properties. Shepherds, Weimaraners, Great Danes. Going to cost
me three thousand a week for meat, for Christ's sake. But
we let them sniff bags of human blood and keep them froth-
ing. Wouldn't like to roam around on any of my own
goddam properties."

"They want much money?" Kirk Abbott asked him.

"The dogs?" Carlson said. "Oh, you mean these lunatics.

This morning after the tanks blew, I got a phone call. They wanted a quarter of a million dollars. For two months' peace. Can you believe it? For Christ's sake, my wife doesn't even cost me that much. And they blew them. They blew them. I moved my lawyers' asses so fast they couldn't think straight. Had the cops, the FBI, the lawyers, the insurance men. All of them telling me not to worry. And I've got to ship my regional sales managers home, after shipping them in. Do you know what that costs? And we get nothing accomplished except hearing them say the company prayer a cappella. This explosion wasn't in Kuwait, mind you, it was fucking New Jersey. Everyone's still telling me not to worry. Can you imagine, for Christ's sake?" He gulped his bourbon. No one else spoke. "I tried to keep the guy on the phone," he continued, "but he had none of it. Gave me instructions and hung up. Well, the FBI and the cops go into a frenzy. All of them have ideas. Does Peerless Oil have any enemies, they want to know. I tell them no! Other than the millions of Africans, radicals at Harvard who don't like Peerless in the portfolio, assorted unhappy stockholders, most of the other oil companies. No. We don't have any enemies. The authorities huddled again. They want me to go along with the demands and they'll back me up; pounce on the bastards when they pick up the package. Who are they? What is happening here? If I knew somewhere safe in the world, I'd go there. Anyway, they keep telling me don't worry. They're the ones who can't stand still."

"This is ridiculous," Abbott said.

"Well, of course it's ridiculous," Carlson said, "but you didn't lose four million in property this afternoon." Everyone else at the table muttered and sipped their drinks. "So I get in my Cadillac with the driver. And we go to a shopping center in Queens, like the phone call said to do. On my lap I got a briefcase loaded with two hundred and fifty thousand dollars in tens and twenties. Know what it weighs? Two hundred and fifty thousand in cash? It weighs like nothing at all. All that money. I put it on the scale in the washroom off my office and it's like nothing. I go to the middle phone booth in a bank of five and it rings when it's supposed to. Same voice, new instructions. He says if I'm followed, my ass is grass. I tell the FBI what he said and they decide it must be a Vietnam veteran because 'your ass is grass' is an old army expression."

The clam chowder plates were cleared and roast beef was brought in with Yorkshire pudding and horseradish sauce and green beans with almonds.

"We head out for Connecticut," he went on, "on the Merritt. And all the time I'm thinking that I can't believe how I'm spending the day. Right after the Lincoln Road exit in Scarsdale, we pull off into a rest area. In the middle barrel of three trash barrels I put the briefcase with a quarter of a million. They told me not to worry because cops and FBI guys are all over the woods with all kinds of equipment watching the barrels. We go back to New York and the Feds pick me up at the Peerless building because I want to be in on the arrest when they grab the sons of bitches. I go off again in an unmarked Ford that looks like a government car ten miles away because it's stripped down bare, no frills. A cheap, simple Ford. Except it's got phones in it and the biggest aerial in America."

Everyone at the table laughed because Lou Carlson was a tale-teller from way back. And they weren't sure whether there was going to be a punch line or whether it was a shaggy dog story. Carlson managed to cram two huge mouthfuls of roast beef into his mouth and gulp a gulpful of Burgundy.

"While I'm hustling back to New York," he went on, "evidently a cab comes by the rest area. The cabbie picks the package out of the trash, makes a U-turn and goes back to the shopping center in Queens. Definitely a high-class operation if they keep going back to Queens. FBI figures they've got to live near there. The cabbie goes into a coffee and doughnut shop in the center. And I'm hustling in the unmarked Ford, with the clean-cut Feds who got senses of humor like a deaf-mute, to be in on the arrest. We get to the doughnut shop just as the troops move in. I kid you not: state cops with gas grenades, New York police with revolvers, FBI with sawed-off shotguns, sharpshooters on the roofs of discount stores. They grab the cabbie who spits coffee all over himself and claims he was to be paid fifty bucks on top of the meter to pick up the package and wait in the coffee shop until he was contacted by a phone call. A black man gave him the fifty and the instructions. The police check everyone in the center but no sign of anyone suspicious. Other than the hundreds of suspicious people who probably shop in Queens every day. So we got the money back and the insurance company is screaming bloody murder and I step up security on my properties and my dinner is cold."

Two men applauded. Simon Ehrlich, president of the Mercantile National Bank, whom no one ever talked to without an excellent reason, and Roger Damon Dinsmore, chairman of Omni Credit Company, whose blue plastic card was as good, or better, than money in every country in the world.

Before they took up the business of the evening, the gentlemen present all agreed that although the nation was in terrible shape, the dissident elements reached their peak of frenzy in the late 1960s.

"Without Vietnam," Kirk Abbott commented, "there's no cause to unite all of the havenots. They can just bicker among themselves. I'm sure it's business as usual these days, and about goddam time." The others tapped on their glasses with their spoons in approval. Simon Ehrlich, being a banker, brought the meeting to order.

"Now you all knew Wicky Warren," Ehrlich said, "whose name the center is to bear. He was a sweetheart of a man who inherited almost a billion dollars and who almost pissed it all away on good works. Not that we assembled are not among the most charitable men in the country. God knows we all give our money and our time. Because we want to."

The men tapped their glasses with their spoons.

"Now we can raise all we need for this proposition. It's exciting, it's New York. It's now, and it's then also. That's the beauty of it. But we need to have controls. A budget. We need to bring in someone who knows how to run a business before he knows how to give a concert with Lennie Bernstein."

"I'm for this character from Santa Fe, who was in *Time* last week," said William Farley, chairman of Federated Utilities and whom the *New York Times* dubbed "Brown-out Billy." "You know, that half Chinese who they say has brought culture to the Southwest. Anyone who takes their minds off football has got to take New York by storm. And if he's really half Chinese, the women who have got to get this project off the ground socially will eat him up."

"How about each of us submitting our choices, and getting on with it," Kirk Abbott said. "There's too much democracy in this country, and at this point in our history, it's hindering progress."

"That's well and good, Mr. Abbott," said Ehrlich the banker. "After you've got yours, close the doors. Correct?" The others laughed and the door to the private dining room opened, admitting a club steward in a dinner jacket.

"Mr. Carlson," he said. Carlson raised his cigar. "Message for you, sir."

Carlson glanced at the note. "They've done it," he cried out, his usual flush draining from his face, as if wiped off with an eraser.

"What?" three or four of the others asked, thinking first of heart attacks for Carlson, then thinking about themselves.

"The terror," Carlson said to them. "My oil farms: Jersey City, Bridgeport, Worcester. They blew them up. God, I can't believe it. Seven million dollars in damage. God, I can't believe it." He dipped his napkin in his water glass and wiped his face. "This is no fucking joke, gentlemen," he said. "You're going to have to excuse me." Carlson rushed out.

"We'd better adjourn," said Ehrlich. "This is incredible. I hope to God they keep this out of the papers. Every nut in America will be trying it."

Kirk Abbott didn't move. He doodled on a pad of paper and kept shaking his head. Farley patted him on the back. "You have to be optimistic, you have to cope," Farley said. "But the markets will be sick tomorrow if the news does get out."

Kirk looked up. "I suppose things could be worse," he said. "I could be in the oil business." Farley smiled briefly and left the room with the others.

Kirk Abbott waited outside the University Club for his wife. The cross streets in New York on the West Side after ten o'clock were quiet. Kirk's mind had not been quiet since he was seven and sick with scarlet fever. His thoughts now raced over possible moves, probable events, and he never saw the two men who slipped behind him and stopped. They were black. They didn't give a damn about probable events. The taller of the two put a choke hold on Abbott and the other put an eight-inch switch to his heart. "With your hands, you silly faggot," the man with the knife said, "empty your pockets on the ground. Pluck your wallet out slow. Like you're paying a bill. Any hero thoughts and your ticker will be lying next to your keys. It's real easy to cut on a heart. And you don't have to be no doctor. It comes out in one piece."

Kirk, lifted up on his toes by the hammerlock, reached into his pocket and carefully dropped change, money clip, and personal men's-room key onto the concrete. For an instant the knife man glanced down, and Kirk blocked his knifeblade arm high into the air. Almost in the same motion he bent down, quickly forcing the chokeholder over his back and hard onto the sidewalk. He kicked the blade man heavily in the left ball and again, right under the nostril on the way down, crashing bone into the mugger's brain and killing him before he had time to worry about his pain-ridden testicle. The man on the ground got the point of Kirk's shoe in the side of the neck and the heel deep in the solar plexus, which should have been enough to burst the muscles supporting the heart. A few people in the darkness scurried to the opposite side of Fifty-fourth Street and continued toward Fifth Avenue. Kirk put all of his change and bills and the key in his pocket just as Grace drove up in the Mercedes limousine. Ted Bronson jumped out of the back seat. "Jesus, what happened?" he said. "What can we do? Call the police? Who'll stay with Grace?"

"Get in," said Kirk. "It's all taken care of." Kirk pushed Bronson into the back seat where Bronson's wife Lisa sat, gasping and craning her neck to see the sidewalk.

"Are you all right, Kirk?" Grace asked him from the front.

"There's a hunk of old sweater in the glove compartment," Kirk said. "Give it to me, quickly." Kirk took the rag and calmly tied it over the rear license plate, obscuring identification. He got into the driver's seat, moving his wife over and patting his dog, who sat on the floor panting with the excitement of seeing his master. Kirk drove the limousine toward the Avenue of the Americas. The bodies of the muggers lay in front of the University Club, sprawled in patent high heels and leather raincoats and wide-brimmed hats, like fancily dressed mannequins who had fallen off of the back of a truck, bound for a department store in the Bronx.

"You've got to report that, Kirk," said Bronson. "What the hell are you doing? Where's that sweater?"

"Just my sense of humor, Teddy," Kirk said. "In case anyone was watching, they'll think it was a professional job. I don't want anybody to know about this."

"You've got to call the police. What happened there anyway?"

Abbott moved swiftly in traffic up Sixth to Fifty-ninth Street, hesitated, then turned right, heading toward Ungerman's, United Stores's most fashionable and profitable outlet, on Lexington Avenue. "Look," he said, "you call the police and tell them I was jumped by muggers after my meeting. Keep my name out of the papers. I don't want any creeps threatening my family. Take Grace home; I've got to stop at the office. I've borrowed Swiss francs. The dollar is bound to weaken in the face of all this terrorism. I'm going to call Singapore since they won't get the news until morning. If I short dollars now versus Swiss francs, it's a good hedge. If there's anything I need now, it's a good hedge." Kirk pulled up outside the store. "You're not talking, Grace." She had been silent throughout the ride, and still said nothing. Abbott shrugged.

"Teddy, you drive," he said. "I'll take the late train home and the cab from the station. I'm sorry about Mabel Mercer or wherever we were going, but first things first. "Sandy," he said to the dog, "be a good boy. Befriend our friends, confusion to the enemy." The dog panted again and Teddy Bronson got behind the wheel. His wife sat alone in the back admiring Ungerman's window, which was full of women and men mannequins dressed in the current designer look, thc mcn in high-hcclcd saddlc shocs, pastcl suits and sporty wide-brimmed hats.

Kirk walked behind the Mercedes, removed the old sweater from around the license plate, and, with his brief-case, walked toward the side entrance to his store.

The Mercedes pulled away with Lisa Bronson asking her husband if he thought she'd look good in big hats. "Big hats are back," she was saying.

In his office, Kirk Abbott made one terse phone call and went quickly to his washroom, using the key he had re-trieved from the sidewalk in front of the University Club.

Trains seem to move faster at night than in the day. In the darkness one's missions seem aimless, one's destination obscure. Louis Carlson nervously dealt cards in the last car, which was empty except for his assistant Dick Donnelly and four other men, who paced and drank from a flask.

"A fine time for me to win every hand," Carlson said. "I don't want to be on a train for Hartford. I don't want to be on a train for anywhere. If I had five minutes alone with those bastards who are ruining America . . . By the way," he added, "gin."

"We're outside Greenwich now, Mr. Carlson," one of the four pacing men said. "Time to go onto the platform." The four went out onto the rear platform of the train. Carlson and Donnelly stood watching at the window of the car. Minutes passed, and the clickety-clack of the wheels flashed sparks into the darkness along the railroad. Eyes strained not to miss what they looked for. More minutes passed. Sud-denly a red signal light flickered on once, then twice, from a stretch of trees they were passing. The four men on the platform pushed a metal box over the guardrail and watched briefly as it bounded down an embankment. The wheels clattered on and the moment was past. One of the men spoke frantically into a portable telephone, issuing directions. "Don't worry, L.C.," said Donnelly to his boss. "They know exactly where the drop is. They'll get 'em."

"The world is upside down today, Dick," said Carlson, suddenly looking very old. "The more important you get, the more they think they can shit on you." The four men on the platform talked excitedly to each other, then into the phone. Carlson's problems were nothing to them. Communications and electronics were everything. The train shot through Darien station without stopping.

Again there were two cars and six people. Alex and Boaz had picked up the box, broken the lock and transferred the money to a schoolchild's green bookbag. Boaz placed a small plastique charge and a manual timer in the metal box, closed it and left it in the woods. They had fifteen minutes on the timer. Quickly they ran through the woods to the cars, where Alex counted the old crumpled tens and twenties into six piles of fifty thousand dollars each. He handed the piles over, one to each person. They transferred the money into currency belts worn under their clothing. The cars sped away in opposite directions. The entire process had taken seven minutes from the time the metal box had been tossed from the train. Only two words had been spoken. As Alex counted the money, he said to the others, "Sweet." And he repeated — "Sweet." He patted Boaz on the ass in congratulation.

A taxi let Kirk Abbott off at his front door. He took half a glass of milk and half a brownie and went upstairs. Grace was reading in bed and flicking the automatic television controls back and forth from a late movie to the end of Johnny Carson. "Are you hedged?" she said.

"It's fairly complicated," Kirk said to her. "I've got to go to Geneva tomorrow."

"You should not only be hedged, you should be bushed. Come to bed, darling."

Kirk started to get undressed and the phone rang. "I'll get it," he warned. Grace looked at him quizzically. "Yes?" Kirk said. "Yes, Teddy. Don't you ever sleep?"

"Sorry, Kirk," Bronson said. "Thought I should tell you. Peerless Oil paid the ransom."

"That's a very bad precedent."

"I would have paid in Carlson's position. You figure the cost against the risk, against the losses, it's cheap."

"I don't figure cost against risk," Abbott said. "It's blackmail. And blackmail should never be paid. But I hope the papers play it down for once. I'm going to Europe tomorrow."

"We'll manage to hold things together."

Kirk hung up. "There's never been a more holier-than-thou, tight britches than Teddy Bronson," Kirk said.

"He's hungry."

"He's also boring. The obvious is always boring."

"Speaking of boring," Grace said to Kirk as he slid in next to her and turned out his light. "You're getting to be like Santa Claus."

Kirk laughed. "Santa Claus?"

"Yeah. He only comes once a year. And that's down the chimney."

Kirk made love to his wife in self-defense, able to stay for a long time, moving for moments against each side of her, inside of her, against the bottom, against the top, until she came and cried the name that she always used when she came. "Kirky. Kirky," she said.

Kirk stayed for minutes longer while she played with his balls and the opening of his rear until he shot into her with a rush of relief.

"We'll always have the best sex," she said. "No matter what, we'll always have the best sex."

Watching her sleep, Kirk marveled at how much she softened. Her face relaxed; the small lines on her forehead disappeared. He touched her hair, brushing it over one ear. Her smell was clean, peaceful.

It was a long time before Kirk could force himself to think ahead. And when he thought ahead, he was unable to sleep. Grace breathed easily beside him, a leg sprawled out to touch one of his. He jerked his away and imagined himself alone.

I don't think he was
nervous. I think he
believed all the Stories
he told me. Daddy will
love his ambition; Mother
will think he's beautiful.
I think he's beautiful.

From Grace Mason's
college diary

6

The idea of being more than one person first occurred to Kirk when, as a college undergraduate, he was driving up Route 1 near Boston looking for a motel room. He chose one that had individual cabins and signed the guest register while the girl waited in her car. Peter Runnels was the name he used. Springfield, Mass. Pete Runnels was the name of a player for the Boston Red Sox at the time. The rest of the night, Kirk played the role of big league ballplayer out for a tryst with the owner's daughter. The girl got bored with the act. But Kirk played Pete Runnels even in the morning, telling her to drop him at Fenway Park and to meet him after the game in the lobby of the Kenmore Hotel, where all the teams stayed. "I want you, Kirk," she said to him. "But I think you're laughing at me. I think you're laughing at everyone."

He shrugged and told her that he was sorry, but that he had been having trouble hitting the curve.

Later, at business school, his classwork on case studies was superior. Instructors marveled at how he could anticipate the problems of corporate officers. Kirk anticipated the problems because, during his study of the cases, he became the officers. He imagined that he lived as they lived, drank what they drank, thought what they thought, played the games they played.

"Abbott, you should have gone to medical school and become a psychiatrist," a professor told him.

"I never want to be in a position where I charge by the hour," he answered. He graduated with honors and very few friends. They always thought that Kirk mocked them.

New York was the only place most of his classmates even considered working. Kirk agreed and found a sublet in MacDougal Alley where various women tried to convince him to join the theater.

"You've been onstage so long," one Off-Broadway actress told him, "I think I'd be disappointed in the real person. If I ever met him, that is."

"Sour grapes," Kirk said.

"It may be sour grapes, but I think you're wasting time in business. You belong somewhere you can get paid for fantasy. I can't take it anymore, Kirk. Everything is Strindberg with you."

He remained a loner, determined to become independent enough to act like a Hughes, spend like a Getty, imagine like a Hearst.

In response to the business school's request for information about careers, Kirk wrote a long reply, ending with:

P.S. Best Bet. Kirk Abbott will spring free from all this and continue the Quest.

P.P.S. Is it true that in the year 2001 a nude skydiver will be devoured by a gaggle of ravenous owls?

He won Grace Mason away from the former stroke of a U.S. Olympic crew by his ability to change character and mood as his whims dictated. When he was introduced to the oarsman the same night he met Grace, Kirk said:

"Far dearer to me than my leisure,"
The heiress declared, "is my pleasure.
    For then I can screw,
    The whole Harvard crew.
They're slow, but that lengthens the pleasure."

The former stroke didn't know whether to laugh or to punch Kirk in the mouth. By the time he decided, he had lost Grace.

"You shouldn't have done that," she told Kirk later. "He was defenseless."

"If you probe the weaknesses of people," Kirk told her, "you can make them your own."

"You may fly too close to the sun," Grace said. That touched Kirk. He called her the next day.

Throughout their courtship Kirk was faithful to her. Even in his fantasies. And after their first meeting, Grace never considered marrying anyone else. But she never stopped trying to reach through and beneath his retreats, his illusions.

"Every woman wants that from her men," Kirk would tell her. "And when you find out what simple souls we are, you won't want us anymore."

She had to admit to herself that this special quality of Kirk kept her wanting him long after most of her friends had ceased to want their husbands. And, of course, there were the homes, the vacations, the possessions, the life her parents had said that Kirk could never provide.

Early in his career Kirk had had a succession of jobs. He whipped through Bloomingdale's training program in a summer and then left to become comptroller of a midwestern chain of seventeen department stores. By the time he was thirty, Kirk had a background of successful management positions, a reputation for tough-minded financial planning, and a flair for fashion unusual in a money man. At night, Kirk would pore through the Standard & Poor's industrial manual as other men might read the want ads. In this way he discovered United Stores, a Big Board company with a book value five dollars a share higher than the current market price. It looked too attractive to be real, with aging management, prime store locations, a fine name and some four million dollars' worth of investments and cash. After a month's intensive checking, Kirk quit his job and set out to pluck United Stores from its current owners. He figured three and a half million shares would swing control. At approximately fifteen dollars a share, he would need to borrow about fifty million dollars. On his reputation he might raise five million between New York, Boston and Philadelphia. In a runaway bull market, which he did not have, he might raise ten million, maximum. But only in a financial atmosphere where dollars were meaningless against the frenzy for action at any cost. A banker in Boston, renowned for his dealings with film companies, his capacity for Scotch and his extramarital situations, told Kirk, "If you want the money badly enough, I know a few names in Geneva. I know a good name in Paris. I know a bad name in Singapore."

"What rates?" Kirk asked him.

"You'll pay dearly for it, of course. But if it's what you want, you won't mind paying for it."

Kirk went to Paris and met the man whose good name he was given, a banker who had fled Egypt about the same time as Farouk. The banker listened to Kirk, looking out his window over Kirk's head onto the Place Vendôme, where people strutted in the sunshine, secure in the feeling that Paris was the center of the world. "Mr. Abbott," the banker said, when Kirk was finished with his story, "you go back to the Georges Cinq, you go to the theater. You go to the Louvre. You go to the Ritz bar and have martinis very dry. Amuse yourself and look at the French women. I shall call you within three days. Fifty million U. S. is major money."

The banker called him on the third day.

"I have arranged things for you, Mr. Abbott," he said. "And I have taken the liberty of bringing in some acquaintances in various other locations. Geneva, Singapore, Hong Kong. One does not mind traveling, Mr. Abbott, if there is a destination."

"You have the entire sum covered?" Kirk asked him.

"Come over in the morning after a good breakfast. We can arrange the transfer of funds to you and you can describe how the shares will be delivered to us for custody. You have some most interesting partners in this enterprise, Mr. Abbott. I can't wait to tell you about them."

"You Egyptians always sound as if you're still in the bazaar," Kirk said to him.

"It is not happy being forced from one's home, Mr. Abbott. We do what we can to remind us of happier days. In the morning then?"

Kirk knew the price of United Stores was undervalued. But after he gained control the market began to undervalue everything. Stocks declined in the face of inflation, energy crises, the fact that the American markets were a wasteland of neglect. Fear and indifference had replaced greed at a time when Kirk Abbott needed greed on his side. United Stores slipped from fifteen, which was Kirk's average cost for three and a half million shares, to twelve on light volume. Lack of interest and occasional panicky sellers lowered it to ten and five-eighths.

At that point, Kirk pledged the stock in his name, enabling him to acquire two and a half million additional shares at what he knew to be a bargain price. But the market continued to deteriorate.

Business was fine in the stores and, despite an itchy Board of Directors that resented the young entrepreneur, United

Stores received favorable comment from industry leaders and Wall Street analysts.

In the midst of five-year cost projections one morning, Kirk received a call from Chicago which his secretary said was urgent.

"Call a flunky and you never get through," the voice said. "Call the president direct and you get action. What do they say? Always do business with a busy man? That's what they say."

"Who are you?" said Kirk.

"I am Franco Bertelli. You can call me Franco, Mr. Abbott."

"What can I do for you?" Kirk said. "Shirt too small? Suit the wrong color? I'm a busy man, as you said."

"I believe you've dealt with a man in Paris," said Franco, "an Egyptian, I'm told. His bank's name is on a loan to you. And, if I understand the situation correctly, I and several of my associates are in fact the people responsible for providing the funds for that loan."

Kirk said nothing.

"Are you there, Mr. Wheeler-Dealer?"

"I'm here."

"I and my associates do not like the trend of the stock market, Mr. Abbott. Nor do we like the liquidity situation of six million shares when United Stores traded a total of forty-seven hundred shares last week. And, need I add, the shares were traded in the wrong direction."

"I don't like it any better than you do."

"I suggest you take a little trip to Chicago, Mr. Abbott. I have a sudden yearning to meet a captain of industry."

Kirk had his hair cut in his office at five-thirty that evening. And caught a commercial flight to Chicago at seven. Out of Kennedy.

Kirk was unusually calm when he left Franco. He had the

irrational belief of the winner that somehow everything was going to be all right. He had been impressed with Franco the way American children are impressed with the villains of our history: Jesse James, Billy the Kid, Legs Diamond, Al Capone. Kirk swaggered into his taxicab and said, "Airport. TWA," out of the side of his mouth. He smoked a cigar, impressed with a sense of being outside the law. He thought himself suddenly to be a gangster and enjoyed the fantasy. In first class he ordered the way he felt Franco might order: "Scotch, rocks, splash of water."

But after the second Scotch he felt the crawl of fear, starting in his spine and moving up his back. Fifty. Million. Dollars. They were squeezing him for the fifty million and the stock was ten and five-eighths.

"Is something the matter, Mr. Abbott?" the stewardess said. "Would another Scotch help, or were two too many?" She smiled at him, since meeting men like Kirk Abbott was the reason she had become a stewardess.

"I need help," Abbott told her. "How do you get hold of a lot of money in a hurry?"

She sat on the edge of the seat and let her arm rub against his body. The lights were down and people slept in first class. "You know what I do when I need money?" she said. "I go to rich people. Rich people usually have what I need. And they've got so much of it. You know," she said, "much too much of it."

Later that night the stewardess took Kirk into the first class john and told him, "If you get laid up here, you're a member of the mile-high club." She hiked up her skirt and told him to sit down. Then she squatted on him. "It's easy," she said, "if you've been doing it for a long time. I like to do it in narrow places."

Kirk insisted that she take fifty dollars and she tucked it away. "Dirt poor in Texas," she said. "My daddy told me that if I grew up beautiful, a beautiful girl from Texas could always have it from rich men. 'Too many rich men,' he'd say, so I'm never in trouble."

All the rest of the flight and all the next day, Kirk wrote personal advertisements for the unique people he needed. Advertisements for *Hump*. Advertisements for *The Atlantic*. Advertisements for the *Wall Street Journal*. Advertisements for *Flying*. Advertisements for the *Village Voice*. "Need experts for experiments in fear and greed," one of the ads said. "Unique opportunities for the enterprising. Must possess special physical and emotional characteristics. Rewards commensurate with ability. Reply box number."

United Stores closed at ten and one-quarter the next day. Kirk Abbott mailed off the ads and the fees, in cashier's checks, at six-thirty, just after the Pacific Coast Exchange had halted trading.

Then he called in Ted Bronson, who seemed hesitant and tense. "I told you so," Kirk said. "I warned you."

"I made a big mistake extending those markdowns," Bronson admitted. "You did warn me and you were right. What now?"

"Nothing. Life goes on, Teddy."

"You didn't tell the board?"

"I told them it was my decision."

Kirk went back to his papers and his comptroller left him alone.

"I'm coming home for dinner," Kirk had told his wife earlier. "It would be nice to have some good meat for a change. A steak. I feel the need for some good meat."

Grace Abbott instructed the cook and, although it was only the middle of the afternoon, she decided to have a drink.

┌─────────┐
│   7   │
└─────────┘

RIGHT-HAND MAN
LEGAL BACKGROUND PREFERRED. ASST. TO A HEAVY
HITTER. COMPENSATION OPEN. NO MARRIED NEED APPLY.
Box 1546 Wall St. Journal

Michael Cagnina read the *Wall Street Journal* every day. And he read the *New York Times* every day. And he believed that there was great inequality in the United States that could be alleviated by distributing monies from large corporations and individuals to the under-privileged. He believed in democracy and he believed in the busing of schoolchildren. Michael Cagnina was a lawyer who found his life's work at the Democratic convention in Chicago in 1968. Using the vacation time from his law firm, Cagnina went to Chicago out of outraged principle, and he was never happier in his life than when he was beaten to the ground by a nightstick. He stayed up for forty-seven straight hours then, swapping stories, drinking wine and blowing grass. He went back to his law firm to collect two weeks' salary and quit, resolved to spend his time educating the poor, telling them what lay beyond the ghetto. He had been married but it didn't last. She wanted . . . things. He wanted to strip himself of . . . things. He had been a tennis player, a scuba diver, but he gave up sports. He worked as a storefront lawyer in Spanish Harlem, walking tall, with sandy hair, a gift from his mother who had been an actress. From his father he inherited a sense of quest. His father, American-born of an upper-class Italian family, had been killed during the war, an officer and hero.

Michael Cagnina labored for McGovern in 1972 and became increasingly committed, after the election and Watergate, to improving the conditions of the poor. He wandered the country, listening to people, doing odd jobs, becoming frustrated at what he was unable to accomplish. He was drawn back to New York the way people are drawn back who need the city. "The legal profession is the hot area of the seventies," a Kansas judge told him. "You want to help people? Go home and practice law and help people. Get yourself cleaned up. You can only do good when you're strong."

When Michael Cagnina answered the ad in the *Wall Street Journal* he was desperate. He was committed to service, but he needed a breakthrough; he needed a leader.

After listening to Alex for an hour, walking through Central Park (they met in front of Rumpelmayer's), he was embarrassed to find that he was becoming physically excited. Alex spun stories for him of building black businesses, funding Puerto Rican little leagues, bankrolling birth control centers in major cities. He told him of his dreams for America, working within the fabric of the founding fathers. "The land, the people, are all here," Alex said. "We just need redirection and leadership. The Panthers never got any support from the people. The yippies were clowns. We need a man on horseback, the way every people's democracy has needed a man on horseback. What would you do, Michael, if I suddenly kicked you in the balls?"

"I'd get off the ground and beat in your head. In any way that I could. I'd stay at you until I wore you down. Any way I could."

Alex aimed a kick at Michael's balls, hard and fast. But

Michael jumped aside, catching the force of it mainly on his left thigh. He was tall but he was very quick. Years spent playing tournament racket sports taught him to move. He was on Alex in an instant, chopping him hard in the neck before Alex could kick him away. "Okay," Alex panted. "I had to know what you believe — and how much." Alex hugged him and took him to a bank near Seventy-ninth Street and Central Park West, and gave Michael a cashier's check for one thousand dollars. "Cash it," Alex said. "It's as good as money. Consider it an advance upon entering a new profession. There is ultimately enough to set you free to do as you choose. What every man wants. I only warn you, the people with whom you share the next two years are not all as motivated as you. Some want revenge; some want evil. If you want good, that's your problem. But we shall be a means to each other's end."

"What do you want?" Michael asked him.

"I want it all," Alex answered him. "I want different things every day. I want to see if brains are still enough in this country."

"Then why did you kick me in the balls?"

Alex shrugged. "Brains aren't enough. Go cash the check."

Michael Cagnina cashed the check.

"You spend your life working your ass off," Louis Carlson said, "so someday you can sit in the sun and go fishing. But something always happens. Maybe the kids are right. Don't work your ass off until it's too late. Go sit in the sun when you're young." Newspaper reporters furiously penciled down his words.

"We know all about philosophy," one of them said. "What we want to know is, did you pay the ransom?"

"Of course not. Who said millions for defense but not one cent for tribute? Who said that, Roosevelt? It's not important. What is important is that every generation has its Jack the Rippers. You cannot knuckle under to this kind of shit. Otherwise, you might just as well pack it in."

Carlson's office was crowded with people: police, FBI, television cameramen, insurance people, banking people. They all looked as if they wished themselves elsewhere. The familiar excitement of dogs smelling death.

"We heard you paid the ransom," said the same reporter, pressing for direct answers.

"The *New York Times* hasn't been right in twenty years," said Carlson. "And you can quote me. Anybody in business who works hard for something, they're ready to tear down. Peerless Oil has not and *will* not pay a dime to any terrorists. If I have to hire a private army to protect property, I'm ready to do it. You can call me a tough old bastard and maybe that's right. But no one is going to push me around."

Several Peerless employees applauded and the red light on Carlson's phone flashed a call. "I said no phone calls," Carlson yelled, and his secretary rushed in to apologize. She worried about Mr. Carlson not coming through on promises he had made in the past.

"It's them, Mr. Carlson," she said.

He wanted to wave everyone out of his office, but the issue had become like an army physical: everyone holds his breath and drops his drawers in front of everyone else.

"Admit it," said the voice.

Carlson hissed into his phone. Cameras whirled, FBI equipment taped, flashbulbs popped, reporters pressed into Carlson's desk and strained to hear. Horror stories belong to everyone in America.

"I can't do that," Carlson said. "Why don't you go bother Exxon for awhile, or Gulf? Everyone's dumping on Gulf."

"You being a funny man, Mr. Carlson? I imagine we'll get around to your competitors. But we thought we'd start with you, because of your fine sense of humor. Suppose we call the newspapers and demand immediate evacuation of all people from oil farm areas? Let's say every oil farm you got? Let's say a half-mile radius?"

"You're bluffing. I can tell you're bluffing. How do I know you're not just some NYU graduate student sniffing glue?"

"Stay cool, Mr. Carlson. Better save the sports page to fan yourself with." The connection was broken.

Outside the Peerless Oil building Michael Cagnina signaled thumbs down from a pay phone. Enrico Boaz, eating a hotdog and standing next to an umbrella cart on Madison Avenue, pressed a button on his electronic signaler and, straining his ears, heard a brief pop far above him. Forty stories up, on top of the Peerless building, the air-conditioning apparatus splattered, returning the building to conditions that stitchers labored in forty years before in the women's garment district: no air conditioning, no fans, no relief from the summer's oppressive smell. Again Carlson was called to the phone.

"Admit it," said Michael Cagnina from a phone booth in a bar on Sixty-first Street. "Admit it or you and your happy family of employees will walk down forty floors. Blowing elevator banks is much more complicated than air conditioners. But life must be a challenge, right, Mr. Carlson? Admit it." Cagnina hung up and went back to finish a beer.

Men at the bar talked about the explosion. "Them people from Con Edison. They live to fuck everybody up. They wait till it's summer. They wait till it's hot."

"Con Edison ain't up on a building," someone else said. "They're in the streets."

"Con Edison's everywhere, shithead. It's power, ain't it?"

"It's power but they're goin' broke."

Louis Carlson looked around at all the people in his office. They were quiet. The sudden loss of cool air made everyone look ruffled and uncertain. "We paid it," he said softly to the room. "We paid it hoping to hell that they're picked up soon. We can't have millions of dollars in stock values go down the drain by stockholders selling Peerless. Not to mention the property loss. And what if people get hurt? Anything could happen. We paid it and we hope you newspapers will be responsible for once. And that you police and smart Federal guys will stop bugging men's rooms and get off your duffs to find these bastards. And get out of here. I've got a business to run. Donnelly. You stick around. I want somebody to stick around."

William Farley became president of Federated Utilities by playing it safe. Superefficient in the accounting department, he eventually became comptroller. Dealing with the City of New York, Nassau and Orange counties, he became a subtle administrator, ruffling no feathers, making no waves. He kept his nose clean, made no enemies, and was mistaken numerous times for Warren Burger, whom he resembled, a resemblance which did him no harm. He was the perfect president of a large utility. He wasn't surprised at all to receive a letter from the People's Revolutionary Army asking for one million dollars in exchange for six months of peace. He quietly called his Board of Directors into emergency session and read them the letter.

"You called me away from Nantucket to listen to that?" one of them said. The other directors all agreed. "They're going to give us a demonstration," the first director said. "Then they'll call back to hear a decision. The demonstration is free, I assume. What are they going to do, parade in front of City Hall with signs saying Federated Utilities is unfair to people who want something for nothing?" The directors laughed. But William Farley didn't laugh. He knew that Louis Carlson had paid two hundred and fifty thousand dollars and that the damage of precedent had been done. The directors voted unanimously to ignore the demand and they filed out of Farley's office in annoyance.

"Basically, Bill Farley's got a clerk's mentality," one of them said. The others agreed.

"You do one of two things with crank letters," another director said. "A, you toss them out, or B, if they are particularly clever, you bring them home to show your wife the kind of drivel we put up with on a daily basis."

They were waiting for the elevators when the power flickered and died in the building, on the block, up and down the length of Eighty-sixth Street. Reports came filtering back to the executive offices of businesses shut down, people trapped in darkness on trains, in elevators. People inconvenienced and angry. People frightened. The directors wandered back into their conference room, holding onto one another for direction, like circus elephants leading each other in a parade. They buzzed in unison around the table. "Blew two major generators; destroyed a power station. In the city, mind you. Not up the Hudson, but in the city, in broad daylight."

"What about people in iron lungs? I always think of that."

"What about lawsuits?"

"What about the stock?"

"I called. It's down two and a half, heavy trading. One of those bastard funds in Boston dumped their entire position, I'm told. Those guys don't care, just dump it on the market. Those Boston guys wouldn't give shit to the crows."

"If it'll stop a panic, maybe a million is cheap."

"You think like that or talk like that, and we're all in the crapper."

Farley asked for a new vote in the darkness, with candles stuck in ashtrays. The directors looked like members of a coven, shrouded in shadows that they never made. A phone call was passed through to Farley during the meeting. By that time the police and FBI were present, their flashlights focused on the conference table, giving everyone there the appearance of being interrogated, with direct spotlights in their faces. The voice on the phone was amplified on an adapter to the entire room; tape recorders took down every word. "I assume you're prepared to pay," the voice said. And without waiting for an answer it continued: "You will send out for the money and place it in a soft leather case. One that will not split when dropped from large heights. Your messenger will proceed to the Suffolk County Airport on Long Island. Without any company, please. Your messenger is to charter a plane and fly due west. I'll call you back. Wait for the call and enjoy yourself. Think of the pilgrims who made candles to while away their time."

The voice was studious, almost kind. It was Michael Cagnina, calling from the lobby of the Museum of Modern Art. When he finished, he had enough time to wander through the upper floors, spending long minutes on Monet.

A state police pilot in an American Yankee Traveler flew west from the Suffolk County Airport. A little man with eyes narrowed from a lifetime of squinting sat next to the pilot, squinting at the countryside below them. A rifle with a telescopic sight lay across his lap, a soft leather satchel from Mark Cross sat between his legs. "I'm itching to shoot a head off a body," the little man said. "With some altitude and these steel-jacketed motha's, this baby can send a head into orbit if you catch it right. Got to be exceptional grouping on the neck. But it can be done."

"You're a big hero, Fly."

"I told you, don't call me Fly."

"Okay, Fly," said the pilot.

They were over Westchester and the pilot knew that squads of police, four helicopters, and several small planes were strung over the route heading due west from Suffolk County Field. The radio crackled on. "Change course to 270 degrees, over."

"Roger," said the pilot.

Michael Cagnina was giving instructions by phone to the
control tower at Suffolk. The tower relayed the messages to
the Traveler. Bill Farley and several of his directors sat in
the control tower. They stared at the telephone. It rang and
Farley answered. He listened and hung up. "Change the
plane's course to due south and immediately ground all
helicopters and light planes in the area. Tell all state police
to stay where they are. At least six cars have been spotted."

"Change course to 180 degrees," the radio operator spoke
to the messenger plane.

"Look," Farley said, "we want to grab these guys more
than you do, but we don't want anybody killed. No blood
can be on the hands of Federated Utilities. We want a
benevolent, kindly image. No violence. We are prepared to
pay. I do not want the police causing bloodshed and blam-
ing us for it."

"It's out of your hands, Mr. Farley," said a captain in the
state police. "We're gonna waste these guys."

Farley shook his head. The phone rang again.

Instructions were relayed to the pilot and he swung the
plane back to 270 degrees, dropping his altitude to 0400.
The plane banked as it came down, flying across the road
that led to a forest, green and thick. "You think this is it?"
Fly asked the pilot. "Or you think them sum-bitches still
fuckin' around?"

"You are approaching a pasture," the radio operator said.
"Repeat: a pasture. Drop the bag in the pasture and continue course 270, altitude 0400. Hold course and altitude for
ten minutes, then return to this airport. Do not try to detain
terrorists. Repeat: do not try to detain terrorists."

"There's the pasture," Fly said to the pilot. "I don't see
nothin'."

"Open the canopy."

The plane swooped low and the little man swung the
Mark Cross bag out, sending it down, end over end. Fly

looked back, his rifle pointing toward the ground. *Kareee, kareee* — he loosed two rounds after the bag in frustration. Then he fired two more shots aimlessly up into the blue sky. "Those ought to surprise any sum-bitch who's around when they come down."

"Shut the canopy and sit down," said the pilot. "I don't give a shit about you, but I don't want any trouble."

"You don't believe I can take a man's head off with this thing?"

"Come off it," the pilot said in disgust, picking up altitude and holding his course. The pasture disappeared in the distance and the leather bag lay alone in the empty field, looking like a giant cow flop in the yellow summer grass.

Two men raced onto the field, one of them carrying a metal detector, the other a canvas laundry bag.. First checking the Mark Cross satchel carefully, they shook the contents into the laundry bag, left the satchel on the ground, and raced for the cover of the forest.

Alex had paid twenty-one dollars cash for a tent site with a platform at Wildwood State Park on Long Island. Seated at a camp table, he waited quietly in a bathing suit for the others. Six bridge chairs were grouped around the table. Alex felt like a Civil War general. He could see himself in Union uniform in a Matthew Brady daguerreotype. His briefcase lay closed on the table in front of him.

"We got it," Scott Dutton said, entering the tent. Edwards, the black man, came in behind him carrying the laundry bag. Then Boaz, Michael Cagnina, Higgins and Glory Cohen pushed into the tent.

"This is a lot of money to be paid for fun and games," Alex said. "I reiterate that we are deadly serious; that any breach of security or awareness will result in immediate punishment."

"We ain't in school, man," said Enrico Boaz.

"Well, I'll correct you on that one, Mr. Boaz. You *are* in

school. And I'm the headmaster, the principal, the boss."
Alex counted the money out onto the table and stacked it
into six piles. Then he took six envelopes from his briefcase
and passed them out. "Two hundred thousand dollars split
six ways is thirty-three thousand, three hundred thirty-three
dollars and thirty-three cents apiece. Not bad for opening
week. David Merrick could learn a lot from us."

"We'll kill 'em on Broadway," said Boaz.

"You have a sense of humor, Mr. Boaz. A good thing in
a partner."

"You call this partners?" Boaz said. "Give us ten percent
and you keep ninety? A million for you. You ain't a leader,
you a pig." The others said nothing. They concentrated.
The odor of new canvas filled their nostrils. The paper bills
were old, worn soft by many fingers. None of the bills were
in sequence.

Alex pushed his briefcase toward Boaz. "You want it all,
Mr. Free Spirit? Take it. Our deal was 90–10. No one quits
for two years and I have absolute control over operations.
What you do with your money is your business. Give it to
charity, buy an El Dorado, piss it away. Anyone want out?"

No one spoke. They took their envelopes and watched
Alex. "Glory," he said, "you haven't been to a beach in a
long time. We may as well use the water as long as we're
here. Right? Saltwater is a great restorative and I've already
paid a dollar to use the parking lot. Waste not, want not,
gentlemen. Remember that slogan for any groups you may
join. I'll be contacting you all in the usual way. I expect it
shall be soon, so stay close to your neighborhood pubs."
Alex left the tent with Glory, and the others scattered.

It was Friday afternoon. With thousands of people flock-
ing to Long Island and away to Connecticut, the police
would not dare set up roadblocks to stop every car. No
American would stand to have his summer weekends ruined
in such a way.

Alex and Glory swam for a while. Then they lay down in the sand and looked out to sea. "When this is over, I would like to live by the sea," Alex said. "What does Glory Cohen want to do?"

"I'd like to be able to stop fucking everybody I feel attracted to. And I'd like to stop running. The country was angry when we ripped off the bank; I thought there was a place for me in the new order. My professors taught me that, and I was smart."

"You'll have enough money to go away. Change your face; change anything."

"It's going to get worse, isn't it, Alex? You don't just want money, you want to change things, don't you?" Alex smiled and kissed her. She opened her mouth immediately. Glory's mouth was a constant surprise; she engulfed people with it. She wanted to take people entirely inside her when she kissed.

"You always come right from the office to the beach?" a voice said in back of them. It was a security policeman patrolling the park. His uniform was three sizes too big, all that the Park Commission could drum up for summer employees. "You always bring your suitcase to the beach?" he said.

Alex sat up. He reached for his briefcase and opened it up. "Ham sandwiches," he said. "Chopped egg salad. Some ham and cheese." The briefcase was full of sandwiches wrapped in cellophane bags. "It's a picnic," Alex said. "Want one?"

The security guard was bored. He was tired of walking through sand and water in his heavy black shoes. "Throw me a ham and cheese," he said. "I'll eat it and get out of your hair. We got the word to check everybody." He took a big bite of the sandwich. "You gonna make someone a good wife, lady," he said, and he walked off along the sand, his black shoes digging deeply into the wetness.

Alex smiled and tasted her again. "Glory," he said at last, "I think you invented the tongue."

It was dark in Grace Abbott's bedroom, although the last traces of sun peeped around the closed window shades.

"Can't you do something about that damn dog," Teddy Bronson said, peering outside through a crack in the shade. Kirk's dog scratched on the bedroom door, whimpering.

"He'll stop in a while and go away," Grace said. "Don't be so nervous. Kirk's off for Europe and the kids are sleeping at friends'."

"I hate to use another man's bedroom."

"But it doesn't matter about another man's wife?"

"It sounds stupid," said Bronson. "But you draw lines somewhere. Kirk seems even stranger than usual. Totally preoccupied. Federated Utilities paid a million dollars' ransom today. Kirk is against payoffs."

"What does he care about William Farley?"

"Kirk owes fifty million and his stock is pledged for collateral. The more terrorism, the worse the stock market acts. He's got to be up against a wall."

"He's built all the walls himself."

"Will you stay with me when I'm running United Stores?" Bronson turned and looked at Grace.

She balanced an ashtray on her belly and flicked ashes from her cigarette into it. "I'll probably take up with the new comptroller," she said. "It seems I'm always fated to be number two."

"That's not very kind."

"What's kind?" she asked.

Ted Bronson came over to the bed and removed the ashtray.

"I told you the dog would go away," Grace said. "You ignore people and animals long enough and they always go away."

Kirk had the edges of magazines lined up exactly upon coffee tables, his suits hung in closets like guardsmen, his lawns were cultivated perfection. Nothing was out of place on his desk, in his drawers, in his life. As easily as he could tell which pencils needed sharpening, Kirk was immediately aware that Grace had betrayed him. His discovery of her infidelity shattered Kirk's sense of precision, his trust in order.

He had returned from visits to the southern stores: Memphis, Atlanta, Little Rock. And he wanted to linger with Grace over a long dinner in the bar at "21." He wanted people to see them together, to see that an ordered business life could extend to marriage. A good marriage, a beautiful wife.

Even in the cab on the way to dinner Grace was preoccupied. She tried chatting happily about nothing. Kirk knew instantly that something was wrong. He interrupted her gossip.

"What happened with the children?"

She knocked on a wooden handle of her pocketbook. "Nothing. They're terrific."

"Something's wrong. I haven't even had my kiss."

"I kissed you at the airport."

"You brushed my cheek. You know I can't stand fake kisses. Christ, I'd rather shake hands than have anyone brush my cheek."

She kissed him then and opened her mouth. But the evening was spent mostly in strained small talk which lapsed into silence.

Grace Abbott was a poor actress and a worse liar. Growing up, she had been given everything. She had no need to lie. But after her marriage she needed assurances. She desperately needed the feeling that she was loved not for her image but for herself. She controlled Teddy Bronson the way she never could control Kirk. And Bronson adored her.

Kirk found out because Kirk could find out anything he wanted to know. He never accused Grace. He merely became cool, withdrawn, lost in the running of United Stores. He was not a modern man. Alone, he brooded about someone else possessing his wife. It gnawed at him when he had moments by himself: on planes, in hotel rooms. It obsessed him on the way to meetings and in the early hours of sleepless mornings.

One night he arrived home to find his dog had been cut and bruised seriously in a fight. "The vet says it was a raccoon," Grace told him.

Kirk ignored dinner and sat up the night with his cocker spaniel, talking to him, soothing him, until the dog slept. At dawn he came in to Grace and woke her gently. She sat up immediately.

"What's wrong?" she said. "Christ, you're dressed."

"I wanted to tell you. Sandy's all right."

"You woke me to tell me that?"

"I want you. I really woke you to tell you that."

She lay back. "I'm asleep," she said, and rolled over.

Kirk watched the dawn in Greenwich, Connecticut, and cried for the first time in years.

Kirk was not a modern man.

del escritorio de
Antonio Figueroa

June 15th

He loves me. He loves
me not. I saw a
scruffy American girl
waiting in line at
Kennedy. She wore
jeans and was with
her husband who
carried both their
tennis jackets. She had
a patch ironed onto
the rear pocket. "Pussy
Power", it said. I
wonder if she knows
what it means.

A. will be pleased
with what I bring.
I think he'll be pleased.

From the scratch pad
of Gena Reynolds

8

Kirk Abbott was checked quickly through Customs at Heathrow Airport outside of London. He carried one hanging suitcase with two suits, a toilet kit and enough shirts, underwear and accessories to last him anywhere from several days to a month. Kirk could carry the bag on board and hang it up inside the cabin. There was nowhere in the world he hadn't traveled, and he knew all the tricks of easy exit, off hours, and simplified arrangements.

Before he stepped out into the daylight, Kirk put on a pair of horn-rimmed dark glasses. Some people cannot wear dark glasses without looking uncomfortable. Kirk looked as if he wore them in theaters, in the rain, anytime. In dark glasses he looked as if he were constantly on the verge of making a deal.

The nasal horn of the yellow Humber Supersnipe blew at Kirk as he waited outside the terminal. A young woman rolled down her driver's window and yelled at him. "You have all your luggage?"

Kirk nodded.

"Trunk's open," Gena Reynolds said. "Have a good flight? London's been hot as hell this week. The air just hangs, you know?"

Kirk got in on the passenger side and settled into the

comfortable leather cushions. As Gena moved with the traffic toward London, she reached with her left hand into her shoulder bag, which lay between the seats. Extracting an envelope, she tossed it into Kirk Abbott's lap. He tore open the seal. "Good girl," he said, "you've got it." Kirk looked at the picture of himself with horn-rimmed glasses staring out at him from a Costa Rican passport. The name across the face read Costas Anastos. "What they lack in stability, they make up in color," Kirk said. "South America, Central America. Lands of opportunity. What about the bank charter?"

"Someone as vain as you should have contact lenses," Gena Reynolds said to him. "Why don't you have contact lenses, Mr. Anastos?"

Gena shifted gears smoothly, moving through the Hammersmith Flyover, in and out, with no effort and along the Great West Road. Her auburn hair was tucked under a leather peaked cap. She looked tweedy, smart, right out of advertisements in *Queen* or *Elle*. She even smelled as if she had been recently scrubbed down in a giant tub with sensible English soap, lightly scented with lavender. She smelled like confidence.

"The bank charter I'm working on," she said. "It will take some time. There are lots of people and lots of money in Costa Rica. And they want lots of things."

"I know you can do it. You're from California," Kirk said. "Have you met the minister of banking and commerce yet?"

They were slowed up by a double-decker bus moving in front of them into London, at Hyde Park Corner.

"I've done better than that," Gena said. "I've beaten him with flyswatters and switched him with a bamboo cane."

Kirk laughed. "You're serious?"

"It's the only way he could make it. Mostly all over the floor. But occasionally he got around to me."

"Is that a problem for you? The involvement?"

"Not as long as I do the whipping."

Kirk watched her while she drove down Piccadilly and on to Nelson's Column at Trafalgar Square. Tourists were taking pictures of other tourists; German youth tours walked in the sunshine, shirts off, packs on their backs. The pigeons grew fat eating bread crusts on the ground and gawoomping noisily from the roof of the National Gallery.

"Drop me at the Savoy," Kirk said, "and take the luggage to the apartment. I imagine I'll be there by four this afternoon."

"You must be exhausted. The time difference."

"I'll nap at the apartment if I get everything wrapped up today." Kirk got out in the Savoy turnaround, near the entrance to the Grille. He touched his palm to Gena's face and then signaled good-bye. She moved out slowly in the Humber behind a row of sober cabs.

Kirk took the Grille elevator to the eleventh floor and walked down a corridor to a suite of rooms where a dapper little man sat behind a Louis Quinze table writing notes on hotel paper in the large flowery script often used by little dapper men.

"I'm sorry your itinerary did not include Geneva this time, Mr. Abbott," the man said. "I dislike leaving Switzerland in the summers. It does not increase my fondness for you at all. I understand you want an extension?"

"Mr. Péter, I'm on the verge of achieving everything I want to achieve. I need time."

The banker smiled. "Everyone needs time, Mr. Abbott. You can imagine I hear that story. In many different languages, I might add."

"I assume, however, you didn't come this distance to say no."

The banker put his pen down for the first time. "With a standby fee of three million dollars, added to the face amount of the loans, we will extend the loans for thirty days. United

Stores, I see, is now eight and a half. The value of the collateral is now fifty-five million dollars."

"The stock is cheap," Kirk said. "A great buy. Have you talked with Singapore about this?"

"We have. I want to tell you that they are not at all happy about it. Reluctantly, they have approved. It seems the gentleman in Paris has taken a liking to you. God knows why. The French are whimsical."

"And the Swiss can be a pain in the ass."

"Don't add the black mark of rudeness to your growing list of deficiencies, Mr. Abbott. I was supposed to be on Lake Como this week."

The banker pushed papers at Kirk. He signed without reading them. "Have an exciting life," Kirk said, as he left the dapper little banker still seated quietly behind his Louis Quinze table.

"Not exciting, Mr. Abbott," he answered to his back. "But — as you Americans say — a sure thing."

Outside, Kirk put on his glasses and took a cab to Basinghall Street in the City. Kirk entered a brokerage office, a branch of a New York Stock Exchange member firm. Showing identification, he was led to a rear office, past the chattering teletypes, past the ticker tapes flashing prices from New York. He stopped momentarily at a broker's desk machine and punched UNS, the symbol for United Stores. Eight and five-eighths, it said to him. An uptick. He quickly erased the symbol and the price.

A jolly man jumped to his feet in the office Kirk entered. He was fat and florid-faced and looked as if he would be at home in lederhosen, yodeling between steins of beer. Yet he was turned out meticulously in a glen plaid summerweight suit, made for him on Kowloon Road.

"Mr. Abbott," he said.

"Mr. Rhinelander," Kirk said to him. "A pleasure. The

impression one gets over many phone conversations and letters is often so different from reality."

"You find me a shock?" Rhinelander laughed.

"I said a pleasure. I meant a pleasure."

"You have some souvenirs of your country for me." Rhinelander closed the door to the office. "I came in from Switzerland only this morning," he said. "Not a nuisance at all. We have enough legal business in London to make the trip worthwhile. Other clients." He shrugged. "I hope you don't mind a stockbroker's office, but I trade with these people in Geneva. I am a favored account. Commodities mostly. And they always kindly provide me with office space. Comfortable and cheap, no?"

"You're my kind of lawyer," Kirk said, snapping open his briefcase and removing the false top section which contained crossword puzzles and two back issues of *Punch*. Kirk counted out one million eight hundred thousand dollars in Treasury checks and pushed the pile to the fat lawyer. Treasury checks could be issued in large denominations and were as good as cash anywhere in the world.

Rhinelander counted the small pile himself and reached the same total. He leaned back in his chair and let his stomach grab for air. Rhinelander felt happy in the presence of cash. "Ahhh," he said, while Kirk waited. "As you wished, Anastos, S.A., has been incorporated in The Netherlands Antilles, with broad corporate powers including banking, investments and mutual funds. It has qualified in Costa Rica. All the stock is owned by a Dutch parent corporation with the same name. The sole stockholder of the parent is a friendly Dutch lawyer. Friendly because he is a distant cousin. I have distant cousins in every European country. All attorneys. Our grandfather was an admirer of the Rothschilds. Much smaller scale, of course, but an admirer, nonetheless. My cousin lives in Amsterdam.

"You own an option to buy all the stock for ten thousand guilder. A bit complicated perhaps, but excellent for taxes. We shall deposit the money in the Credit Suisse and hold it pending further instructions. Yes?" Rhinelander beamed as if he were praising a favorite child.

"Yes," said Kirk, "excellent. Now I want a second corporation set up. A parallel. Call it Gena, S.A. Use another bank, not the Credit Suisse, and another Dutch lawyer. You must have another cousin in Amsterdam. There will be further funds shortly. Very substantial deposits."

Rhinelander signed a receipt with a flourish and handed it to Kirk. "I like you cowboys. I honestly do."

"I'm no cowboy," Kirk said. "Just a struggling businessman. Trying to stay ahead of the Joneses."

"All Americans are cowboys," said Rhinelander, standing up and escorting Kirk to the door. They said good-bye and Kirk walked through the board room. He couldn't resist checking United Stores once more on the quote machine. Eight and three-quarters, it said. Up another eighth. A good morning.

Kirk awakened from a long nap in the apartment he had rented in Smith Square, a narrow court of townhouses that reminded him of stories from Sherlock Holmes: fogbound small places of mystery and fear. He had let himself into the apartment earlier in the afternoon, found a note from Gena saying that she was off to the Silver Vaults to look for a coffee service and that there was food and Whitbread Ale in the fridge if he were hungry. Kirk had an ale with some cheese and a few slices of cold roast. Then he collapsed into a deep, jet-lagged sleep. When he awoke, slowly and with great effort, he found it difficult to remember where he was. Kirk looked at his watch. Seven o'clock. He stretched and felt himself in a delicious limbo, without memory.

"Feel better?" Gena had come quietly into the bedroom

and turned on a small lamp near the door. She was wearing a simple, short cotton dress and looked elegant. Clean. California. She came over and sat on the bed.

"I always used to like naps," Kirk said. "Needed them. It seems it's been years since I could afford the time. So much to do." He sat up.

"Here," Gena said, handing him a glass. "It's cheap Chablis on ice. Couldn't find anything American in the cabinets." Kirk smiled gratefully and took a long swallow. Gena had mixed it with soda.

"What's your real name?" she said to him, folding her legs beneath herself in an unashamed lotus position.

"How can I answer questions when that's looking at me? Is it red? I can't tell." Kirk reached out and touched her softly, experimentally. He brought his hand back wet. "It must be the wine," he said, and reached for her. She came to him.

"It's red, Mr. Anastos," she said. "Believe me, it's red."

Later they split a bottle of champagne at the Garrick Club, where Rhinelander had given him an introduction. Seated beneath a portrait of Edmund Kean, they both felt enormously comfortable, wonderfully privileged. An ancient waiter brought them another bottle and they luxuriated in every sip. The waiter disapproved of them holding hands, but he made no sign. He merely looked away and attributed their foolishness to the fact that they were American. Kirk paid in cash.

For dinner they walked to Soho, where they dined next to the upstairs window of the Dumpling Inn. Rich Peking dumplings with rice wine, pressed duck, apple fritters for dessert.

"It's difficult to believe we don't know each other very well," said Kirk.

"We're getting there," Gena said. "What's your real name?"

"My passport says Costas Anastos."

"What about your other passports? You certainly don't screw like a Greek."

Kirk rubbed her cheek and leaned forward to kiss her lips. Softly. "There are times for disappointments," he said. "And times for happiness out of all time. You'll know when you have to know."

2, 2 5 0, 0 0 0.0 0
2, 2 5 0, 0 0 0.0 0 T

.0 0 T

.0 0 T

.0 0 T

From the tally sheet
of Kirk Abbott

9

At Scarsdale High School, Glory Cohen was generally considered to be an ugly teenager with big tits. She spent her junior year with a French family in Toulouse, summers at camp in Maine, and school vacations doing volunteer work in drug rehabilitation centers on Staten Island and the Bronx.

Because of Glory's dedication, her mother gave up May, her black cleaning lady, who had taken the train out from 125th Street for years, three days a week. Glory's mother hired a weekly cleaning service of uniformed men and began to criticize her friends who maintained live-in help. Glory's father gave money to Grambling and the Southern Christian Leadership. He was thrilled when Glory brought two black girls home for Thanksgiving from her first year at Brandeis. When she heard the term "lip-service liberal" for the first time, her reaction was — not me. She thought she proved it when she went to bed with Ralph Chadwick, a campus hanger-on from Boston's Roxbury district, who became the rage at Brandeis because he had been given a five-hundred-dollar advance from a New York publisher on a novel. It was the first boy for her who hadn't been Jewish. "I just love your tits, Glory," Ralph used to tell her.

"Will you put me in the novel?" she'd asked him. And he'd just grab for her tits and laugh.

Things were always serious for Glory, but Martin Luther King's assassination and Kent State triggered such anger in her that she joined the SDS and soon outgrew their demonstrations in her eagerness to rip off and destroy. On night marches in Harvard Square and through Boston she would become frenzied: a dark, lusty, latter-day Madame Defarge. She threw bricks through windows. Screamed slogans. Jumped on policemen's backs, her nails grabbing for the flesh of their cheeks. Afterwards she was always violently nervous, hyperkinetic. She would demand to be screwed by the most daring, the most destructive of the young revolutionaries. A rock group wrote a song about her called "Rutting Mama." She was the one who challenged three of her lovers to knock over the Cambridge Savings Bank. "No one will fire into all those kids," she said, planning the robbery. "Not after Kent State. We just mix with the street people, they'll protect us."

They did it in broad daylight, just like that, at lunchtime with a borrowed Mustang and four old M–1 carbines stolen from supply at Fort Devens by a friend of a friend who later deserted to Canada. An ancient security guard, who couldn't take retirement from Boston Edison and went to work standing up in the Cambridge Savings Bank seven hours a day, thought that Glory and her friends were a joke.

Glory thought he was a joke and killed him with a clip of World War II ammunition at very short range.

She was shaking so hard with excitement that the others had to slap her to get her to leave the body. They abandoned the Mustang in Central Square and scattered to various crash pads around the city. Within a week Glory was in New York City and on the FBI's ten most wanted list, the youngest female ever to achieve that distinction.

Several times in the next few years she felt that she would be taken. She was sure that certain people she met were either informers or jealous enough to tip the authorities. But the underground kept her on the move, kept her changing appearances and jobs and homes. After the bank, she broke all contact with her family. As far as Glory was concerned, they were people she had never known.

A friend sent Glory the ad in the Boston *Phoenix*. Passed along by the underground network, it reached her in Columbus, Ohio, where she lived in a house near the Ohio State campus posing for life classes and waiting for action. "Looking for the New World?" the ad said. "Action to change the course of history? Unusual and dangerous opportunity. Male or female. Black, white or yellow." Glory Cohen answered the ad and the next week hitchhiked to New York.

Roger Damon Dinsmore had built a small loan company in Providence, Rhode Island, into the Omni-Credit Card Corporation, with annual sales of two billion dollars, a listing on the Big Board, offices in every principal city in the world, and over one hundred thousand employees. Dinsmore could never get over the fact of his success and took great pleasure in hopping around the world, watching people pick up their mail and their money at Omni-Credit offices. He found it difficult, if not impossible, to delegate authority. He supervised as many facets of Omni's operation as he was physically able to, initiating all major new changes and all promotions, including direct-mail envelope stuffers. Thus he was at first surprised, and then angry, about a rumor his secretary told him concerning a free merchandise offer for new credit-card holders. Everyone knew that an Omni-Credit Card was the Rolls-Royce of credit cards worldwide, and that the screening of applicants was complicated and selective. Omni certainly never gave away free merchandise.

Dinsmore fumed at the rumor and told two assistants to check it out. "Your wife's on the phone, Mr. Dinsmore," his secretary said.

"Good," he said. "Little mother will know what's going on."

Roger Dinsmore couldn't delegate but he consulted his wife in everything: sought her advice on whatever the company did; whatever he wore; whomever Omni hired at world headquarters in Providence. "Little Mother," Dinsmore said into the phone, smiling at himself for feeling better already. "How funny you should call. I've just been thinking of you."

"Roger Damon Dinsmore," she said. "What in hell and damnation is going on? I've just gotten an Omni card in the mail. An honest-to-goodness blue and white Omni special card with a stuffer saying it's good for a hundred dollars' worth of free meals or merchandise or travel. It's made out in my name and the flyer says it's an introductory offer to housewives. Who the hell needs housewives? You never cleared this harebrained thing with me. And if you sent out more than two of those cards, you're crazy."

"Help, Little Mother," Dinsmore said, feeling himself ready to be sick, knowing the cards were not his cards. "You'd better get down here," he said. "It's those people who threatened us a few weeks ago. I can't believe it. There's no telling how many of those things are out."

"I'll throw on some slacks and be right down. Better call the insurance companies and the FBI."

"Jesus, what do I look under?"

"U.S. Government, and take a pill, and I'll be right over. I'll check with the girls in the neighborhood."

The Omni-Credit Building pointed like a blue and white steel finger at the foot of College Hill in Providence. In Brown University territory it looked like an advertisement for Yale. When Mrs. Dinsmore arrived, she found her hus-

THE KING OF TERRORS 91

band and four of his chief officers slumped in their chairs in the conference room.

"Are you guys gonna roll over and die?" she said.

"They want two million dollars for the cards and the plates," her husband said. "They only wanted a million a week ago, and we ignored the threat."

"Well, I talked with the girls," she said, sitting down at the head of the table. Alice Dinsmore loomed. In a steel-gray pantsuit and iron-gray hair cropped closely to her surprisingly fine-featured head, she looked at the men as if they had all just fouled their trousers. She snorted and tossed five credit cards at them, all made out to her female neighbors, all with identical offers with one hundred dollars' worth of free purchases. "Half the girls have already bought things: clothes, shoes. One bought a sewing machine for two hundred twenty-five dollars. She said she'd never have to pay because the Consumer Protection Law, which covers the sending of unsolicited credit cards. I had to grab her pocketbook to take the card away."

"They've got two hundred thousand cards out now," Dinsmore said, "and they are perfect. Laminated, stamped and dyed perfectly. Two hundred thousand times a hundred dollars is twenty million dollars. And you say people are charging more than a hundred dollars' worth of stuff?"

"How do you know they've got two hundred thousand cards out?"

"They called. Or rather, *he* called. Same guy on the phone two weeks ago. Says they want two million now for their second printing. They've run off ten million cards. Can you believe it? We're ruined."

Alice Dinsmore looked at the men still slumped in their seats. She felt sorry for Roger Damon, who got such pleasure out of seeing people collect their mail at Omni offices in Tokyo and Paris and Rome.

"What do we do, Little Mother?" he said desperately. "We're ruined."

She sighed and reached for a cigarette. "We're not ruined," she said. "We've got the money in Treasury bills. We can write the goddam thing off. Roger Damon Dinsmore, call the bank."

His face lit up and he was pleased he didn't have to make the decision. He came over to her and, in front of his corporate officers, kissed her lightly on the cheek. Two million dollars is jelly beans compared to peace of mind.

The main telephone communication center in Noroton knew no seasons, knew no changes of night or day. Operators worked four shifts of six hours each, groping around their switchboards to keep the systems running until they could grow old and retire, or marry and retire, or make supervisor.

"You know, I never see my husband. It's beautiful," said Ann Duffy, a telephone operator on long distance, serving New York City and upper Connecticut on the midnight to 6:00 A.M. shift. "He's driving the cab in the days and he sleeps at night. He has a beer occasionally with the eleven o'clock news, when I'm having Special K or sometimes All-Bran for breakfast. It's a perfect marriage. Christmas we get three days, we drive to Pittsburgh to visit my mother. Big deal! But for me it's getting away. Long distance, may I help you?"

"May I help?" Ann Duffy said again, thinking of her ten-minute break.

A gloved hand from behind reached over Ann Duffy's shoulder and broke the connection, pulling dozens of wires out of dozens of holes. "You broads always want to be so helpful," the man's voice said. "Help yourselves to a night off. On your feet slowly and leave your bags. Put your hands on your heads and march single file in front of us just like you was a bunch of ducks. No one gets hurt if you act like ducks — stupid and follow the leader." Two men with Uzi submachine guns dressed as telephone linemen and wearing stick-on handlebar mustaches led the operators to the parking lot and into a yellow school bus where they were seated two by two. They were joined by a dozen others several minutes later: servicemen, supervisory personnel, union representatives seeking grievances in the night shift.

When everyone had been cleared out of the building, Michael Cagnina addressed the people in the bus, who all sat in silence, terrified. "We're not out to hurt you," he said. "We're only here to discourage the institutions that exploit you all. When I leave, we shall padlock the doors to this bus. We shall then spray the outside with gasoline. If anyone moves to bust out, or crawl out, one of my men will ignite the fuel. It's a lousy way to die, especially to protect the telephone company. Stay on the bus and sing songs. 'You Are My Sunshine' is a good one to start with. Eventually someone will let you out. If you hear loud noises, don't panic. You're out of range and we're just giving you a few weeks' vacation. With pay, I sincerely hope." Cagnina paused at the door. "Now sing," he said.

They began haltingly and kept it up as the doors were shut and Silver Wheels Edwards pumped water on the windows of the bus from a portable insecticide spray can. Several minutes later, the communications center was blown into that great directory assistance in the sky. The employees on the bus sang "Nearer My God to Thee" and put their heads between their legs, cushioning themselves against shock and doing what they were told to do.

At three forty-three the following afternoon, the telephone company paid two million dollars to the People's Revolutionary Army, behind the Brooklyn Heights Casino. Two million dollars was like so many jelly beans compared to peace of mind.

Flowers, Flowers, Flowers
and The auction

Call police abt. being away.

**From the daily lists
of Grace Abbott**

10

Summer mornings in Greenwich, Connecticut, seem richer, softer, than summer mornings in other towns. Grace Abbott had gotten up earlier than usual, to make her husband breakfast. It was annoying to be married to someone like Kirk. For lots of reasons, she thought. One of the reasons was that he never appeared sleepy in the morning. He always looked fresh. Shining.

"What did you do? Sleep standing up last night?" she said to him. "You look as if you stepped out of a dry cleaner's."

"Did you get up early to abuse me, or make me breakfast?"

Grace poured coffee for both of them and sat down opposite Kirk. "You look fabulous, darling," she said. "But I'd like to know what's going on."

"Strong coffee. It's good," Kirk said and stared at her eyes. "Nothing's going on. I'm trying to run a business and provide for my family's security. This seems to be taking more and more time."

"I called you in Geneva at the Richemond and you weren't registered."

"I went to London," Kirk said. "Geneva came to me; it was more convenient. I telexed the office. They knew."

"It's the idea, Kirk," she said. "I don't want a cliché scene about what's happening to us. But the children see Ted Bronson more than they see you."

"The children will fend for themselves," he said. "They'll make their own way. You never saw your father, for Christ's sake."

"Kirk, I'm not interested in arguments. I want to know what's going on in your head."

"I thought we weren't going to have any clichés." He took a bite of English muffin. "The truth is that I drive home and see all this"— he swept his arm around, indicating the house and everything in it — "and know I'm responsible for it all. And I say to myself, I wonder who lives here. I wonder who's responsible for all this. It's unreal."

"You've been traveling too much. Teddy and I think that perhaps a doctor would be helpful. I mean, you can't seem to talk to anyone close to you."

"Ahhh. Close to you. That's the rub. So you and Teddy think I should see a shrink. It's not enough that I have to contend with the son-of-a-bitch in the office; his shadow is all over the walls of my house."

"I only want everything to be happy. I don't like living in a stage set any more than you do. But I need things. Emotional things, not possessions."

"You know what United Stores means to me, Grace. I don't have to tell you how much thought and work has gone into getting me this far. No one has suffered too much around here. Just me. And I've busted my ass."

"You didn't have to. My money . . ."

"Your money only brings two things with it: strings and money. I want clout. I want everyone to know Kirk Abbott."

"I know. At least, I used to know."

"Look. I want everything happy too. As much as you do. I promise we'll go away this summer with the kids. Martha's Vineyard or the Cape. If you're so friendly with Lisa Bronson, I don't care. Invite them, too."

"It would be so good for you, Kirk. The sun, the saltwater. Yacht club dances, if we go to Nantucket."

"You make the plans. I've only got one more trip abroad this summer. Five days to the Orient."

"Are you planning to open a store in Japan? Why can't I go?"

"Too much hopping around, too many appointments. I'm trying to cover all the bases. With the stock market the way it is, I've got to make sure of long-term money. That's as much as I can tell you."

"I told you a long time ago, I won't push."

"Terrific. Because if you weren't pushing in the last fifteen minutes, then I'm home free."

Beep-beep-a-beep-beep came the rude noise of an automobile horn.

"That's Skelton. I'll have to get into town."

"He blows the horn with more disrespect than any chauffeur in America," Grace said.

"If he thinks he's getting away with something," Kirk answered, "and he stays on the job, that's all I care about. It's the only way to keep help. It's a lesson you might learn." Kirk got up from the breakfast table and leaned down to scratch his dog, who rolled over on his back and whimpered with pleasure. "Something special about you, dog," Kirk said, continuing to play with Sandy.

Honk-honkity-honk-honk went Skelton on the horn.

"Everybody wants a piece of me," said Kirk to the kitchen in general.

"Your trouble, darling," Grace said to him, "is that you can't differentiate between people. You try to treat us all the same."

Kirk touched her breast lightly. She looked mildly annoyed.

"I'm learning," he said. "Thanks for getting up for breakfast. I appreciate it. I really do."

Kirk went out into the Greenwich summer and was driven

down Round Hill Road, past swishing sprinklers and orderly stone walls.

Kirk was in his office working on projections for back-to-school business when his secretary told him that Ted Bronson was outside.

"Are you aware that things are coming down around our ears?" Bronson said, as he entered Kirk's office. "There hasn't been much in the papers, but there isn't a business-man in the country who doesn't know that these ransom requests are knocking the shit out of the fall. No one's ordering goods. People are scared."

"Don't be ridiculous. No one's been killed."

"You've got your head in the sand, Kirk. Some of your best friends are shitting their pants."

"Have I heard that line before?"

Bronson sighed. His earnestness made him impatient. "Something I want to clear with you." He handed Kirk the thick folder of an insurance policy.

Kirk read the title out loud. "Terrorist Act and Business Interruption Direct Damage Insurance Policy. A mouthful," he said. "What is it?"

"A new wrinkle. Something we can use; we're so goddam vulnerable with our stores."

Kirk said nothing and Bronson spilled out his pitch, certain he could get Kirk to rubber-stamp something about which he had already made up his mind.

"It's a fifty-thousand-dollar deductible that will cover ransom demands," Bronson explained. You get a threat, you report it. You get a ransom demand, you report it. Either the insurance company pays the ransom itself, less the deductible, or they refuse to pay. In this case, they are unconditionally liable for all direct loss from terrorist acts and all interruption of business."

"Up to how much?"

"Without limit: all loss of profits, all loss of inventory value. All continuing expenses if you are shut down. In addition, on top of everything else, you get one million dollars of insurance per head on the lives of key executives."

"What kind of fly-by-night outfit came up with this?" Kirk said. "Christ, for everyone's misfortunes there's a hustle."

"Come on," said Bronson. "Look what's been going on. It's four dollars per hundred in premiums. A million dollars, that's forty thousand a year. The idea of running a business is the bottom line. For ten million dollars' coverage, which is what we would need, that's four hundred thousand a year in premiums. Look, I'm a financial man, too. But we've got to move with the times. It's deductible. It has to be. Half of it isn't even ours. The government will pay."

"Who are these people? They can't be Travelers or Prudential."

"Some new London firm. They check out with all the banks and I hear there's big dough behind them: Paris, Geneva, Singapore." Only Kirk's eyebrows betrayed his reaction.

"I'll be going to Singapore this trip," Kirk said. "Let me give it some thought."

"Singapore. What the hell are you doing there?"

"I'm going for the baths."

"There are no baths . . ." Bronson stopped himself. He would never be able to figure Kirk out. He needs help, Bronson decided. Watching him, he thought of making love to Grace, and he had an overwhelming desire to tell Kirk, to watch it hurt him, to see the cool façade turn to anger.

"We're going to spend a few days together, I understand. At the beach, Grace tells me."

"It'll be good for you, Kirk. You've been under a lot of strain."

"Don't believe everything you hear," Kirk said. "Now let me get back to business."

"Just promise me you'll think about that insurance," Bronson said. "It's too good to pass up. All this uncertainty . . ."

Kirk cut him off. "I'll give it a thought."

Bronson left the office.

Kirk stared out of his window and watched the roofs below him. It was a steaming summer's day in New York and a young man and woman stretched out below him, several buildings away, sunbathing on the top of an apartment complex. The woman had taken off her halter and pointed her pert, small breasts at the sky. Occasionally the man rubbed lotion over her front. What do they care? Kirk thought. All these problems are just pissholes in the snow. He imagined Gena Reynolds and felt a twinge of longing for her. Brutal honesty, he thought. She can care the way I care, and not be afraid of it. Still watching the sunbathing couple, Kirk direct-dialed a number, using his private line.

"Mr. Franco Bertelli, please," Kirk said, making the connection. "Kirk Abbott calling from New York."

Franco came to the phone. "Mr. Abbott," he said, "you can't be calling with a little good news? Like your check's in the mail? All I can tell you is that I hope your chair fits my ass. I always wanted to be president of a Big Board company. And as long as you got me, you can do me a favor."

"A favor for a favor," said Abbott.

"I'll always scratch your back, Mr. Abbott."

"You know anything about an insurance company in London? Terrorist insurance?"

"Great minds on the same wavelength," Franco said. "Yeah, I know about it. And something that United Stores can use. As a matter of fact, several friends of mine are involved with the company. I got a lot of friends. I've been outside of Chicago once or twice," he added.

"That's no new business," Kirk said. "It's the old protection racket you guys have used for years. I thought you were smart. Tip over a few fruit carts, break a few windows, steal pennies from the blind news dealer, and everyone on the block will pay. Once a punk, always a punk. No matter how you dress it up."

"Well, that's bullshit, Abbott. We're not in on this terrorist stuff. We do nothing political. The President has called up the National Guard, for Christ's sake, to protect property. We didn't get where we got by being crazy. Tell you what — I'll give you two extra weeks for free, if you look at this insurance. We wouldn't want anything to happen to United Stores."

"Beautiful," Kirk said. "You wreck everything, then turn around and insure it. That's what I call a vertically integrated business."

"You need the insurance. It will show your good faith."

"If there's anything I want to show you, Franco, it's my good faith."

"If there's anything I want you to show me, Mr. Abbott, it's your money."

"Good-bye, Franco."

"I'm the one who says good-bye," said Franco. But it was too late. The line was already dead.

Abbott stared out at the couple on the roof. The man was trying to pull the woman's bathing suit bottom over her hips. She resisted him, clawing at his face and eyes with her nails. Kirk buzzed his secretary. "Get Ted Bronson in here," he said.

Bronson came in, annoyed. "Jesus, Kirk, I've got the auditors with me. At least I care about United Stores. It's my wife and mistress."

Kirk smiled at him. "I like you go-getters," he said. "While I'm away, go ahead and present the insurance plan to the directors."

"Christ, look at that," Bronson said, staring out of the window at the couple struggling on the roof. The man had gotten the girl's bathing suit bottom around her knees; he had taken off his own shorts and was rampant in the noon sun. They looked like an erotic puppet show, far beneath Kirk's office. He could not tell whether they were sweating or not. But he supposed they were.

"Okay, Bronson. Out." said Kirk.

"Are you kidding?"

"They're entitled to their struggles in peace without you slobbering over them."

"We should call the police."

"Do whatever you want without watching them in secret. Out!" Kirk ordered.

Bronson left in a hurry, and, while Kirk continued to watch, the woman on the roof was making it clear that a piece of ass would cost her companion dearly.

Kirk watched alone, until it was over.

Book
2

11

   Scott Dutton told me long ago when we met
that the army taught him one important thing:
always act as if you know perfectly what
you're doing and no one will stop or question
you. "Keep movin'," Dutton told me. "An'
look like youall certain it's right." He is
right. We are able to accomplish anything by
being organized and never hesitating. Why
is it that Americans are so trusting? Or is
every people this way? But if we're so trusting, then we must be inherently good. It is
our country's leadership that makes us selfish,
mean spirited. Alex tells the others it is
the leaders in politics and industry, the
people who wield the power and the money.
   So what else is new? I have known this all
along. Eventually the people will rise to
help us, feed us, hide us. In the meantime,
Alex says it is important to build a reservoir
of fear.
   He has the clerk at the Saudi embassy
bagged. The man, Louis Bakhash, begs daily

to join us. Alex has told me it will never
happen but perhaps he will change his mind.
Bakhash and all his cousins went to Harvard.
They roomed together, ate together, went
to films and concerts only with themselves.
Alex asked him what he hated most about America
and Bakhash has answered, Harvard. The man
has arranged everything, issued permits, hired
security, made the appropriate clearances
with Swissaire. They question nothing because
it comes from the embassy. The airline ads
say, "Switzerland still remembers when people
traveled for more reasons than just getting
somewhere." For once, advertising does
not lie. They are happy, the Swiss, to assist
caution.

We have managed to get in at least 30 jumps
apiece over the last month, with Higgins pi-
loting the Cessna 180. No reports that we
know of yet to the FAA and Boaz could use at
least 20 more jumps, but we've cut it as close
as we can. Be jumping between 1200 and 3000
feet, probably on low side of that, with quick
ejector hardware and paracommanders, the
Papillon. French-made canopies and safe.
Has to be rear-door exit. Side doors too much
risk of hitting wing or stabilizer. Three
seconds free fall will clear us. Try for 180
degree turns and track away from each other
to avoid canopy collision. Hope is to land
within 30-50 yards from each other. Flotation
gear military 6 inch by 3 inch packs, unfold
to rubber duckies. If one leg and one
chest strap loosened in air, water should

```
bo no sweat.  Jump schools exit ten bodies from
Noorduin Norseman cargo plane.  We should
not worry with six.  Water will be 60 to 65
degrees.  Everyone an athlete and swimmer.  The
excitement is general.  A feeling that suc-
cess will bring recruitment level way up.  If
Alex wants it.
```

Extract from the journal of Michael Cagnina

"The fucking Arabs and the Jews are giving me seven hours of overtime this weekend," said a Pinkerton guard assigned to Kennedy Airport.

"My father's Jewish," said his partner, as they walked to a boarding gate at the Swissair terminal.

"I didn't mean nothin'. It ain't your father's fault I work overtime. But the Arabs got all the money in the world. More oil dollars than you got pimples on your ass."

"Tell me something I don't know."

"The Arabs think it's the Jews blowing up oil tanks. The Jews think it's Arabs blowing up property."

"Tell me something I don't know."

"Right now we watch a sheik's family going first class to Geneva. Six people they take the whole first class. You know what that costs? Thousands. For six people."

"Just don't say anything against the Jews. I'd have to punch you in the mouth, even if you are my son-of-a-bitch partner."

"Give me a Jew anytime. Jews ain't niggers." That satisfied the other guard and they moved out to a private gate, away from where the regular passengers were boarding the Swissair 747.

All the travelers were waiting in their seats. First class had additional curtains placed between it and the tourist section and people were curious. "I realize that first class is first class," said a woman to one of the stewardesses. "But why all the fuss? Who's coming on board? Jackie Onassis?"

"Just some Arab businessmen," the stewardess said. "They've got the whole first class. Their religion won't allow them to sit with other people, or something."

Faces were pressed to every window as the two limousines pulled onto the tarmac and proceeded slowly to the foot of the first class ramp. Arab dignitaries in long white robes emerged from the back seats. A woman walked between two of the men wearing a veil and carrying a baby wrapped in the same white cloth as the robes. Two of the Arabs dressed in burnoose and dark business suits carried sidearms and looked all around before allowing the others to board the plane. After the group was safely loaded, the two passed their weapons over to the Pinkerton men and double-timed up the ramp without looking back. The door was shut and the giant plane began taxiing almost immediately. It took off moments later.

The Arabs were silent. They spread through first class, seating themselves separately and, shaking their heads, refused all refreshment. The veiled woman held her baby close to her breast when the stewardess approached. The girl shrugged and went back to demonstrate the use of the life jackets to the passengers in economy.

"*Ce que je ne peux tolérer, ce sont les voyageurs grossiers,*" she said to another stewardess. "*Si vous voulez passer en Première pendant ce voyage, soyez mon invité.*"

"*Vous pouvez les avoir,*" she was told, "*mais j'ai une surprise pour vous. Il y aura une fête à Genève demain soir. On m'a dit que le frère de l'Aga Khan y sera. Quel prix!*"

"*Aujourd'hui j'aimerais mieux servir La Classe Touriste que me marier avec l'Aga Khan.*"

The other stewardess shrugged and her companion

climbed the stairs to the first class section. She picked up a
baby's bottle in the galley, determined to offer service
whether or not it was appreciated. She went up to the Arab
woman, who still held her baby closely to her chest. The
hostess pointed to the bottle and smiled.

Glory Cohen removed the veil from her face and smiled
back. As the hostess reached for the child, Glory pulled a
Ruger 22 Bearcat revolver from her robe and stuck it against
the side of the hostess's nose. "Freeze, you sweet frog bitch,"
Glory said. "One move or sound and you get a nose job
without paying for plastic."

Glory threw the baby up into the air. It came out of its
covers, a rubber and acrylic creation, and fell to the floor
under the seat. It uttered one brief "waa" from the shock
and Glory kicked it out of the way. The other Arabs produced weapons from under their robes, sawed-off shotguns
and Colt Cobra pistols. They took off their headdresses.
Alex and Glory escorted the stewardess to the pilot's cabin.
"Tell them you've got a baby that needs an emergency ap-
pendectomy," Alex whispered to the girl. She knocked on
the pilot's door and told him. The first officer opened the
door immediately and Boaz shoved his way inside, pushing
the shotgun's muzzle an inch into the man's belly. "Tell the
passengers what's going on," said Boaz. "You are being
hijacked and held for ransom. We shall not hesitate to kill
the passengers — one by one — until the ransom has been
paid. After you inform the passengers, tell them to stay cool
and not try to be Bruce Lee. Break open the bar and give
free drinks to everyone who wants them. All seat belts must
be fastened, and anyone wanting to use the facilities should
be prepared to piss under the watchful eye of one of our
people. We don't want anyone dying for nothing on this
trip. Only for money."

"What course do you want us on?"

"Stay on your normal course for ten more minutes. Then

head north toward Canada. We'll check you out with our pilot, so don't try to be anything other than a sensible Swiss."

The pilot announced the situation to the seventy-eight passengers in the economy section. Immediately, Edwards, Boaz and Scott Dutton covered the cabin with their shotguns. Sean Higgins had requested assignment to the lounge in advance, and Alex allowed him to sit on a barstool against the door. "Drink up," he told the people at the bar. "If you lift a few glasses, you never mind being inconvenienced. Get to know each other. Drink! If you're lucky, you'll be able to tell your grandchildren about it. Talk to me if you want. I love to talk." He raised his shotgun and sighted along the barrel, pointing it at the mirror over the bar. Everyone ducked. Higgins laughed and lowered his weapon. "Drink, goddammit," he said. "Be good company so I don't get bored."

Alex had the pilot radio New York to alert the authorities and to tell Swissair to assemble two million dollars in Swiss francs, pounds sterling, dollars and deutsche marks, and to have the funds ready at Kennedy Airport awaiting further orders.

Swissair officials did not hesitate to order the money gathered and ready. "We don't want the reckless spirit of William Tell," one of the directors said, speaking to the others. "We want to carry on our business and be left alone. The pattern of these people has been to accept ransoms and move on to other victims. They have yet to strike the same company twice. Two million is easy for us. After this flight, if no one is harmed, we publicize that Swissair will probably not be touched again. 'Fly Swissair,' we can say. 'We've been through it already.'"

"What is the world coming to?" one of the other directors asked him.

"Ah," he answered. "People have said that since the wheel. Since fire. What's the most important thing?"

"That we survive."

They gathered the ransom and sat in an office at Kennedy with the money on the table between them. They took turns touching it, counting it, until they received their instructions.

A Cessna Citation raced to Portland Airport in Maine with the money in a footlocker. The plane was cleared immediately for landing and allowed to taxi to within several yards of the jumbo jet. Maine National Guardsmen, state troopers, five U.S. district judges, and one congressman waited in half-tracks surrounding the plane. Several FBI sharpshooters lay on their bellies peeping through telescopic sights at the plane's huge tires. Their fingers squeezed and relaxed, squeezed and relaxed. But nobody risked early retirement. The pilot of the Cessna lugged the footlocker underneath the open baggage compartment of the 747. He attached the trunk's handles to ropes which dangled down from the fuselage. When the footlocker was secured, hidden hands pulled the trunk into the plane.

Scott Dutton and Enrico Boaz were counting the money when a nervous FBI man squeezed his trigger just a fraction too hard and one of his rounds pierced the left rear tire. Immediately, the Maine National Guard contingent opened up with their M–14s, and two Maine federal judges fired 45s in the general direction of the cockpit.

"Okay, you downeast bastards," Alex said on a bullhorn over the noise of the firing. "I'm sorry to have to present you with reality." A halt was called to the gunfire and a nervous silence fell over the field. The footlocker was dropped with a sharp thump back onto the runway. Everyone watching saw it drop; everyone watching saw that a body hung out of the empty trunk. As they watched, a red stain spread across the asphalt like beef gravy leaking around the sides of a plate.

Scott Dutton had cut the man's throat without a second thought, and dropped him on his ass inside the footlocker and kicked it out of the open hatch. And cut the ropes connecting the handles. And shut the hatch door. And felt badly that the man never knew he was being killed.

Scott Dutton was the youngest of four sons of Andrew Aspinwall Dutton from Charlottesville, Virginia; the youngest grandson of Andrew Aspinwall Dutton, manufacturer of fine finished fabrics; the youngest great-grandson of Colonel "Flaming Andy" Aspinwall of the First Virginia Cavalry, who lost an arm and all his inhibitions at Antietam in 1862.

Scott Dutton was a second-string halfback at the University of Virginia and a lacrosse All-America at midfield like his three brothers before him. Scott was a good boy, a good son. He had a Z branded into the sole of his left foot, a naked lady tattooed into the sole of his right. He got the tattoo when he was drunk, the brand when he was sober. He belonged to the Secret Seven at Virginia, something the world would never know until he died, when a wreath of flowers in the shape of a giant seven would appear on his coffin. The wreath would have been sent by the Secret Seven Society, more exclusive than Skull and Bones at Yale, more selective than the P. C. at Harvard. Scott went through army ROTC the way his brothers had gone through army ROTC, at the head of his class.

"You-all lucky as hell, little Scott," his daddy told him on his graduation from Virginia. "All your brothers had a crack at a war, and you got a crack as well. You shoot the shit out o' them little slope-heads. The way your brothers shot the shit out of the Japs and the Koreans. Man, you boys been lucky. I hope you-all appreciate it."

Scott was trained as a jungle fighter in Panama, learning

survival among the thickest groundcover in the world. He learned how to eat snake and lizard, how to make fetid water drinkable, how to treat tropical diseases and sudden wounds. Most of all he learned to kill, with M14s, M16s and bayonets. With throwing knives and the garotte. With fingers and thumbs. And with feet and teeth. But his buddies were there: through Fort Gordon, Georgia, through Panama. It was a game.

But once they were shipped to Vietnam it was no game. It was no game when his best friend fell into a spider hole near Sangin and another onto punje stakes sharpened to a point and rubbed with human excrement. The South Vietnamese shot him because they couldn't get to the infection and his convulsions were too horrible to watch. It was no joke when a fragmentation grenade took down two of his fraternity brothers, and Scott went berzerk trying to find three deserters from Detroit in the back alleys of Saigon. He searched for four days, drunk on Biere 33 Export, to no avail.

The day he walked into the village of N'Goy, fifteen kilometers from the DMZ, and he saw the VC use children with explosives wired to their bodies as human sacrifices, was the day he truly graduated from the University of Virginia. The villagers smiled as a jeep full of good ol' boys, mostly from the border states, flew into the sky. Scott Dutton wasted the village. He ordered his men to waste it. He himself fired, reloaded, fired and reloaded until he suffered second-degree burns of his hands and forearms and there was nothing or nobody standing in N'Goy. Not an old woman, not a baby. Not a hut, not a tree, not a dog.

After three years in Leavenworth at hard labor, Scott was dishonorably discharged and turned over to his family. He was in and out of institutions after that: the best institutions, with the best care and doctors. "He's become antisocial," the doctors said. "With psychopathic tendencies." He assaulted orderlies, nurses. He tried to strangle animals. And when he attacked two of his brothers at the Aspinwall Mill when he believed they smiled at him, a family council voted to put him away. They also voted to tell everyone in Charlottesville that Scott was traveling in Europe for an indefinite period, to learn about the world.

A week before the papers were to be signed, Scott had just come back from running six miles, a daily routine to stay in shape despite the battles in his mind. A letter was waiting for him, offering him a job in New York if he were the military weapons expert the newspapers had claimed he was. The job offered unlimited pay for doing what he loved to do. It was signed "A friend of the Confederacy."

The next morning Scott threw a foreman of his daddy's gentleman farm down the concrete stairs of a storage cellar when the man tried to stop him from leaving. He left a note giving his lacrosse sticks and army uniforms to the Deke House at Virginia, and he hitchhiked to New York with no trouble at all. Being raised so nicely, Scott Dutton was extremely polite.

He met Alex in the living room of a townhouse on Eighty-first Street. On a long table in the middle of the living room floor were hundreds of parts and ammunition from Thompson submachine guns, Czech Skorpion machine pistols, U.S. M14s and 45 automatics, Israeli Uzis, Chinese AK 47s. "Go ahead, hero," Alex said to him. "Put them together in fifteen minutes, loaded and ready to go. If you do it"— Alex gave him half of a ripped thousand-dollar bill —"you get the other half. If not — see if it buys you a bus to Virginia."

Scott assembled all the weapons in nine minutes. Then he took them apart and dumped the pieces back onto the table. Then he tipped over the table, with all the pieces, onto the floor. He snapped the other half of the thousand out of Alex's fingers. "Where can you get some good chili in this town?" he said.

Alex took him to a place on Second Avenue in the Nineties and told him about his ideas for straightening out the people who had fucked up the country. "Including the pricks who have destroyed our domestic textile industry?" asked Scott.

"Including those pricks," said Alex.

"Do I get a title?" Scott asked.

"You can be a colonel."

"Hot damn," said Scott, wolfing down his chili and sucking on a beer.

The jet's engines fired into life and the plane prepared for takeoff. No one on the ground moved. They just stared at the trunk and the juices falling from it onto the hot tar of the runway. The first kill had happened so easily that it was almost a relief and the Swissair 747 disappeared into cloud cover.

12

Yarmouth, Nova Scotia. It is lazy here.
Alex told me that I would probably feel guilty
sitting in the sun and waiting. Of course,
he's right. At the Grand Hotel, there is an
old man who drinks at the bar each night.
Something he calls Pile Drivers . . . vodka
and prune juice. I could get very lazy in Yarmouth. All accept the fact that I am a sport
fisherman. I know boats; I know the gear.
Have chartered a 30 ft. Bertram . . . wanted
a Hatteras with twin 350 diesels. Had to
get same in Wedgeport, $65 per day at boatyard
of Fidelis Boudreau, a philosopher if there
ever was one. Many tourists. I come and
go as I please. Two more days to wait. Everything is so simple here, easy not to leave.

Not sure I trust the others. Without Alex,
we would wither away. Two more days.

From the journal of Michael Cagnina

It wasn't long out of Portland that all passengers were ordered into the emergency crash landing position. The crew was given flying orders and Sean Higgins informed Alex, as he requested, when the plane was nearing 46 degrees 07 minutes west longitude, and north 43 degrees 15 minutes latitude.

"Keep your heads between your legs," Alex said through the bullhorn to the passengers. "It's good for your circulation and your brain. I can assure anyone who sits up that it will not be good for his circulation."

"That means you, Grandpa," Higgins snapped at the old man, who sat straight up in his chair. Higgins raised his arm but the old man never flinched.

"I've done too much to be pushed around now," the old man said. "I want to see where I'm going to die."

Alex stepped between them, restraining Higgins.

"No one is going to die," Alex said gently, so gently that the Irishman wondered at him. He saw Alex put a hand on the man's shoulder, a quieting motion. "Stay up," Alex said. "Shut your eyes and imagine good times."

"Jesus," Higgins began to protest, but the old man shut his eyes and Alex moved on up the aisle.

The pilot had been told to fly at fifteen thousand feet with a maximum air speed of two hundred knots. Alex gathered his team, in jump suits and parachute packs and flotation gear, near the rear door. Then he opened it. The rush of air wrenched the giant plane suddenly, but not enough to prevent the group, holding hands, from jumping through the opening. They had trained together as skydivers, so it was easy; the passengers screamed at the plane's lurching, certain that it was all over. A young priest, just out of seminary, dared to look around and go to the cockpit to inform the crew that the hijackers were gone. The first officer and the navigator couldn't get near the door to close it so they slowly eased themselves back to the controls. The plane banked, turned back to Portland, and the young priest led everyone in a prayer of thanks.

The terrorists landed in the sea near Tusket Island off the coast of Nova Scotia, less than two miles from the target area. They were picked up in a thirty-foot Bertram which Michael Cagnina had chartered weeks before in Halifax. Boaz hated the water and was a weak swimmer. He had to be cut out of his suit by Sean Higgins and hauled aboard the Bertram by his feet. "I thought all wetbacks knew how to swim," Higgins said to him.

The Bertram moved toward Yarmouth through seas that were calm. The jump suits and flotation gear and weapons and parachutes were weighted with lead and dropped over the stern.

Enrico Boaz had said to Alex on the boat, "I want to go with you and Glory. It's time we talked without the others."

"I don't like it," Alex said. "I want everyone going back to New York separately."

"Glory and I have talked about it. I think you better listen."

"If you're determined to fuck things up, all right."

"It's not that. It's about Glory."

"I see."

They looked at each other without talking, the dark man with the desperately piercing black eyes and the black-haired Alex, looking cool and unruffled.

"All right," Alex said again. "Get two staterooms. Don't let me see you until we board."

They traveled almost thirteen nautical miles to Yarmouth, coming into harbor along with a small fishing fleet and the flagship of the Cruising Club of America. No one noticed or bothered them as they wandered away from the waterfront on foot. And, indeed, what was there to notice?

The motor ship *Prince of Fundy* leaves Yarmouth every evening at eleven o'clock for Portland, Maine. Fourteen fifty is an adult fare one way. Forty-six dollars buys a stateroom, which, in a pinch, can sleep as many as four. Alex boarded at ten o'clock and locked himself in his cabin. His stretch wig itched his scalp and had been terribly hot most of the long day. He stripped it off and gave himself a shower and shampoo, massaging his hair for a good five minutes. He toweled himself vigorously and lay down on a bunk. He was not able to relax. He was never able to relax. But at least he could let some of the weariness drain off. Alex slept through the sailing. He awoke, refreshed and starved, at one in the morning. Carefully he shaved, dressed, and pulled on his black stretch wig, combing it out over his ears, so that no hint of his sandy hair peeped through the artificial thicket.

Alex found Boaz and Glory Cohen in the casino, seated side by side at a blackjack table. They were losing hand after hand. But the stakes were small, and it looked as though they didn't care. Alex stood in back of them. "Play the slots," he whispered, nodding at the machines that lined the walls of the casino.

Boaz ignored him and continued to gamble like a fool, drawing cards when he had fifteen or over, not keeping track of what cards were out. Alex smelled a pungent odor around Boaz's shoulders. The man was stoned. "Let's get some coffee, a sandwich," Alex said, still standing behind Boaz's back.

The casino was almost empty, except for an attractive American couple who sat at the next blackjack table sipping club soda, smoking Players and betting conservatively to make their money last the night. They seemed determined to make the trip without sleeping. They had the heavy, defiant air of people trying to win a wager with friends.

A fat woman went up and down the rows of slot machines, dropping in Canadian dimes, pulling the levers methodically, the fat on her upper arms jiggling with each pull, throbbing to the occasional small jackpot.

Boaz ignored Alex's instructions, although Glory swept her chips into her purse and got off her stool to cash in. Boaz pushed five dollars out onto the green felt table. The dealer flipped him a card face down. Boaz peeked at a corner of it: ace of diamonds. The dealer then turned up a deuce for Boaz. "Hit me," Boaz said. He was dealt a six. "Hit me," Boaz said. The dealer flicked him the five of hearts. "Hit me again," Boaz said. Simultaneously, Alex rocked him from his seat with an extended knuckle behind Boaz's ear, and the dealer shoveled him a queen of spades. The dealer collected the twenty-five dollars Boaz had bet on his hand and Alex carried the unconscious man out of the salon to the aft deck of the motor ship. Glory stayed behind for a few minutes. "We're all friends," she told the dealer. "He has a bad gambling habit. We're trying to break him of it one way or the other." The dealer cashed her in and shrugged.

"Whatever happens on this tub," he said, "I could care less. Ordinarily, you only find me in Tahoe this time of year, and I'll be back there soon enough."

"Sure you will, Jack," Glory said, and walked from the salon past the fat woman, who was crawling on her knees, groping under a chair, for two dimes that had rolled away.

"I can control people as well as you can," Boaz said sullenly to Alex. They sat on deck chairs in the stern watching the boat's wake shuffle away from them in the moonlight. "There's no reason you get all the money, you have all the women. I probably have had more women in my life than you got hairs on your head."

"That's probably true, Rico. But that's because I have never gone with whores." The Mexican tried to get up, but Alex pointed an ugly little Colt 22 at his forehead. "No one could run this show or plan it the way I can," said Alex. "You can do all right with hippies and losers. But if you keep your eyes open and stay off grass and tequila when you're working, we'll be able to put it all together. This team does not need prima donnas. It doesn't bother me if you want to get rich or you want to die. The others would gladly split up your piece. You want to play nickel-dime blackjack on a ferry? Want to flip baseball cards against some stairs for pennies? You let me do the thinking. You stay pissed off, that's fine. But let me do the thinking."

"I'll get some sleep," Boaz finally said. "What about Glory? She likes me. She likes me better than you."

"I don't doubt that either, Rico," Alex said. "I'm not in this to be loved. But as it happens, I need her tonight. After tonight, she's yours. Or anyone's until I need her again."

"You are a true cocksucker."

"That's where you're wrong," Alex said. "I'm your leader. Glory is a true cocksucker."

Alex escorted the Mexican to his stateroom, then turned and entered his own, carefully bolting the door.

"You weren't too hard on him," Glory said from behind him. "He's such a beautiful animal."

"Just kept the tension level up. He performs best when he's got someone to hate. It's not enough for him to hate the system. He needs people. He needs a person to hate now. It might as well be me."

"Would you do me a favor?" Glory asked. She had put her hair up for the jump and the day's activities. Now she shook it out and brushed it vigorously, her full breasts bouncing as her arm moved, her nipples standing out like tiny fingers of a baby.

"What's the favor?"

"Let's do it on the floor, Alex. I want to root around. Those beds are so small."

Glory finished brushing and faced him. She slid out of her black bikini pants and, balling them up, threw them at Alex. Then she began brushing the luxurious coat between her legs. Alex shut the light in the cabin and came to her on the floor. They did more things to each other than they had ever done before to anyone. Afterwards, Alex climbed into his bunk. Glory stayed on the floor and hummed to herself.

"You were very wet," Alex said.

"Was it bad?"

"It was fine. Just not as tight as usual. So wet."

"Must have been the long day. Plus the fact that I fucked Boaz before we went to the casino. I thought you'd want to know."

"I knew," said Alex, turning onto his side.

The engines of the *Prince of Fundy* soon put him to sleep.

"Always leave 'em laughing."
Football 1, 2, 3, 4. Hockey 1, 2, 3, 4.
Latin Club 1. Glee Club 1.

From Sean Higgins' biography in the
Boston College High School Yearbook

13

Sean Higgins was born on Day Boulevard, South Boston. He grew up in the middle flat of a triple-decker, in a row of wooden triple-deckers, where the people kept the peace and voted Democratic. Sean remembered work in his childhood better than he remembered anything else. He sold papers at the end of Summer Street near South Station until he was old enough to work at Flaherty's Pool Hall, where he racked balls, shined shoes, went out for pint bottles of whiskey and ran numbers for "Big Vinny" Walsh, who controlled everything in Southie from congressional elections to bingo at Hibernian Hall.

Sean was a middle child and avoided the violence that his brothers and sisters welcomed. He became a favorite of the nuns in school, never getting black eyes, never being a truant, never being returned to his house by fat Officer Joe Charlton to be smacked around by his father, who would be pissed on Dawson's Ale at four o'clock in the afternoon. Sean Higgins developed the ability to talk his way out of anything. "He's got the gift of the blarney, Sarah Higgins," Officer Charlton told Sean's mother. "Either he's got to be on the Boston School Committee or in the seminary."

Sean did well enough in grammar school to be invited on scholarship to Boston College High, where his life was changed. He was caught in a teacher's conference room with a Latin teacher in an unnatural act, and, before being sent back to his family's three-decker, was given a switch across his knuckles for two and a half minutes. He never got over getting caught. "The bastard said he'd give me an A if he could also give me a blow job. It sounded like a good deal to me."

Every generation in South Boston has its angle man. Sean filled this role for his contemporaries. He knew how to get a hot Raleigh bike for ten bucks. He knew how to distract the ticket-takers and sneak into Fenway Park; he knew how to sucker older boys into games of eight ball and progression, and clean the table on them. Because of this, he also learned to take a beating and come off the floor swinging a pool cue.

Sean organized the first gangbang on Day Boulevard, with sixteen-year-old Peggy Flatley, whose cousin was a political reporter and later won a Pulitzer Prize. At the time, Sean took two dollars and a Bing Crosby album of Christmas songs from the cousin before Sean would let him screw Peggy Flatley. "Learn what people got in their closets," Sean always told anyone who sought his advice. "That's when you get them where they live."

Tradition on Day Boulevard meant marching in the St. Paddy's Day Parade with the politicians and enlisting in the Marine Corps. Sean enlisted, doing boot camp at Parris Island and hoping someday to become a drill instructor so he could kick ass. Instead, Sean became the orderly for a platoon leader, Bradley Hoag, a Princetonian gifted from birth with an inheritance of five million dollars and larceny in his soul.

Bradley Hoag came out of the Marine Corps with a knowledge of weapons and two desires: to live in Paris and to have a manservant who anticipated his needs. Sean Higgins went with Hoag, preparing his clothes, driving his car, buying him bourbon at three in the morning, finding him girls at any time. "Higgins," Bradley Hoag told him, "you've got red hair like every other mick. But you've got the sense of survival. We can help each other, protect each other." Hoag bought flying lessons for the Irishman. They took karate together. Hoag bought warehouses of weapons from the Pentagon through Marine contracts. He bought mortars, recoilless rifles, grenade launchers, surplus M1s. He bought three antique B29s, Korean War Sabre jets, outdated Hawk missiles, 45-caliber pistols by the boxcar. He bought half-tracks, LSTs from World War II. He bought Walker tanks. Using Sean Higgins as a delivery boy, and occasionally as a negotiator, he sold his products to African nations, mercenary colonels, royal pretenders, Greek Communists, gangsters in Marseilles, Arabs in transit. Sean Higgins marveled at his own life and experiences, and thought it was the luckiest break in the world that he was caught receiving an unnatural act in the teacher's conference room at Boston College High School.

"I don't like flying to anybody else's territory," Higgins told his employer one day, as they flew in a Helio V/STOL aircraft to a clearing in one of the San Blas Islands off the coast of Panama. "You never know when these jokers turn on you. The Arabs, no problem. But these spics; they ain't gentlemen."

"As long as we have what they want," Hoag answered, "we're in great shape. I learned that at Princeton, believe it or not."

Higgins set the plane down in a clearing ringed by coconut trees and Colombian rebels with cartridge belts slung over their shoulders and machetes in their hands. "They're the sorriest-looking bunch of bastards I ever saw," Higgins said. "Including the winos in the White Tower on Washington Street at four on a Sunday morning. I don't trust sorry-looking bastards. That's what I learned in South Boston pool-rooms, believe it or not."

Hoag was determined to pick up what the rebel chief had promised him: stolen pre-Colombian art, treasures from Henry Morgan days in Panama. Behind the seats of the V/STOL were stored two cases of Korean War smoke grenades and a case of brand-new Russian SKS 7–62 carbines with a thousand rounds of ammunition.

Hoag jumped down from the plane, carrying one of the grenades and one of the rifles, and held them out for inspection. The rebel leader chopped off the hand holding the carbine and the rest of his crew surged toward the plane. Higgins, who needed virtually no taxiing room, took off immediately. He buzzed the clearing several times, but by then it was all over for Bradley Hoag from Princeton. A bullet shattered Higgins's windshield and, cursing and frightened, he headed out over the ocean. The rebels left Hoag's body in the middle of the coconut grove for the San Blas Indians to find and bury. Sean Higgins was in business for himself.

But he was lost without Hoag's direction. He discovered after several months that he was a great sergeant but a terrible officer. Higgins could not close deals with the diplomatic weasels who peopled the international weapons trade.

Broke and panicky, Higgins returned to South Boston and, day after day, lay naked on the beach at L Street, dreaming and plotting. Drunk one night, he almost reenlisted in the Marine Corps. In the morning, terrified at what he had so nearly done the night before, Higgins began to read the want ads in the back of a *Flying Magazine* that he picked out of the trash at the Park Street subway station. He read, "Pilots of Fortune — Wanted for Rewarding, Possibly Hazardous Assignments. Twenty years ago, this sort of person would have joined the Foreign Legion. Answer this ad."

Higgins flew Alex upside down over Westchester in a Piper Aztec; took him for a Sunday helicopter ride, fifty feet off the ground, through the canyons of Wall Street; and landed a Lear jet on a dime at Islip in fog as thick as hot Ralston.

"I want it understood who runs the show," said Alex, giving Higgins half of a five-thousand-dollar bill.

"The man who runs the show got the other half of this," Higgins said. "Even the sisters taught me that."

"I'll buy you a drink," said Alex.

Higgins smiled the smile of the crafty servant. His red hair and large white teeth made him look, for a brief moment, like the choirboy he once had been. For a very short hitch.

National Guardsmen bitched and moaned as they walked the streets of New York. Called to special active duty by the governor, squads worked two days a week guarding businesses and stores. Then they were allowed back to their own jobs, law firms and garages, brokerage offices, ball parks. New squads took their place, and mutiny was kept to a minimum by these staggered patrols.

Four guardsmen leaned on their rifles outside of the big Mercantile National Bank branch on Madison Avenue at Sixty-first Street. There was a specialist fifth class in charge of them who, in civilian life, was an eight-dollar-an-hour plumber on the East Side.

"I don't mind eight dollars an hour if you do the goddam job so it lasts," said one of the others to the specialist. "I mean, the icemaker breaking in the middle of a dinner party when you supposedly fixed it the week before."

"Your wife probably didn't do what I told her."

"I want you back tomorrow morning before nine o'clock," said the other guardsman, an investment banker who held the rank of private first class.

"That shit's all finished now, soldier," the plumber said to him. "You're in the army."

The investment banker searched the plumber's face for the joke. And he couldn't find it.

A military police car pulled up at the curb in front of them. A National Guard major with a white MP helmet jumped out of the back seat. The four guardsmen saluted involuntarily.

"You want to get your asses back to the Armory spending the weekend cleaning rifles?" the major asked. The four guardsmen stiffened. "Leaning on your weapons and shooting the shit when you're on guard duty. What goes on?"

"Sorry, sir," said the specialist, "but this is such a waste. There's nothing going on except a guy selling pretzels without a permit. We called the cops."

"Well, that's just peachy, soldier. For your information, this bank has just been robbed."

"That's impossible."

"What's your name, soldier?" the major asked the plumber.

"Munson, sir."

"Well, Munson, get your ass inside the bank. With these jokers, too. Let's give the people some help."

"Boaz," the major said to his aide, a master sergeant, "take down this man's name."

"Have a heart, major," the plumber pleaded. "I've got kids at home to play with this weekend. I got to make a living."

"This is no weekend drill, lardass," said the major. "Get in that bank."

Alex, dressed as a major in the MPs, left Michael Cagnina at the wheel of the MP squad car, and, with Boaz, Edwards, Dutton and Sean Higgins carrying M16 rifles set on automatic burst, went behind the other four guardsmen into the bank.

Simon Ehrlich was the president of Mercantile National Bank, the fourth largest commercial and lending institution in the United States, with assets of over ten billion dollars. He was in the habit of visiting branches unannounced, feeling like the caliph who would visit the Baghdad bazaar in disguise to hear what his subjects had to say about him. Partly for this purpose, every branch of the Mercantile had a balcony constructed over the main marble banking floor where Ehrlich could observe from above, watching the tellers, the lending officers, the hustle-bustle of his empire.

Simon Ehrlich was a small, self-satisfied man who had played golf every weekend for twenty years and who had his soft white hair trimmed daily in his office while he sipped cranberry juice for his kidneys and read the statements from his banking interests around the world.

"Jesus," he said to the branch manager of his Sixty-first Street office, as they looked from the balcony onto the floor below. "This country has come to a pretty pass when troops march the streets of New York City."

"It's sickening, Mr. Ehrlich."

"And to see them in the bank. My God, it's the end of democracy. I never thought I'd see it."

"I'm sure you're right, Mr. Ehrlich, but the troops make the customers feel better. We have more guardsmen than Chemical's branch in the next block and we've opened seven percent more accounts in the last two weeks."

"Look at that," Ehrlich said, pointing below him. "God, they're carrying weapons into the bank. Look at people smile and salute them. We're ready for a dictator."

Alex had his men spread out around the main floor. "Munson," he said to the specialist-plumber, "let me see your weapon." The man handed it over. "Filthy," roared Alex. "Boaz, check out the other weapons of these men. I'm going to have you on KP so long, Munson, you'll think you're an automatic disposal." Boaz picked up the rifles of the other three and stacked them in the middle of the floor. Using the specialist's rifle, Alex shot him in the foot.

"What's going on?" Ehrlich yelled from the balcony. The blue-uniformed guards ran to the center of the floor where the plumber lay, rolling and bleeding and moaning from shock. "I didn't know these guardsmen's weapons were loaded," Alex explained to the chief policeman on duty. Everyone gathered around with advice. All the guards had come down from the balconies, out from the vaults. "All right," said Alex in a loud voice, dropping the rifle and pointing his own M16 at the balcony, "everybody: weapons on the floor and into the center of this room. We are making a withdrawal and I am not fucking around. Come down off the balcony you head honchos up there, or I will perforate a few of your customers."

Ehrlich and the manager came down to the main floor, careful not to trigger any of the alarms. Terrified customers lay prone on the cold marble, as Edwards, Higgins, and Scott Dutton, in full battle gear, shoveled cash into knapsacks and shouldered the bags, leaving their hands free to sweep the tellers' cages with their M16s, daring anyone to move.

"You are a little pompous man," Alex said to Simon Ehrlich. "I want you to take off your pants." Alex held the M16 to Ehrlich's buttoned vest and pushed him backwards until the bank president undid his pants from their suspenders and dropped them to the floor. "Now the shorts, little pompous man." Slowly, Ehrlich complied, and stood naked and shriveled in the midst of his most productive office. Employees and customers sneaked looks, praying it wouldn't also happen to them. "Outside," Alex commanded his men. They backed up toward the bank's main entrance. "I suggest you all lie on the floor for a while," Alex said. "There are a lot of National Guardsmen walking the streets and a few outside the bank. Several of them are ours, and they have instructions to shoot to kill anyone leaving this building for fifteen minutes." Alex and the others put their weapons at port arms and escorted the money to the patrol car. Cagnina put on the siren and they screamed up Madison Avenue. At Seventy-fifth Street and Park they abandoned the patrol car and scattered in different directions, flagging taxis when they could to drop them at designated locations around the city.

Simon Ehrlich had ordered his branch manager to remove his own pants and give them to him. But not before a *Post* photographer took what was generally regarded to be the picture of the year.

Outside on the streets, police were asking every uniformed guardsman for identification. Rush-hour traffic was unbearable.

ROCKS AND SEAWEED

IF YOU FEEL ENERGETIC WHILE YOU ARE AT THE BEACH, HELP IN GETTING STONES OFF THE LO-TIDE LINE AND PULLING UP SEAWEED WOULD BE GREATLY APPRECIATED.

Ted Bronson
for the Beach Committee

14

*E*veryone in Atlanta knew that Creed Edwards would be a professional ballplayer. Even when he was a kid he could throw a ball farther, jump higher, and run faster than any of the other children around Cain Street. Creed grew up being adored for his athletic prowess by his parents, his brothers and sisters, and by most of the people in the neighborhood. "If you're a black hero, it doesn't matter to you that you're not white. You can have it all, Creed Edwards," his mother used to tell him. He got meat for dinner when everyone else in the family ate cereal. He was excused from family chores and allowed to play basketball with the older boys, to shoot one-handed jumpers from the key, from the corners, until long after the sun had gone down. Creed grew into puberty with an ugly face that pouted at the first sign of disapproval or neglect. He was All-Georgia at halfback in high school and received the nickname "Silver Wheels" from a local reporter who saw him, in his junior year, break the state schoolboy touchdown record of twenty-one, which had been held since 1944 by Charlie Trippi. Kap-Kola, one of the largest bottlers in the country, offered Creed Edwards a full four-year scholarship to the college of his choice. And the choice included at least fifty-four major universities, including Dartmouth, which was about to field its first all-black backfield. Edwards stayed in Atlanta to play for True College, where he could pull the hometown fans who worshiped him, and where, as he told *Newsweek*, "I could stay close to my personal foxes, which was important."

Atlanta businessmen treated him better than they had ever treated Ty Cobb. They gave Silver Wheels Edwards a silver Lincoln, free wardrobes, a new job for his father. He had never known a bad day, never a disappointment; his knees were in great shape, and he could run the forty-yard dash in nine seconds flat with full pads and football cleats. His freshman year at True he ran a kickoff back one hundred and three yards against Alabama. As Bear Bryant said, "The kid shows me more at his age than any football player I ever seen. All he needs is time. And, of course, a little instruction from Bear Bryant." The True freshmen lost only to Auburn, by a last-minute field goal, and Edwards romped the winter away with whirlpool baths and scrimmage basketball. Professional scouts were already visiting the Edwards house and Silver Wheels was forced to hire an attorney suggested by the Kap-Kola Company to negotiate any future deals.

In his sophomore year he was named to several All-American teams before the season began. He started at setback for True that year and, midway through the season, he had gained almost eight hundred yards, pushing Hank Aaron, who was approaching eight hundred home runs, off the front of the sports section. On a Tuesday, after Silver Wheels's picture had been on the cover of *Sports Illustrated*, his coach commended: "He still remains a fine example to Christian youth. Creed Edwards is a God-fearing intelligent young man who loves his family and his school and respects his coach. I wish I could field ten more like him."

The following Saturday against Wake Forest, after a play was whistled dead, he was blind-sided by a 6–6 redneck linebacker from Wheeling, West Virginia.

"Everytime you thinkin' that you about to become a white man," the linebacker said, "this will teach you to remember that people deep down know you nothin' but a nigger."

The play lost Wake Forest fifteen yards but it broke Silver Wheels's left leg in two places and he was out for the rest of the season. The bones healed badly, and in February they were rebroken and reset. In July, trying to work his way into shape, Creed found he could not cut, could not put any pressure on his left leg. X rays showed a deterioration of cartilage surrounding his left patella, and he was operated upon in August. He missed the entire football season his junior year and paid no attention to his studies, which centered around human relations, the big jock major at True College. The doctors told Silver Wheels, and his coaches, and his parents, that he could not absorb any punishment, especially tackles to his left leg, ever again. The Kap-Kola people were told as soon as possible. Creed Edwards refused to believe the prognosis, but found himself, by April, barred from spring practice, on academic suspension, and the recipient of a letter from the directors of Kap-Kola, withdrawing his scholarship.

Creed drove to Nashville that night with three fraternity brothers. He belonged to a Jewish fraternity at True, Sigma Alpha Mu. They went to Nashville to drink Boilermakers, listen to country music, and to go to a whorehouse. Edwards had brooded during the drive, silent and dangerous. Later, as he got drunk, he became more silent. Until finally he threw a bottle of Kap-Kola through the glass mirror in back of the whorehouse bar. When his fraternity brothers attempted to restrain him, he lashed out and punched one of them, hard and fast, directly in the Adam's apple.

Silver Wheels Edwards was totally unprepared to be anything but a hero. He dropped out of school, refused to work, grumbled about society in general and honkies in particular.

He hit the streets of Atlanta and fell in with the wise guys, who used Edwards as runner, bodyguard, and armed robber, for which he received a suspended sentence from a judge who had seen him play in high school and who believed in the socially redeeming aspects of athletics.

Creed went to New York, as thousands of people go to New York every year, believing that the city's aura of wealth and success would trickle down to him. He went to try out for the New York Giants as a free agent. Creed was the third fastest man in camp, but when the hitting began he couldn't make it through the day. He left before the coaches came around to knock on his door. Like the thousands of others, he stayed in New York, waiting for the goodness to come on down. He stayed. And he answered the same ad in *Hump* magazine that Enrico Boaz had answered.

When Silver Wheels met Alex, Alex challenged him to a race along the Hudson near the Cloisters. Then he made Edwards arm wrestle, first one hand, then the other. Then he asked him if he could kill. "I don't see no reason not to," said Edwards. He took Alex's thousand dollars, bought some clothes, and moved into a residential hotel on the West Side near Lincoln Center.

That night, near his apartment, some kids were playing buckbuck up against a tree. They stopped to watch Edwards walking by. He was dressed up and feeling fine.

"It's one a' the Jets," said a kid. "I seen him against Green Bay."

"Come on," said another. "He's too tall. Gotta be a Knick."

"Which one are you mister?" a wise guy called to Edwards. "A Jet or a Knick?"

"I'm b-a-a-d," said Edwards. "An' don't you ever forget it."

He was happier than he had been in years.

There were twenty letters in all and they appeared from the outside to be invitations. The stationery was blue and had been purchased at Neiman-Marcus in Dallas. The handwriting was formal, the script done in white ink, as if a little old lady had been hired to do the job, painstakingly using a small ruler. All the letters were identical and said:

How much is your President worth? It will cost you one million dollars to keep him alive and healthy. Do not RSVP. You will be contacted.

They were postmarked from Nantucket, Massachusetts, and were mailed to the presidents of twenty of America's largest corporations.

The Abbotts and the Bronsons picnicked on the beach at 'Sconset with their children: Bloody Marys, vodka and tonics, stuffed eggs, submarine sandwiches, beer in a cooler, watermelon. A lustrous Labor Day weekend in Nantucket with the sand and sun smells of childhood. Kirk Abbott lay on his back with his head on a towel. His eyes were closed. "Is this what it's all about, Grace?" he asked his wife, who was slicing watermelon in her two-piece bathing suit and drinking vodka over ice. Grace never wore a bikini, although her figure deserved one. She wore handsome one-piece suits or conservative two-piece suits, seemingly left over from the forties. "Fine people do not wear bikinis," she had told Kirk years before. And he had let it go at that.

"Oh, it's so good for you, Kirk, the sand and the salt. If your doctor could scare you enough, he'd make you do this every three or four months."

"You ought to listen to your wife, Kirk," Ted Bronson said. "God only gave you one body."

Kirk got up onto an elbow and opened his eyes. Even in

the harsh sun, no redness crisscrossed the whites of his cold blue eyes. He was beginning to tan.

"I'm really lucky to have so many people caring about me," he said. "Lisa," he added, speaking to Bronson's wife, who did wear a bikini and had her hair streaked as well, "do you worry about me, like Ted and Gracie do?"

Lisa Bronson worried about her children and her husband's career, in that order. "Of course I care about you, Kirk." Lisa found it most difficult to answer a direct question. She had spent her life backtracking, trying never to make a mistake with anyone who counted. Her father adored her and called her "Precious Jewel."

"Good," Kirk said. "Because you know I have big plans for Teddy. He can go a long way."

"Let's not talk shop now, Kirk," Grace said. "I want you to forget for at least a weekend."

"Stores don't close for the weekend, Grace," Kirk said. "They have a life like real people. Stores have a pulse and a heart. People need them. I don't leave United Stores for the weekend, and I don't leave her when I go abroad. If you ever go into Bloomingdale's on a Saturday or any of *our* stores on a busy night, you'll see what I mean. Teddy's a money man. He's a controller, not a lover."

Grace put a glass to her lips and Bronson drew circles in the sand with his big toe.

"What do you want the company to do if we are threatened?" Bronson asked.

"We hire more security people and tell the terrorists to shove it," Abbott said. "You know how I stand on this, Teddy."

"But the people who have paid ransoms all own their own companies. Look at the cost-effectiveness ratio. Ten detectives at twenty-five dollars an hour is six thousand dollars a day, times three hundred sixty-five days a year, is two million one hundred ninety thousand dollars, plus room, board, transportation and equipment. And who says it will stop in one year? If the companies don't pay, who knows what will happen. Ehrlich, that bank president, going bolliky in his own bank. You've got to be really sick for that kind of scene. More people are going to get killed."

Kirk watched his two children trying to body surf and getting bounced around by the waves. They were laughing with the Bronsons' children. Unable to beat the waves.

"I'm afraid that unless people are killed," Kirk said, "there's not going to be much done about it. Who cares about Peerless Oil or Federated Utilities being vandalized? Not many men on the street care if the chief executive officers are tarred and feathered."

"You're saying that public companies shouldn't pay," Bronson said. "I absolutely agree with you. Big Board companies should set an example. My cost-effectiveness study says you can't pay. No public company can absorb the cost of guards. Or the cost of ransom if the company isn't insured. The stock would be dumped so fast you wouldn't believe it. Even IBM. They'd stop trading. No single executive is indispensable. Does Geneen matter if ITT is under selling pressure from institutions? Of course not. So United Stores would not pay ransom, right?"

Kirk was trying to build a castle out of wet sand as Bronson talked. Grace watched them and sipped her drink.

"God," Lisa Bronson said. "I wouldn't want United Stores to get tough if Teddy were threatened. You can't measure life in terms of dollars."

Abbott smiled. Lisa had been eating her submarine sandwich and tomato seeds dribbled down her chin. She wiped her mouth on the back of her hand.

"I believe in the fairness of the courts," Kirk said. "There should be a mandatory death penalty for extortion leading to terror. And twenty years to life for anyone caught paying off. That would end it soon enough."

"Why don't you men leave it alone?" Grace said. "Come on, who wants another Bloody?"

Kirk pushed himself up in the sand and jogged easily down to the shore where his children were still trying to body surf. He grabbed them both and wrestled with them. At first they were surprised, then delighted, to have a roughhouse with their father, who had always seemed so distant. "Watch me ride a wave," he said. "You keep your body very stiff and wait for the big one."

Kirk paddled out beyond the wave line and slowly eased back toward shore, letting small breakers wash over him. Spying the right one, he swam faster to be there when it broke. Catching it, he stretched to meet it and was carried along with a whoosh of noise and foam. The wave brought him to the feet of his children. "You look like a torpedo, Daddy," his daughter said.

"That's what you're supposed to look like. Come and try it with me."

"It's too far where you were. We'd be frightened."

Kirk tried to convince them to take a chance. They refused and he left them to play again by themselves in the shallows, to be buffeted around by smaller waves that crested early and spent themselves into the sand.

Falmouth, on Cape Cod, like so many American towns, has features to recommend it and features that do it discredit. It has old money and estates that remind one of simpler, grander times. It has condominium developments and summertime honky-tonks that line the Main Street and the roads approaching the town. It has sleepy Cape Cod winters and noisy, crowded, rowdy, good-time summers, where the best jobs of all, if you are young, are those of singing waitress and part-time cop. There are some crummy housekeeping cottages near Old Silver Beach that serve the purpose, if you don't have much money, and the weather is favorable.

Enrico Boaz rocked in an old wicker rocker on the weathered front porch of the cottage. Scott Dutton and Michael Cagnina played backgammon on the steps. They played for big money, using the doubling cubes often. Sean Higgins had worked in Falmouth in the past, a wise-guy bartender at a Route 6 bar that sold five hundred Budweisers a night on good nights. He had been gone since early morning searching out old friends who, in Massachusetts, worked the same restaurant-bar circuits for years. Silver Wheels Edwards was off running on the beach, getting hot, plunging into the water, getting out to continue running. Always getting into shape for the season, judging the calendar by the football year.

Alex pulled up in front of the cottage in a Volkswagen. He looked tanned and relaxed. "Where's Glory?" he asked.

"She went shopping," said Boaz, still rocking in the creaky rocker, and looking out in the direction of the sea.

"She think this is some kind of fucking summer vacation? Where's Higgins? Where is everybody?"

"Your superstar team is all around you," Boaz said, holding his arms out and still rocking.

"Let's go inside," Alex said, walking up the steps of the cottage and kicking at the screen door. "Jesus, where's Edwards?"

"He's working out," Cagnina said. "He's okay. He's getting ready."

As Alex was talking, Glory walked through the door with several packages. She emptied a bag on a round table in the living room. Six yellow T-shirts and one red T-shirt fell out of the bag. They were all size Large and all had superhero cartoons on the chest: Captain America, Ant Man, Plastic Man, The Hulk, Scorpion Woman. "Nobody can touch us," she said. "It's like we're invisible. I thought the team should have uniforms."

"I don't want anyone letting down," Alex said. "We've gotten this far without mistakes because you were all on edge. I can tell you this: there are probably fifty qualified people behind every one of you who would love to take your place. Keep looking over your shoulders."

Edwards came in, sweating heavily. He smiled at Alex. "A little roadwork," he said. "Never can tell when I'll want to run away faster than the others."

"You get a bonus, Creed. Spirit award."

"Spirit award for the spook," said Scott Dutton.

"I'll spook your ass," said Edwards stepping toward the southerner.

"Jesus," said Alex. "I leave you people alone for a few days and I've got chaos. Don't tell me you're all rich enough already?"

"You're the one who's rich, boss," said Boaz. "We just work for a living."

Higgins walked through the door wearing a flowered bathing suit and carrying a case of beer. For a minute he did not see Alex, who walked up behind him and violently tugged his bathing suit down around his knees. Caught totally by surprise, Higgins grabbed for his suit and the beer cans all went crashing to the floor, rolling around the linoleum. Alex pushed him hard, and his legs, caught in the fabric of the elastic suit, tripped him. He fell heavily onto several of the cans. The others laughed hysterically.

"You got lousy reflexes, Higgins," Alex said. "You're getting soft."

"No Irishman expects a sneak attack in Falmouth, Massachusetts."

Alex picked up a can and noted a local brand. "Also, you've got shitty taste in beer."

Glory handed Alex the red T-shirt she had bought. It had

Captain Marvel embossed on the front, and the word
"Shazam" under the picture. He took it and asked her, "All
right, Glory, what are the totals?"

"Out of the twenty letters, eight are paying. They've
agreed to the amounts and the arrangements. Eleven gave
no answer at all."

"What about Ehrlich the banker?" Alex asked her.

"The only answer. He told us when we called him that
we could go screw ourselves."

"Now that's not nice language, even for a banker," Alex
said. "Someone in charge of all that money should be a little
more humble about his responsibility to the common people." He held up five fingers. "I want five out of the twelve
expunged from the records. I want Ehrlich to be the first,
and I want him dead, with no mistake."

Michael Cagnina frowned. "I don't know, Alex. What
happened on the plane happened. Once we get started on
killing, it's a problem. Property and corporations are one
thing, we even get sympathy from some big sources. A lot
of the newspapers have pretended to see our side. But assas-
sinations? We'll never get near our drops, let alone our
targets."

"You're a lawyer, but you're emotional," Alex told him.
"If you weren't emotional, you'd still be practicing at One
Chase Manhattan Plaza. Property stays still. It can be pro-
tected. People move; you can get at them. And we can get
much more money from people. If it's a million dollars for
a factory or a million for a son or a daughter, where do you
think the easy mark is? Notice I did not say wife."

"But cold blood?"

"Listen, Cagnina, what do you care about a few capitalists,
more or less? You know what you got yourself in for." Alex
spoke to the others. "This guy wants to fuck up the Golden
Goose."

"Let's put him in the electric pig," Silver Wheels Edwards said, "chop him up fine."

"You're kidding," Cagnina said to the black man.

"Man," said Boaz, "you pull this shit. We'd just as soon waste you as look at you."

"I want you people unanimous," said Alex, "before we move on."

Cagnina looked around him at the others. "It's unanimous," he said. "If it's necessary, it's unanimous."

"Good," said Alex. "You stay put. I'll call you in two hours with the story on banker Ehrlich, Lord rest his grubby soul. Higgins, empty out that beer. If I find you had any, or that this operation screws up because of you, you better grab your rosary in a hurry. Because that's about all the time you'll have."

"I want to follow him," Boaz said to Glory, after Alex left the cottage.

"Don't be foolish," she said. "We'll have our chance."

"I want you," Boaz said to her.

"I know," she said.

Labor Day morning was a brilliant testimonial to a summer gone wrong. The eastern half of the United States, in the circles of power, had spent the preceding months looking over their shoulders. The weather on Labor Day, hot and languorous and record-setting, made people throng to the beaches and the lakes, seeking shadow in the cool and long iced drinks on boats, and on porches, and in dark, air-conditioned bars.

Simon Ehrlich had blueberry pancakes with Vermont syrup and lots of butter. He had three cups of coffee in his summer house in Hyannisport, looking out onto Squaw Island.

"You shouldn't eat so much before you exercise," his wife Virginia said to him. "Pancakes sit so heavily in the belly."

"It doesn't matter. We're taking a cart. It's the only way they'll let me play."

"The bank should have paid the demands."

"Bullroar, Virginia," Ehrlich said. "The board was right. Because I told them they were right. The buck stops here."

"Do you think it's wise to go out so soon after the demands?"

"It's all bluff. They can't afford to get the whole population up in arms. The reward money soon will be sufficient to have a stool pigeon on every street corner in America. Besides, I've played golf every weekend for twenty years. I'm not about to be intimidated. Let's face it. Nobody dared attack Kennedy down here and nobody's going to attack me. We've got enough security for six presidents, let alone one banker. And I know everybody in my foursome — all they want is my money."

"That's all the terrorists want."

"A two-dollar Nassau I can afford." He looked thoughtful. "You wonder sometimes what your life has been worth. Now these guys put a million-dollar price tag on it. Ironic."

"Why ironic?"

"I showed you the books, Virginia. I'm worth more than a million, closer to three. Two million six to be exact. It'll all be yours."

"Simon, don't be morbid. It's bad for your golf."

Ehrlich got up and knocked on the dining room door. It was opened by a security guard carrying a sawed-off shotgun. "Ready to go, Mr. Ehrlich?" he said. "Windy day, down by the water. Got to keep the ball low."

"If I could do with the ball what I'm supposed to do," Ehrlich snapped, "the game wouldn't be any fun."

The guard, an off-duty policeman, shrugged. He wasn't paid to make conversation.

"Darling, I don't want you wasting time after you play,"

his wife said. "We're due at Filoons' for lunch. And you know how impossible they are if we're late."

"One beer. I'll have one beer."

"Just don't linger over it. I want to be on time. And Simon . . ."

"Yes," said Ehrlich, walking out the front door.

"Be careful. I'm scared for you."

Ehrlich was driven to the club by the off-duty policeman, who kept the shotgun in the front seat beside him. Another car followed them, containing two bored protection agency men with .38-caliber pistols and white socks. Ehrlich's foursome was already waiting to tee off. Another security man had checked out the golf cart, along with Ehrlich's clubs and bag.

"One thing about being a marked man, Simon," his partner said, "there's no waiting and there's no one playing through us."

"It's what happens when you go to heaven," one of his opponents said.

"Always the needle, Charlie," said Ehrlich. "How about raising the ante today? A three-dollar Nassau? Automatic presses?"

"You take the heat pretty good, Simon," the man said. "You want to lose all the money you didn't pay off?"

"You could talk the pants off the pope," Ehrlich said to the man. "Tee off, for Christ's sake."

The man held a ball in his hand tightly. "Odd or even?" he said.

"Odd," said Ehrlich.

The man smiled and showed a Maxfli Two in his hand. "Our honor," he said. "And we intend keeping it all day."

The man teed off, a partially dubbed, smothered hook, ending up on the left side of the fairway about one hundred and fifty yards out. People watching in back of the tee booed good-naturedly. The man's partner boomed one down the middle about two twenty. "Catch us," he said to Ehrlich.

Ehrlich's partner put a ho-hummer down the right center and gave an exaggerated yawn, as if to say that he could hit the same shot every time. Simon Ehrlich hit a big ball. But it had a bigger tail on it, slicing into the rough near the woods that lined the right side of the first fairway.

"Want your Mulligan now?" his opponents chided him.

"It'll play, Simon," Ehrlich's partner assured him. "Let's take a look."

"I want to check out those trees, Mr. Ehrlich," the ex-policeman said. Two of them whipped off in their own cart to check the rough and the trees. Two other guards trotted alongside Ehrlich's cart. They were being paid twenty-five dollars an hour and the flaps on their holsters were unbuttoned.

Watching with binoculars from the bell tower of St. Andrew's Church overlooking Hyannisport Golf Club was Scott Dutton. Next to him, looking out to sea and watching one of the last races of the yacht club season, was Enrico Boaz. The small Beetle Cats shimmered on the sea. "Look at those sailboats out there," Boaz said. "What do those people care? No work. Nothing but money. I wish we had shit planted on every one of those boats and that when I pressed a button, they'd all go 'poof.'"

"Get ready," said Dutton, watching Simon Ehrlich get out of his cart and go to his bag to select a club for his second shot. The guards all watched Ehrlich, already bored with the prospect of wandering after a hacker for seventeen more holes.

Ehrlich pulled out a three wood. "Too much club," his partner said.

"Maybe you're right," said Simon Ehrlich, and he put it back in his bag and moved for his five wood, the dependable weapon. Ehrlich had made so many fine shots over the years with that club. Using it, he had eagled the par-five fourteenth at Dorado Beach, his shot carrying the water guarding the green and jumping on two bounces into the cup. With that wood he had made his first hole-in-one, the par-three fifth hole at Belmont Country Club's Tournament of Champions.

Ehrlich took two practice swings, feeling as comfortable with the club as a carpenter would with his favorite chisel. He stepped up to the ball, thinking only of his second shot, and saw it in his mind's eye, nestled in the center of the green, when his limbs flew from his body, and the last thing that flashed through his brain as he died in a thousand pieces was —"Keep your head still. Look at the ball."

"Jesus," said Boaz, high in the church tower.

"No Jesus about it," said Dutton, the professional. "Fifteen ccs of nitroglycerin, poured into the hollow shaft of the club."

"Golf is a stupid game."

"Takes a lot of time," Dutton agreed, still watching through the binoculars. "And it's dangerous."

15

Alex and I had words. He says ten right
deaths will save thousands of lives eventually.
When I'm with him, I believe; when I'm alone,
I doubt. I have accumulated almost two hundred and forty thousand. The others talk
of nothing but the money; of nothing but doing
for themselves. If I must carry out my work
alone, without them, still it must be done.

"Get a poison gas for us," Alex says to me.
"You're the lawyer; the chief of staff. Go
to a library. Do some research. You're along
for your brains and your soul. Use your
brains . . ." He should know that titles
mean nothing to me. Titles are meaningless,
like brokerage house vice presidents.

I called Arthur D. Little, Rand Corporation,
McKinsey, cold, out of the blue. Asked for
Research, Chemical Research. Three calls.
Last call, I get put on hold twice, finally
shifted to eager voice. Eager voice sounded
just like me in Law School.

"My name is Michael Carling," I told him.
"I'm writing a mystery. Had fourteen published
under different names. Could use some help
with a gas. I know nothing about gas."

"Sure. I need a break anyway."

"I won't take too much time."

"No sweat," he says. "This is great. Like
doing crossword puzzles for us. Enter-
tainment."

"I want to gas somebody to death in an
elevator. Can you fix that?"

"Sure. How much time do I have?"

"What do you mean?"

"Can I stop the elevator? Or does the elevator have to be moving?"

"You can stop it."

"Okay. That's best. There'll be less circulation that way. Fewer air currents moving
around."

"What'll you use?"

"I don't know."

"Cyanide?"

"I could, but I don't think I will."

"How would you use cyanide? If you wanted
to?"

"You'd take cyanide salts, such as potassium
cyanide, and put it with concentrated hydro-
chloric acid. First, you'd chill the acid
with liquid nitrogen. Freeze it in a glass
ampule. Then add the cyanide. Then take
a torch and seal the ampule. Then the whole
thing would be safely in glass. Imagine a
25-watt bulb, something about that size. You
throw it down into the elevator and it shat-
ters. Then you replace the trap door quickly

and get the hell out. But cyanide isn't
the answer. I'd use phosgene."

"How would it work?"

"Same way. Get phosgene gas into a liquid
and seal it into a glass ampule. The light
bulb. Drop the ampule. And it's all over."

"You sure?"

"Either dead or in a coma in a minute or
two. We'll use ten times more than we really
need. You only need 90 parts per million
to kill. We'll use a thousand."

"I really appreciate it."

"One more thing."

"Yes?"

"There are probably seventy-two safety steps
with phosgene. Have your killer use 'em all."

"I'll send you a copy of the book. If I
can have your name and address."

"I'll spell it out and, yeah, you want
detail, right?"

"Right."

"Incidentally," the guy tells me, "phosgene
smells like musty hay."

He gave me his name and address. Incredible.

I gave Alex the information while we walked
in the park. Stopped for leak in Men's Room
and there were two fags coming out of a
stall. Alex stopped and looked at them. Two
older men. Pathetic. "You won't call a
cop. We're going," one of them said.

"I won't call a cop," Alex said. "You've
got somebody, hold onto him." Incredible.

Extract from the journal of Michael Cagnina

Kirk Abbott thought he understood human nature. He believed there were only two ways to probe the core of a person. One way was to deal with his money. The other was to confront him with danger.

"Audie Murphy never knew he had it in him to be a hero," Kirk said. "Neither did Sergeant York."

"Who's Sergeant York?" Gena Reynolds asked him.

"The biggest hero of World War I. A backwoodsman from Kentucky. Gary Cooper played him in the movie."

"I met Audie Murphy. I ate next to him once at Chasen's. He didn't look like a hero. He was cute."

"You never know about people until you put them to the wall. They can fight back, or they can roll over and die. Most people are never threatened with violence, so they never know this about themselves. It's a shame."

"How do you react to violence, Mr. Anastos? How do you think I'd react?"

"I react well, like a hero," Abbott said. "It's easy to say. It's easy to tell a beautiful woman. I hope you have a chance to see someday. I need to be praised, to have people admire me. I think you would react solely for self-preservation. I'm being very honest with you."

"Do you know that I watched you this morning? From the hotel window?"

Kirk reacted carefully. "You watched me?"

"Yes. On the lawns. Playing soccer with those children. I'd swear you were their teacher. Not a stranger at all. You do so well with children."

"Perhaps it's just playing soccer that I do so well."

"No. It was with the kids. You don't have to be embarrassed. I think it's fine."

"All right. I admit I lost myself for a while."

"That's a step in the right direction," Gena said, smiling at the man in the thick, horn-rimmed glasses.

Kirk Abbott and Gena Reynolds were dining in the Elizabethan Grille of the Raffles Hotel, still one of the great hotels in the Orient. At Raffles, the sun never set on the British Empire.

"You know," Gena said. "I never had any idea of going to Singapore. I always thought of Japan, and certainly Hong Kong. But Singapore never crossed my mind. I mean, I'm glad because I saw my family in Los Angeles. But twenty-five hours from California with two stopovers . . . that's a long way to go for curry. And it was most difficult to explain to Figueroa."

"Our good minister of finance," Kirk said. "Can't he make do with his wife for a few days?"

"He's gotten used to eating out."

"The trouble with success is that people want to share it. An energy-sapping enterprise."

"You show remarkable restraint, Mr. Anastos," Gena said.

"Anything in particular?"

"You haven't asked me. I have a surprise for you." Gena wore an Indian sari of blue silk bought that afternoon on High Street. It had a Calcutta label inside and was hand-stitched and hand-finished. She looked like the daughter of an Irish spice trader who had intermarried and settled in the Far East. Gena had that quality of looking as if she belonged wherever she was.

Kirk had wired her a ticket in Costa Rica with instructions to meet him. It was uncharacteristic of him. He never did anything on impulse, had never done anything in his life on impulse. It bothered him slightly and he wondered about it — until he saw Gena and knew he had done the right thing. It was good to indulge himself once in a while, he thought; he knew too many things that no one else knew. It was a heavy burden. Gena was his hobby and his escape.

"I know what the surprise is," Kirk said. "You got the bank charter."

"Not exactly the easiest first job right out of business school," Gena said. "No normal working hours, all overtime."

"Then that makes it all time and a half."

"I must tell you, Mr. Anastos," she said. "I've been taking notes for a book."

"You have a beginning, a middle and an end?"

"So far it's all middle," Gena said. She reached across the table and took his hands in hers, rubbing her skin softly against his. Some people are able to hold hands better than other people make love. Gena was a master at both.

Kirk kept his hands folded within Gena's and sensed Singapore around him, the giant ceiling fans rotating quietly, the *whisk, whisk* a counterpoint to the subdued rattling of silverware and plates. Understanding nothing about the Far East, he let the Singapore night surround him, secure in its mystery. "Middles are the most important thing," Kirk said to her. "Beginnings are easy, it's like buying a stock. Endings are usually bad. Meaningful perhaps. But usually bad. I want to keep this going."

Gena took her hands away. "If you want to keep it going, you're going to have to be honest with me. Games have gotten me to this point; money has taken me a little further than I thought I would go. But there's a limit. You know my father was a gardener in Bel Air. He saw a lot of unreality and he taught me about it. I know the difference."

"Ah. But your father made things beautiful."

"Yes, Mr. Anastos," Gena said. "But he made things beautiful for other people."

A Chinese waiter brought them a good, runny Brie, some sliced pears with the skin left on, and a bottle of champagne, a 1955 Pol Roger Blanc de Blanc, in a silver ice bucket. "Fine after curry, sir," the waiter said to Kirk. "A good choice."

The waiter liked Americans. They had begun visiting the Far East in greater numbers after the war and he found them generous, happy. They encouraged him to assist them in ordering. They smiled when he approved their final selection. He could speak with Americans. He could never speak with the French or the British.

Looking across the table at the oddly amused expression on the face of his beautiful woman, and a little high from the drinks and his trip, Kirk made a decision. "I think I'll tell you a lot of things, Gena," Kirk said. "If you can wait a little longer. I know I'm going to be ready soon."

"What's soon?" she asked.

"By the first of the year."

"That's months!"

"We're talking big numbers, Gena. You can't push it when you're talking big numbers. Can you hold out in Costa Rica? Is the finance minister still in the ball game?"

"He's in love."

Kirk looked at her, the slightly pouting lips, her eyes a deep brown with long black lashes, her auburn hair falling over her shoulders, shining with a thousand strokes of a Mason-Pearson brush an hour before dinner.

"I can understand that," Kirk said.

Gena laughed out loud and he poured her more champagne. "Does that mean I can find out who you really are? That I can call you by a name that means something? No one is really named Costas Anastos. You look more like Sandy McTavish than Costas Anastos."

"The glory that was Greece," Kirk said. "One has to live with mysteries. It's a sad story."

"Did you bring me all the way to Singapore to tell me that you're ready to trust me? Almost? Miami would have done nicely, and with much less expense."

"I have business in Singapore in about fifteen minutes. It won't take a long time. I missed your stories of lust and intrigue with the minister of finance."

"I could have sent you a letter."

Kirk got up and caressed the back of her neck. She leaned her face down and kissed the palm of his hand. "I missed you," he said. "Wait for me and we'll take a rickshaw around the island and see the night."

"There's no moon."

"It's all right," Kirk answered. "There are no rickshaws anymore, either. We'll think of something."

Gena wondered about him as he left, and she glanced up at the ceiling momentarily. The big fans went slowly, round and round, and she remembered that tomorrow she wanted to buy a white dress with pleats in the skirt.

The bar at the Raffles Hotel sold more gin than any other hotel in the Far East. The hotel encouraged gin, fostered it, perpetuated it. And gin reminded everyone who ever lifted a glass in the Raffles bar that Rudyard Kipling knew the good life when he saw it.

"After dinner, I drink gin and bitter lemon, with two ice cubes, Mr. Abbott," said Arthur Choa, vice president in charge of loans for the Singapore-Overseas Bank.

"I'll try anything," said Kirk ordering the same.

"I've heard that about you," said the banker, who was tall and impeccably groomed in a summerweight, tan three-piece suit with white shirt and navy blue Balliol College tie. "How are you enjoying our island?"

"I haven't seen much except the hotel. But dinner was delicious. So many people in the streets."

"We are not so civilized yet, Mr. Abbott, that we have ladies' groups passing out birth control information. Our people's lives center around the streets. The outdoor markets. At home, they sleep and eat. That's all."

"Every now and then I think of the simple life, Mr. Choa."

"I'm sure you do, Mr. Abbott. But I know you're not here to discuss the purchase of a waterfront cottage."

"I'm here to pay you twenty million dollars in cash on account. If you extend the balance due for six months beyond the deadline."

The banker drained his gin and bitter lemon. He sucked on one of the two ice cubes until it dissolved in his mouth. "No."

"Just like that?" Abbott said. "Check with your principals."

The banker stared at him. Aristocratic Malays never smile. They think it is in bad taste to show emotion. He took his other ice cube, rolling it from side to side in his mouth. He said nothing.

"I see," said Abbott.

Choa dissolved the second cube. "You see," he said. "What do you see?"

"I see that they are squeezing me, although I have cooperated."

"You Americans and your fair play," said the banker, his face darkening, his lips pulled back to show gums almost black in his mouth. "Your country's innocence has cost you the mastery of the world. You want to be loved by everyone, but your innocence makes you objects only of contempt. I shall pass your words along, but you know the state of your markets. United Stores seems a little lower each day. What is to stop the decline? What is to stop the confusion? We lead ordered lives here in Singapore. I hope you can learn something from your visit."

"I've learned I'll probably pay for this check."

The banker nodded. "Your woman is very lovely," he said. "It must be a consolation. She believes in controlling the population, no doubt."

"Good-bye, Mr. Choa," Kirk said. The banker bowed slightly and turned to leave.

"One thing, Mr. Choa."

"Yes." The banker turned.

"I think gin and bitter lemon is a shitty drink."

The banker kept walking, moving gracefully and carefully out of the bar. He nodded to several people, but never stopped for words.

George Grayson, president of Grayson Construction Company, ate lunch every weekday in the bar at "21." He had the same lunch every day, beginning late, at one-thirty, with a martini made with a dash of scotch instead of vermouth, a tomato and lettuce salad with house dressing, the "21" cheeseburger with a Carlsberg dark beer and two cups of black coffee. Grayson was a widower and usually ate with young ladies possessing ample proportions that he could show off to his friends at the bar. Two bodyguards sipped tomato juice near the door and watched George Grayson. They had been hired by the company after Grayson had refused to pay the million-dollar ransom demanded by the People's Revolutionary Army.

"This is a bunch of bullshit," the bluff, self-made head of the largest private construction company in New York had said. "No chief executive is worth a million dollars to his firm."

"You *are* the company, Big George," his associates told him.

"Don't you forget it," he had said. "Call the cops and give them the note. We've got projects to build. We've got places to tear down. Let's stop with all the bullshit and get the lead out." They prevailed upon Grayson to hire guards. He agreed reluctantly, but he insisted that they make themselves inconspicuous. Grayson always moved at double time, which complicated any security job.

"Honey," he was saying to his current lunch companion. "I know there's no fool like an old fool. But did I give you the ride of your life last night, or did I not give you the ride of your life?"

"George," she said. "People will hear."

"See those two guys there?" He pointed to the entrance of the bar. "They're supposed to be taking care of me. I'm valuable, honey. Think they're big enough to take care of me?"

"Am I big enough to take care of you?" she asked putting her hand on the thigh of his wide-wale corduroy workpants.

"Careful, honey," he said. "I may not be able to go back and tear up Sixty-eighth Street this afternoon."

She had eaten a shrimp cocktail with a glass of Chablis and some cheesecake. Her tummy felt rounded and fine. People stopped by Grayson's table to say hello, shake his hand, tell him a story. "Let's get traveling, honey," he said finally. "They flatter me so much here that I think when I retire, I'll become a waiter."

"It turns me on when all those people notice us."

George Grayson was already noticing a girl waiting to come in with a giant fat man who developed real estate.

"Got yourself a court stenographer, Fat Louis, I see," he said to the man as they passed him. "Fifty words a minute, eh?"

"Fastest hands in the East," the fat man said to Grayson. They nudged each other and roared with laughter.

At least two dozen briefcases and leather attaché cases lay in random disorder on the floor near the hatcheck room at "21." Customers just put them down to retrieve them after lunch. No one objected and the hatcheck girl was too busy to be bothered with executive luggage. George Grayson picked up his thick briefcase, bulging with blueprints and documents, and put his arm around his lady. "Got a little something for you, honey," he said. "Come on over to the door where we can see it in the light."

"George," she gushed, pressing herself against his arm. "You don't have to do that. It's not my birthday or anything. You barely know my sizes."

"This don't matter about size, honey," he said. "And I know all the sizes I need to know. Besides, it's been just a month since we met. Our anniversary." They walked to the doorway, with the security men watching from the hatcheck area about fifteen feet away. Grayson dialed the three-number combination of his briefcase — 7-7-0, the street address of his office. He flicked the release button and the double lock releases on the side. He opened the case to show his shining-faced lunch partner the pearls he had picked out for her at Harry Winston. He never noticed the tiny thread, a switch, surrounding the catch on the lock, which led to the blasting cap in a half-stick of dynamite buried beneath his blueprints. The explosion blew off the door at "21," and locked George Grayson and his new lady forever together in their one-month celebration. The security men were slammed against a wall, and the only tangible proof that George Grayson had been there at all was a receipt from Harry Winston.

Scott Dutton rushed from the bar where he heard the explosion, along with twenty other drinkers and diners. He and three unemployed advertising men who had nothing to lose went back to the bar and ordered fresh drinks.

A month later, the hatcheck girl found four pearls in a corner of the coatroom. She put them in her purse and took them home.

Edward Mahoney lived in Ridgewood, New Jersey, and kept a permanent suite on the twenty-fifth floor of the Regency Hotel, mostly for the convenience of his wife, who hated to go back to Ridgewood after a day of spending money in the city. She had been a famous beauty in her youth, and Edward Mahoney, the largest bottler of Kap-Kola in America, still adored her and still indulged the petty delights of his former famous beauty.

"I'm terrified to even go to Bendel's," she told him, hysterical at breakfast in their suite. "I'm going crazy expecting something to blow up in my face. You've got to do something, Eddie. This is America!"

"Look, darling," he said with no conviction. "The authorities are all working on this thing. They've got everybody digging, from the CIA to the Marines. The New York commissioner himself tells me they're very close to a breakthrough."

"The maid told me this morning that we've been asked to check out of the hotel. It that true?"

"The bomb squad has searched the place from top to bottom and found nothing. I'm afraid the management doesn't like the police and security people crawling all over the corridors and the lobby. I don't really blame them. I've been thinking about moving us to an upstairs floor at the Camden Bottling Plant. You know, fix it up like a luxury apartment."

"You mean a bunker, for God's sake. Let's pay the money," she suddenly screamed. "I can't stand it."

A police lieutenant burst into the room with his .38 in his hand. Two sergeants were in back of him, their pistols also drawn. Mrs. Mahoney fell to the floor behind her husband. "Don't shoot," she screamed, and lay there sobbing violently. Edward Mahoney took two Librium with the remains of his grapefruit juice. "Lieutenant," he said, "I've had it. A million dollars is not worth my marriage and everyone's sanity. Call the newspapers, the radio and television stations, and let them broadcast that we'll pay. Please do it immediately."

The lieutenant didn't bother to argue; he felt nothing but pity for Mahoney. He knew he was looking at a dead man. He had seen too much fear in his life; it always looked the same.

"I feel better already," Mahoney said to the two detectives, who walked him down the hall from his room. "I don't feel a million dollars poorer. I feel as if I've been given a wonder drug. Never forget that money means nothing if you don't have your health."

"I got nothing to worry about, Mr. Mahoney," said one of the detectives. "I've had arthritis for fifteen years and I take home one hundred and sixty-three dollars a week."

"Well, do you blame me for wanting to save my ass?" Mahoney asked. "You guys aren't threatened. You saw my wife. She was out of her mind."

"If you people who have the money didn't have backbones like my kids' fuckin' gerbils, we wouldn't have half the people in the country arming themselves and shivering in their beds."

"What's your name?" demanded Mahoney, whipping out a thin gold pencil and notepad. "You can't talk to me like that." The elevator doors opened on the twenty-fifth floor.

"Sullivan, Mr. Mahoney," the detective said. "Capital S-u-double l-i-v-a-n, and you're a poor excuse for an Irishman. Must be an Orangeman, you must." They got onto the elevator and it hissed shut behind them.

"I'll have your badge, you sorry imitation of a flatfoot. Nobody talks to E. J. Mahoney that way."

Detectives off of the lobby watched the lights mark the changing floors and saw them flicker and go out between levels twenty and twenty-one. They raced for the stairs.

Creed Edwards, two weeks earlier, had broken into the office of ABC Services, electricians, who serviced most of the hotels on Park Avenue. He took nothing but two sets of white coveralls with ABC SERVICES sewn in red letters on the back. The coveralls got Creed into the service entrance of the Regency carrying a small tool chest. He went directly to the top floor of the hotel, where he opened the door to the roof of the elevator shaft.

Creed Edwards had shorted out the circuits. Crouched on top of the elevator car, he pried open the grating in the metal surface just enough to drop the light bulb containing the phosgene gas.

E. J. Mahoney pushed and pulled at the detectives, trying to get them to shield him from the gas. "I'll pay," he screamed at the top of the elevator, "I've said I'll pay. Make it two million. Anything." The detectives frantically put their jackets and hats over the shreds of glass, but the trickles of gas crept from beneath their clothes like the fingers of a ghost. Mahoney was pulling bills out of his pockets and waving them at the ceiling.

The detectives died first, choking and streaming yellow from their ears, eyes, noses and throats. E. J. Mahoney passed on without last rites, and with his pockets empty of everything except a commemorative coin, a souvenir of twenty years with the Kap-Kola Corporation.

Silver Wheels Edwards forced open the doors on the twenty-first floor and proceeded by stairs to the roof. A policeman held a gun to his head the minute he exited and an assistant manager came running out half a minute later.

"I'm with ABC Services," Edwards said. "We're here every week for the electrical systems." He showed the cop his ABC identification card and spoke to the assistant manager. "You know me. I been coming here for years. All this shit about equality. First black face anybody sees, he's the man. He's the *man*. What did I suppose to do?"

The assistant hotel manager, a graduate of Cornell Hotel School who grew up in Long Island's Five Towns, felt terrible.

"He's right," the manager said. "I know him. He works on the electrical systems. Let him go. I'm awfully sorry," he said to Edwards.

"Sure, you're sorry," said Edwards. "Also, you ain't black. This give you a taste of what it's like."

"I'm really sorry. Look," the assistant said. "I'll call your boss and tell him what a terrific job you're doing."

"I was told to hold everyone," the policeman said.

"I'm responsible for our hotel," the assistant said. "This man has been coming here for years. A trusted professional."

"As long as you're calling the shots," said the cop. "What's a Western Union splice?" he asked Silver Wheels suddenly.

"You kidding?" said Edwards. "It's a job where there is big stress, and two wires are to be joined. End to end. Mostly use it for extension cords. Easy."

"You can go," said the cop. Edwards walked to the roof exit door and disappeared, carrying his tool chest.

"You used to be an electrician?" asked the assistant manager.

"Naw, I just thought it up. No idea what the hell it is. But the spade answered right away. Must be legit."

"It's people like you, using words like that, that make him as bitter as he is. How would you like to be innocent of something and always stared at as a guilty man because of your skin?"

"Wise up, chief," the cop said. "You gotta accuse somebody of something. For some reason."

The assistant manager headed for the roof exit himself, without saying anything. The cop would never understand. Dumb mick, the assistant said to himself, sprucing up the white carnation in his lapel.

"Okay, you dumb mick," Boaz said to Sean Higgins over his walkie-talkie. "Do you see him?" Higgins lay prone on a roof looking across at the board room of Champion Electronics. He was carefully putting the chairman, David Nason, in the middle of the cross hairs of a .30–.30 deer rifle with a Norman Ford Texan model telescopic sight. Nason looked as big and as close to Higgins as though he were sitting in a seat directly in front of him. "Goddammit, Higgins, are you there?" insisted Boaz again.

Higgins put down the rifle and picked up his transmitter. "You are such a greasy pain in the ass, Rico," he said. "I'm zeroed in so well I hope the bastard doesn't pay."

"We're calling him now," Boaz said. "No more conversation. I give you one beep, get the hell out of there. Two beeps, you hit him and that's all. Just him. Don't hang around to mop up. They got helicopters out patrolling the city."

"This is your last chance, Mr. Nason," Michael Cagnina said into the phone. "You have ten seconds to give us an answer. If you have not answered in ten seconds, it's sayonara."

"I'll see you all fry in hell," said Nason into the phone. "And Champion Electronics is going to supply the electric chairs."

"Sayonara, Mr. Nason," said Cagnina. From a gas station phone booth on Riverside Drive he signaled thumbs down to Boaz, who immediately gave two beeps on his walkie-talkie.

Sean Higgins lingered on his target, moving his rifle from Nason's stomach to his chest, to his heart, to his brain. So easy.

Nason sat in his chair at the head of a long conference table, facing his assassin directly.

"I don't know, David," Nason's senior vice president, and next in line, said to him. "It's too big a gamble. I'm sure we should pay and have this thing off your shoulders."

"Someone's got to hold the line," Nason said to his board. "All I can tell you right now is that it's going to be David Nason."

"We'll back you up in whatever decision you make, Dave. We're thinking of you."

"Well, think of Champion, goddammit," he said. "If more of you thought of Champion half as much as I do, we wouldn't be selling at nine times earnings."

Higgins chose the chest as his target, and the first shot with his special ammo with hollow points put a tiny hole in the safety glass in Champion's board room and turned David Nason's upper chest into a disaster area. He didn't die immediately, and he was conscious of the phone ringing and somebody answering.

"According to the Annual Report," Michael Cagnina said, "you're the first vice president." All the directors were prone on the floor underneath the conference table. The wind sucked through the broken glass in the sealed wall of the building. "Well?" said Cagnina's voice on the phone. "Are you next? It's an easy way toward building a flexible corporate structure."

"We'll pay," the vice president screamed into the phone.

"We'll pay," the directors yelled at the top of their voices, as the tremendous pressure created by the smashed window threatened to draw them out into the void, twenty-five stories above Third Avenue, from which nothing usually fell save the droppings of pigeons.

William "Willie" Henshaw was a heavy-hitting floor member of the largest institutional house on Wall Street, Henshaw, Freeman & Company. He was a governor of the New York Stock Exchange and a member of the Racquet and Tennis, the Knickerbocker, and the Field Club of Bronxville, where he lived with his wife and four children. His life had been threatened twice before, both times by husbands demanding satisfaction for the horns Willie Henshaw had put on their heads. He shrugged things like that off and had responded to the demands of the People's Revolutionary Army by saying, "You guys are obviously misinformed about the state of Wall Street these days. You couldn't get a million dollars in liquid capital out of anyone down here. Personally, I couldn't raise thirty thousand cash if I had to."

"No snow job, man," he was told. "*Who's Who* says you're the fucking pillar of Wall Street."

Henshaw laughed and went off to play tennis.

He disdained police protection. But, under the mayor's orders, two detectives stayed in his shirt twenty-four hours a day. They even dogged him at lunchtime when, three days a week, he would leave the floor of the Exchange and be driven uptown to the Sherry-Netherlands Hotel. There he maintained a suite by the week, where he would entertain fund managers, pension representatives, and various women who would be sent to him by a madam who lived at Central Park West and Eighty-ninth Street. The women cost Henshaw seventy-five dollars a visit. The two detectives would sit outside on the Plaza fountain and wait. Three lunch hours a week.

Glory Cohen had no trouble entering the Sherry in a black wool suit from Alexander's that clung to her the way Saran Wrap covers a plastic dish. She took the elevator and walked down the hallway, her black patent shoulder bag hugging her side. She looked like an editor for a man's magazine, a confident woman, used to luncheon meetings on business matters.

Henshaw admitted her to his room and looked at Glory, up, down and sideways.

"You're not Puerto Rican," he said. "She's been sending Puerto Ricans practically every time for weeks."

"I'm Jewish," Glory said, unbuttoning the jacket of her suit and hanging it over the back of a chair. "You're not anti-Semitic or anything?"

"Quite the contrary," Henshaw said. "I was married once to someone whose grandfather was Jewish. An exciting woman."

"Why don't you get undressed and we'll talk about it."

At age fifty-three, Henshaw was white-haired, broad-shouldered, and proud of his permanent suntan and flat stomach. He took no time to leave his clothes in a pile in the middle of the floor.

"Now you," he said, watching her.

Glory removed her blouse. She wore no bra. Carefully, she took an ice cube from a glass left on a coffee table by Henshaw, and rubbed her nipples with its coldness. They instantly began to rise. And so did Willie Henshaw, until he stood rampant and expectant, ten feet away from Glory. She pulled down the zipper of her skirt. Then she undid the zipper of her shoulder bag. She dropped her skirt to the floor and stood naked facing the stockbroker.

"Unbelievable," said Henshaw, a moment before Glory pulled a .25-caliber Smith & Wesson with attached silencer from her bag and gave Willie Henshaw the jolt of his life. Henshaw started toward her and she was forced to shoot him three more times: high, middle, low. Knocked backwards, he fell heavily over a chair and died, not believing it could have happened to him at lunch.

Glory checked his pulse. The guy was in great shape, she thought. Great shape for his age.

del escritorio de
Antonio Figueroa

I step through looking
glasses and I'm certainly
not Alice.
Who am I?
Is it Jet-lag?

From the scratch pad
of Gena Reynolds

16

*P*eople around the world were smug about the chaos in America. Ministers of state preached the inevitable results of materialism. They campaigned for office extolling the benefits of a simple society. Taxi drivers said they had known it would happen all along.

Corriere della Sera in Rome quoted five cardinals, who agreed that God was responsible for the events in North America, that God was repaying the unforgivable sin — pride.

The London *Economist* claimed that a second revolution was entirely within the Western tradition. It called for "the second boot to drop, three hundred years after the first, the separation from the mother country in 1776. At last, the United States comes of age."

Der Spiegel, in a controversial editorial that infuriated Christian Democrats, maintained, "The myth of democracy, that all men are created equal, contained the seeds of its own destruction. The lunatics," it said, "are taking over the asylum."

Asians still believed what they had believed for generations — that Westerners lacked the ability to govern themselves. "They have no sense of submission," the news broadcasts declared. "The Americans never cared for the laws of nature, they only cared for themselves." Millions in Asia read the news or heard the stories on radio and television, and they smiled at one another, secure in their feelings of moral superiority. They worked all the harder on assembly lines, in stores, on export agreements. They were submissive and efficient. They had known all along that in the end, in time, the world would be theirs without firing a shot.

Africa was gleeful, and its press was full of stories about the American animals who had reverted to their true nature: savages living in steel and concrete cities that were no better than cages. What was happening in North America was no more than divine retribution.

On October first, the President of the United States arranged a historic dinner for the business leaders of the nation, the sort of dinner that had not been seen since the dark economic days of September 1974 when the stock market was threatened with collapse. But now the Dow Jones Industrial Average stood at 630, and Eliot Janeway was predicting lows of around four hundred before the bottom was touched. United Stores was at seven, its only saving grace being the fact that the really big sellers seemed to have already moved from the stock between nine and ten.

Fifty men gathered with the Cabinet in the White House's Private Dining Room, lit with more than seven hundred candles, to eat from James Madison's china, with silverware that Andrew Jackson had won in a horse race from a Louisiana gentleman. A company of Marines was dispersed in full battle gear around the White House lawn. Each of the corporate executives, from the fifty largest companies in the country, had been driven from the airport in limousines with special steel plating. Secret service men were at the wheel, in the jump seats, hanging onto the sides from running boards. After a dinner consisting of softshell Maryland crab cocktail, beef Wellington, Caesar salad, and strawberry shortcake, the President got up with no introduction.

"Our country," he said, "is in the grips of an irrational fear. And while fear itself is the primary factor, feeding on itself, we cannot overlook the dreadful and shocking destruction of property, the horrifying loss of life of some of our economic leaders, both Republican and Democrat. I think we should all pray for their souls for a minute, and for the integrity of our republic." The President's Cabinet and fifty businessmen stared down into the remains of their strawberry shortcake and prayed for their own lives and the safety of their own families.

"Those men," the President continued, "your brothers at the heartlands, the pulsebeat of this, the greatest country in the history of the world, died because they were principled and stubborn. I want you all to be principled and stubborn. And we shall beat all terrorists to their knees. The time has come for an eye for an eye, a tooth for a tooth. I am declaring war on terrorism and terrorists, and a state of national emergency. I am placing reserve units on alert all across this great land, and offering full cooperation of the armed services to any local authorities. I am announcing a reward of one million dollars, tax free, for any information leading to the capture or death of any terrorist or extortionist. I am declaring a mandatory death penalty for any so-called terrorists, and life imprisonment at hard labor for any pranksters who threaten the fabric of public order. And the courts can cooperate in these matters or I'll shut 'em down faster than a dog can jump on a coon. That's off the record, of course. I want to close with all the assurance of this office that these acts and these people shall be stopped." The President slammed his fist down upon the table. The men rose in unison, cheering and applauding. The President held up his hands. "Refreshments will be served in the Red Room," he said. "And some very good chocolate mints. Cigars for those of you who want to stink up a room etched in history."

The President turned to his secretary of state. "That ought to get this country off its ass and moving again," he said.

A captain of New York police and a detective lieutenant had come down for the dinner, escorting Gerald Kenner, president of Kenner Gas & Fuel. They were talking to a White House security man standing under the brightly lit south portico.

"How do you guys get excused from duty?" the security man asked. "Who's minding the store?"

The New York cops laughed. "Christ, we're making seven hundred a week apiece protecting fat cats and escorting payoffs all over the goddam state. Pinkertons, Burns, Wackenhut: all the protection people are offering us twenty-five an hour to moonlight for them. And prices are escalating."

"They're getting so hard up they're pulling winos off the streets and putting them into uniform. Junkies, too. People are so desperate they don't care who's standing in front of their apartment door as long as he's warm and breathing. It's harder to get a bodyguard than a maid, if you can believe it. Even in Queens."

"We ain't had any trouble in Washington."

"That's because you've got nobody with any real dough down here. Maybe they got power. But nobody's heavy with any money that's important."

"When the hell are you guys gonna catch these bastards? They're making more money than the oil companies."

"If you want to know the truth, the mayor of New York says it's a conspiracy by the President. I heard him myself, coming out of his office at City Hall. He said the President wants to be the first king of America. So he engineers all this fear, and pretty soon the people say, do anything to save us from getting our property and our asses shot up. Then the President throws out the Constitution and makes himself the king. And he calls off his boys who are doing the killing."

"The mayor of New York sounds like he's got his head up his tail," said the White House guard.

"Well, the heat is on him something fierce. If he can't run his own city, he sure as hell ain't gonna be a candidate for dogcatcher anywhere else."

"Who are the Giants playing this weekend?" the White House guard asked.

"Miami," said the detective. "It's a you-pick-'em."

"Want to have a little action when they play the Redskins?"

"All this overtime, I can probably get us fifty or so."

"One thing's sure," said the White House guard. "They take my football away, I'd join the goddamned terrorists."

"The thing that frightens the shit out of me," said the captain of police, "is the false alarms. The papers and the TV give everybody the same ideas. Every fruitcake in the country is pushing out ransom demands as fast as they can get to the telephone or drop a note in the mail. That's what's out of hand, that's what's out of control. We had a stakeout last week on a drop in Central Park, near the zoo: plainclothesmen, police in drag, squad cars, patrols on scooters, all in a big circle. Half a million bucks being delivered to a trash barrel. We get the signal and converge on the trash barrel and we find three smartass kids from Bronx High School of Science. One of 'em going to MIT next year. They thought it was a good idea to bring their parents up from fuckin' poverty, one of 'em said. Can you believe that? You know what the deal cost the City of New York?"

"Plenty."

"You bet your sweet patootie it was plenty. That's what we're facing."

"You've got to get the real ones."

"We should take 'em all. The real ones. The fake ones. We should burn 'em all. This shit is getting to be too much like work."

"Better get the cars," said the White House guard, seeing the doors opening and the guests spilling out, waving their good-byes. "Here come the troops."

The phalanx of limousines moved like sleek, black caterpillars up to the south portico, retrieved their passengers, and eased away from the White House. Gerald Kenner, president of Kenner Gas & Fuel, felt comfortable after the food and wine and the Chief Executive's reassurances. "The worst is over," he said to the captain of police, who sat next to him in the back seat of the limousine. "The President has promised action. It's about time we went back to business as usual."

"Will you need me next week?" the policeman asked Kenner.

"I'll need you until I let you know otherwise," the businessman said.

"I'm spending too much time away from my family. As of now, it's going to cost you a little more."

"Like what?"

"Like a hundred an hour. Cash. In twenties so it's easy to count."

"That's extortion," said Kenner.

"That's tough titty, sir," said the policeman. "Everyone's entitled to make a living." The limousine accelerated when it hit the highway and they raced to the airport on a road deserted by all but racing black limousines carrying wealthy and frightened men.

"I am a woman happy in her work," said Gena Reynolds. "I'm only unhappy in my play. How's that for a puzzle?"

"I took you to the country to solve these problems," Kirk Abbott said to her. "Perhaps I'll solve my problems as well. Isn't it lovely?"

"It's beautiful. I can't believe that they could keep the

country green, considering how many people live in the cities."

"It's an ordered land. The people lead orderly lives. They wouldn't stand for the desecration of the villages. It's their touch with the past; Americans don't give a damn about the past."

Gena and Kirk were driving a rented Jaguar through the Cotswolds. They had taken a morning train from London to Bristol, dozing off to sleep in a comfortable first class compartment. In Bristol, Kirk picked up the Jaguar that had been reserved for his arrival. They hurried to Bath to be in time for a late luncheon at the Hole in the Wall, which at certain moments can be the finest restaurant in England. They talked about nothing special at luncheon, glad to be with one another. They still retained the tension produced by the unknown, the question marks that make for passion, if not love. After lunch Kirk took it more slowly. He had no rigid schedule and there was plenty of time to reach Broadway before dark. Kirk had reservations in Broadway.

"You are the goddammedest businessman I ever saw," Gena said. "It's nice to have whims. But Jesus, this bank of ours is not plastic and shaped like a piggy with a slot in it."

"What's the matter?" Kirk said. "Haven't you been paid every fifteenth of the month?" His tone was bitter, but he was smiling.

"Yes, I've been paid. It's job security I'm looking for."

"Join a union," Kirk said.

"I want to know when you're going to take me seriously. Play games if you want. Or get a new patsy for Costa Rica." Gena leaned against the passenger door of the Jaguar and stared out at the countryside. The leaves had turned russet on the trees and began to blow down and across their path. The October air was smoky and crisp. Kirk pushed the car up to a hundred and twenty kilometers. Gena didn't move a muscle; her mouth was set in stubborn anger.

"A man has to cover himself," Kirk said finally. "If he opens up to everyone, he ends up being defeated. Every man I ever knew who revealed his plans to others ended up behind the eight ball."

Gena turned to look at him. "You have to trust someone," she said. "It has to be part of all success. Sooner or later, everyone lets down."

"We'll see if we can make some progress tonight," he said. "It's the reason I brought you out here."

They came upon Broadway gently, the way it should be approached. Broadway is an ancient town that has scarcely changed since the time of Edward the Confessor. The houses and the shopfronts are stone, with thatched roofs. Everything is well maintained and shines with the efforts of people at ease with their past, people content to live within the confines of a rustic museum.

"I can't believe there's a place like this," Gena said. "We're staying here?"

"Just outside. An inn I discovered not long ago."

"With somebody else? I want to stay in town."

"With no one else. A business conference. Stop sounding like another person."

"You're the only one who's allowed to do that."

Kirk circled her shoulders with his left arm and pulled her close to him. "You'll adore it," he said. "I promise."

Gena snuggled against him and he moved beyond the center of town, accelerating up a steep hill. Again they were surrounded by fields. A farmer was driving cows slowly from pasture.

Kirk pulled off the blacktop onto a dirt road and, a thousand yards down it, took a sharp right turn, clattering onto a cobbled courtyard of an old farmhouse that had obviously undergone recent repairs. The Dorsel House, a wooden sign proclaimed, waving from polished chain links and hanging above thick oaken doors. Kirk registered and sent a boy out to collect the luggage.

"Let's have a drink," he said to Gena, and they walked into a sitting room–library, paneled in dark mahogany with leather-spined editions of sporting chronicles stacked in floor-to-ceiling shelves. The furniture was oak and leather, as you would hope to find in such a place. There was a giant fire in what must have been the old farm's main fireplace, big enough for a man to stand upright in it. "It's perfect, Mr. A." she said to Kirk. "Thank you." She kissed him on the cheek.

"I'd like to sit here and have some whiskey," Kirk said.

"Can I disappoint you and ask for tea?" Gena said. "It's a room we should have tea in."

"We'll have tea another afternoon," he said, "before we drive to Chipping Camden."

"Chipping Camden," she laughed.

"It's about twenty miles away. We're going there for dinner tomorrow."

"With Sir Walter Scott?"

"Scott is always on crusades. I thought a young baron would be right."

"Perfect," Gena said.

A young waitress costumed as a serving wench took their drink order. They had Ballantine Scotch in front of the fire. While they sat, an English couple in tweeds entered, collapsed together with relief upon a heavily stuffed couch, and chatted about vegetables, the price of petrol, and Anthony Powell.

"I think this is a film set," Gena said. "You've produced the whole thing."

"Only people from California would believe that. Is it all done with mirrors? Will it all disappear tomorrow? You never can ask those questions. It's just here and you have it."

After three Scotches Gena asked to see their room.

"The room is for later," Kirk told her. "After dinner, we see the room. First we sing in the bar with the locals, and we feel that we can't keep our eyes open another minute. That's when we see the room."

"I'd like to comb my hair and wash my face."

"Use the loo, luv," Kirk told her. "Don't be so impatient."

"I don't like surprises as much as you do. I don't think I'm as romantic," she told him. "Christ, you are romantic. I wasn't kidding about Sir Walter Scott."

Later, they were conducted to dinner by the owner of the Dorsel House, a spoiled young man in Gucci loafers who had been at Christ Church, Oxford, and came into his inheritance in time to indulge his hobbies: food and antiques. He bought the old farmhouse in Broadway and stocked it with his collection, taking over the supervision of the kitchen and the wine cellar himself.

"As soon as he gets bored with his toy, he'll sell it," said Kirk. "In the meantime, there's not an inn in England done as tastefully, with food as good."

"The waitresses look as good to eat as the beef Wellington."

"That's one of the prerequisites of an inheritance. It allows you to make your forefathers turn over in their graves."

"What are you leaving to me?"

"Ahh. That's my insurance with you. To make sure you go back to Costa Rica and preserve our little bank and our little finance minister. You know about Swiss bank accounts?"

"I know that if you die without instructions, the banks get to keep the money. Horrible for unnamed beneficiaries."

"An extremely civilized way to do business. I want to insure the fact that you stay on my best side. Like a favorite niece."

"Every birthday I'll send you a card. Uncle."

They had smoked salmon with capers, then grouse stuffed with wild rice, onions, raisins and nuts. Cheese and fruit they ate with a port the owner claimed had been bought at auction from the cellar of Winston Churchill. Gena smoked a long thin Uppmann; Kirk an Antonio & Cleopatra, and they each patted their bellies in great satisfaction, like old friends at their club. Kirk looked across the table at the auburn-haired woman. She seemed so relaxed: her full lips drawing easily on her cigar, her blue eyes large and clear, giving no hint of anything but complete honesty, innocence. She blew a smoke ring at Kirk, a slow, perfect oval, and immediately split it through its middle with a quick puff of cloud.

"I might love you," Kirk said.

"It's all right, Mr. Anastos. You can say it without hedging. You're safe; I won't bite."

"I think I might love you, Gena," he said. "Out here with nothing expected. With nothing expected at all."

"You can only love when it's make-believe," she said, pressing him. "What's the story? Who are you? Where do we go from here?"

"I'll tell you this much," Kirk said. "By the first of the year, I plan to join you in Costa Rica. I plan to run our bank and travel and lie in the sun and fish for giant tuna. I put part of the cards on the table for you: financial independence for the rest of your life. And eventually, no more mysteries. Can you wait that long?"

"What are the chances of your making it? Am I supposed to agonize every day over what's happening? Over where you are?"

"I'm leaving a letter for you with my Swiss bankers, which I intend having them burn on January second. When I'm safely with you."

"Figueroa isn't going to like you very much."

"By then it'll be too late. By then I'm not going to be interested in sharing you. Money will reduce the pain of his loss."

"If I'm not there for you," she said bitterly, "what will cover the pain of your loss?"

Kirk ignored her question. "Let's go into the bar for a song and a pint. I've told you more than I intended. More than I ever intended to tell anyone."

"Just tell me one thing more." Gena held onto his arm. "What's your first name? I always knew at least the first name of anyone who told me he loved me."

There was a long silence as he led her from the dining room to the bar. The room had been restored as a long, narrow pub with cushioned benches set into niches in the weathered wood walls. Kirk sat Gena down and went to the bar. "Two pints of the bitter," he said, signing a tab.

Men and women from the town sang old Music Hall numbers, accompanied by a tinkly upright piano. Kirk brought the beer to Gena and sat down beside her. Holding up a pint, he toasted, clinking his glass mug against hers. "It's Kirk," he said. "Cheers." They each took a long swallow.

"It's Kirk," she repeated, her face beaming. "Cheers," she said, clinking his mug in return and again swallowing long and deeply, until a moustache of foam appeared on her upper lip. They sang with the regulars for half an hour, Gena treating the crowd to a solo rendition of the old folk song about Anne Boleyn: "With 'er 'ed tucked underneath 'er 'arm. She walks the bloody tower," she sang. And the crowd, including Kirk, joined her on the choruses. With handshakes all around, they tore themselves away at one in the morning, leaving the owner in his Gucci's drinking brandy by himself in the library.

They walked upstairs. Great elm railings outlined the hall and family portraits scowled down from darkened walls. Their room was practically all feather bed, a fourposter with canopy and velvet curtains to shut out the light and shut in the pleasure. They undressed and fell gratefully into its midst. They wrapped themselves around one another, touching each other, kissing slowly, the urgency building with each discovery. Kirk broke away to pull the curtains all around, enclosing them in a blackness dark as death. "I can't tell it's you," Gena said. "Is it Kirk? Is it my Kirk?" He opened her legs and pulled them around him. Her heels moved up and dug lightly into his back. She arched her bottom, almost lifting it off the bed to meet him.

"It's Kirk," he said to her, entering Gena the way an otter slips into a pond.

Kirk left her sleeping in the great bed in the morning. He dressed, went outside to the Jaguar, and drove into Broadway, parking outside the Lygon Arms, which dominated the main street and where tourists and travel agents usually preferred to book. Built in 1530, it had provided lodgings for both Charles I and Cromwell (on separate occasions).

Kirk wore a trenchcoat and carried a bulging students' green bookbag over his shoulder into the hotel. He walked upstairs without pausing and down a hall to a door. When he knocked, a voice, gruff and hearty, called, "Open. *Entrez.*"

Rhinelander was seated in splendor, eating a gigantic English breakfast. His mouth full, Rhinelander gestured with his fork for Kirk to take a chair. Kirk emptied the green bookbag into the middle of the floor. Money poured from the bag in wrapped packages of U.S. twenties, fifties and hundreds. "There's another bag for you in Paddington Station. Here's the locker key." Kirk tossed it onto a couch. "There's a receipt for you to sign in the locker. Leave it there. I have a duplicate key."

"You really are bloody marvelous, Mr. Abbott," Rhinelander said. "I wish I had your talents, whatever you do.

Come have a banger with me. I'll ring for some eggs if you like."

"Nothing, thank you. I just wanted to make sure that everything was in order."

"Oh. Everything is in order. Quite so. How much is in the bags?"

"To the penny, six million four hundred and fifty thousand dollars. To the penny. No change."

"A shame we don't pay interest on cash balances. Please have a banger. It's worth coming to the country for their bangers. Bloody marvelous."

"You're beginning to sound English."

The fat Swiss wiped his mouth with a large linen napkin. "Wherever I am," he said, "I try to sound like the people of that country. It gives them more confidence in me, what?" The banker went down onto the floor and counted out the money, stacking it into piles around him as if he were a child playing with green paper blocks.

He counted the money three times, whereupon he went to a writing desk and issued Kirk a receipt. "When shall we see you again, Mr. Abbott?"

"I'm not sure. I'm going to be quite busy this fall."

"In the United States?" the lawyer asked. "I'm surprised you intend going back there. A barbaric country. All this terrorism and destruction. We got over that sort of thing hundreds of years ago. Your President has just declared war on the outlaws, I see." He indicated the morning London *Times*. "Like your bloody Wild West. I'd be careful if I were you. We hate to be the recipients of our clients' bad fortune."

Kirk laughed at the headlines and put the paper down. "The irresponsibility of the press in a democracy," he said. "Enflaming people's imaginations."

"Be that as it may, dear boy, it's damned serious," Rhinelander said. "Many of my clients are quite beside themselves."

As Kirk left, the lawyer was once again counting the money. His bangers had been forgotten. His tea grew cold.

Outside the Lygon Arms, Kirk paused, then decided to walk along High Street. He kicked leaves as he ambled slowly to the chemist's at the end of the block. The crisp autumn day, the fallen leaves, made him think of football and tailgating. He felt tired. At the chemist's he bought a package of Gillette blades and glanced at the previous day's evening news. PRESIDENT DECLARES WAR ON TERRORISTS, read the headlines. And in slightly smaller caps below that: TERRORISTS COUNTER WITH OWN DECLARATION. THREATEN TOTAL TRANSPORTATION PARALYSIS. YANKS SHUN TRAVEL. Kirk took his razor blades and walked back to his car. Clouds crossed over the October sun, and the sudden wind caught Kirk in the chest, chilling him.

19.750,000.00
19.750,000.00 T

.00 T

.00 T

.00 T

**From the calculator
of Kirk Abbott**

17

Glory Cohen and Enrico Boaz sat in the middle room at P. J. Clarke's on Third Avenue, the room connecting the long bar to the large dining room in the rear. The middle room was Siberia for the people in New York who knew better. They dreaded being seated in the middle room with the unknowns. But Glory Cohen and Boaz didn't mind. They liked to watch the people file into the back room, to be fawned over by the maître d'. Some people fawned back, slipping bills into palms, going through the New York ritual for survival in the best restaurants and gin mills. "Pretty good London broil," said Glory, mopping a piece of rye bread through the juices on her plate.

"The beer's okay," Boaz said. "Cold. You don't know how many places serve lukewarm beer. Like drinking you know what."

"Piss," said Glory.

"Yeah. I didn't want to say it."

"You've got to get over that, Rico. I'm not like an old-fashioned woman that you have to hold doors for. I like screwing as much as you do. I'm your partner; remember that. No secrets and all trust."

"What about Alex?"

"Look," she said. "I don't know what Alex is all about or

what he wants, except money. All I do know is that we are so far into this thing the only way we get out is to go along. If we don't go along, we're dead."

"I know that. I don't want out anyway. I was a dead wet-back a long time ago. I've been living on borrowed time ever since. Now I've got more money stashed in the floorboards of my apartment than I ever knew existed. But, when I think I've got enough, Alex is going to die. And he's going to die begging me to make it quick."

"He's a bastard. But he's one smart bastard."

"Eat up, Glory, it's almost time."

It was Friday afternoon. Advertising and television and magazine men lined the bar, extending luncheon to three-hour productions and deciding, by three-thirty or four, that it wasn't worth going back to the office. Boaz went to the men's room, taking a long leak onto a steaming ice cake sitting in the bottom of one of P. J. Clarke's urinals. He got pleasure out of pretending that he could destroy the ice cake completely in one urination. He washed his hands and combed his hair slowly. It was still thick and very black. It pleased him that Glory liked his hair. I'll have enough money soon, he thought, to have any woman in the world. Any car. Any home. He paid the check and they left the saloon. Nobody gave them a tumble as they walked out of the bar. The advertising, TV, and magazine men just kept ordering more rounds, talking point spreads for the coming weekend.

It was a quarter to five, and the streets on New York's East Side crawled with early rush-hour traffic. The sidewalks were full of people shopping, walking home, ready for a break from the week's routine. Glory and Boaz said good-bye at the corner of Fifty-fourth Street and Third Avenue. They moved in opposite directions, Boaz toward the East River, Glory toward Lexington. They both looked straight ahead, doing nothing to attract attention. Glory went down the Fifty-first Street entrance to the IRT, heading uptown. She almost had to run to keep up with the surging crowd that pushed and shoved and milled around her. She thought about how safe she was, how incredible that anyone on the FBI's ten most wanted list could be so difficult to find, could remain so anonymous in the most anonymous of the world's cities. It was so easy. She moved down the subway stairs with hundreds of other faceless Friday night people and stood on the platform. She eased her way in front of the people who jockeyed for position and tried to guess at exactly which spot the next train would open its doors. As necks craned down the tracks at an approaching headlight, Glory reached into a Bloomingdale's shopping bag which she had set down at her feet. She quickly pulled the pins from two grenades and held the plungers together tightly, one in each hand. People pressed forward to the edge of the platform, hearing the screech and squeal of the onrushing car. No one noticed Glory release the pressure on the grenades' handles. No one noticed her tossing them gently beneath the wheels of the train. She stepped back as the doors hissed open and the crowd pressed by her.

The explosions ripped up track for twenty feet and blew wheels and undercarriage out and off of the car itself. Oddly enough, no one was injured by the blast. But the ensuing panic caused two heart attacks, one stroke and a broken arm for a teenaged girl who had fallen and been repeatedly stepped on. Glory allowed herself to panic with the rest, and also allowed herself to be saved by two businessmen who escorted her from the subway and offered to buy her a drink and a taxi home. Glory declined the drink but accepted the cab fare. But no one got home via the Lexington Avenue line that night, and National Guardsmen rode every car in New York the next day.

Boaz walked to the East River Drive and watched the automobiles crawl their ponderous way to the weekend. He waited for limousines, Lincolns and Cadillacs, Rolls-Royces

and Bentleys. When a Rolls Silver Cloud with chauffeur
came abreast of him, inching its way alongside a Mark IV,
Boaz lobbed two grenades. The first exploded on the hood
of the Rolls; the second blew the right front wheel from the
Lincoln.

The traffic jam was complicated by the fact that as word
flew back in line that the terrorists had the column under
attack, drivers and passengers either huddled on the floors
of their vehicles or abandoned their cars altogether. Boaz
could have ridden away on the back of a tortoise. He ambled
along with escaping motorists talking and agreeing with
them about sickness and anarchy and the end of the world.

Sean Higgins shot the driver of a trailer truck loaded with
produce at the New Jersey exit to the Holland Tunnel at
5:20 P.M. Then he shot the tires out as the truck jackknifed
and fell over, blocking the exit. He also shot the drivers of
the three cars behind the truck. The noise of the horns in
the tunnel was a chorus from bedlam.

Scott Dutton and Michael Cagnina got onto the Penn
Central commuter express to Westport. When the train had
cleared Westchester and was clacking along toward Greenwich, Dutton shot the ticket taker in the chest. Everyone
else in the car froze.

"Keep your hands on your seats, palms down," Dutton
said. "Anyone moving their hands off their seats goes the
way of the conductor. You'll all be home for martinis if you
cooperate. If you want to be heroes, you can drink your martinis in hell."

The commuters kept their palms down on their seats.

Cagnina stopped the train and forced the crew down onto
the roadbed in front of the engine. Dutton clicked on a bullhorn, then ordered the passengers to leave from all eight
cars by the front exits, one by one. Then he ordered them to
assemble in front of the engine. There must have been almost two hundred people all conditioned to be calm. They

deposited watches, rings, and wallets in an empty U.S. Mail sack, open on a chair next to where Dutton stood. Cagnina lined the commuters up beside the train. Scott Dutton went back through the cars, checking for stragglers.

"What about the conductor?" one brave man asked from the ranks. "You can't leave him in there. It's inhuman."

"Well, mister do-fucking-gooder," said Dutton, who had swung down from the car, carrying a full mail sack over his shoulder. "Why don't you get back on and pull him out of there?"

The man began to ask several others to join him. Dutton clicked back the hammer on his .45 and sighted at the man's head. "You alone, hero. It's your good deed for the day."

The man dragged the dead conductor from the car and held him up, leaning him against the car.

"All right, gentlemen and ladies. Move out." Cagnina and Dutton raised their pistols, cradling them in the crooks of their arms. Cagnina spoke: "Walk down these tracks and be thankful you are a test case. The People's Revolutionary Army does not think that taking trains from now on is going to be a safe method of transportation. We advise you to stay home until your government becomes responsive to the needs of the people. Trains, planes, ships, trucks, buses, and automobiles will be shot at, robbed, sunk or blown up. Unfortunately, people will be killed to gain the greatest good. Pass this information along and thank your God for our mercy. Now move out."

In columns of two the people walked along the darkened roadbed. They kept a ragged step and soon disappeared into the night. On the tracks on the way to Westport, they had left behind the body of the conductor, lying beside his train.

"You didn't have to kill anybody," Cagnina said to Dutton. "They got the idea without that."

"For a smart guy, you're a dumb bastard," said Dutton.

"But you're a guinea, so it figures. You know how to break an Italian's fingers?"

"Let's get this over with and get out of here."

"You don't want to know the answer?" said the southerner. "The way to break an Italian's fingers is to hit him in the nose. Get it? In the fucking nose." It cracked Dutton up and he giggled all during the time it took them to plant enough explosives on the train and around the tracks to blow up a large building. From a comfortable distance they detonated the explosives. The flash was visible from New Canaan to Bedford Village.

Silver Wheels Edwards followed a bus bound for Washington on the New Jersey Turnpike. A mile from the Montclair cutoff he pulled alongside the front passenger door and rolled down his window. He popped six shots through the door of the bus; three of them caught the driver in his neck, arm and chest. As the bus swerved, Edwards accelerated and left the wreckage behind. The survivors had to be pulled out of the baggage compartment, which in turn had to be cut open with acetylene torches. Edwards took the Rahway exit and was soon doubling back to New York. He left his pistol somewhere on the turnpike, where it was crushed beyond identification by the traffic.

Police forces in New York, New Jersey, Connecticut, Massachusetts, and Pennsylvania were joined by the reserves and National Guard troops, regular military personnel, and armed neighborhood vigilante groups. Most of the people in the northeastern United States remained indoors for the weekend, dreading what would come next.

Families had something to talk about; they huddled together. They played Scrabble and checkers and chess and backgammon. Fathers taught their children things they had almost forgotten themselves: how to tell north, how to stop arterial bleeding, how to shuffle a deck of cards with one hand. Grandfathers taught grandchildren dominoes. Mothers baked brownies and chocolate chip cookies by the thousands. And, as a chorus to all the simple activities, television sets stayed on twenty-four hours a day, offering news breaks as news breaks occurred.

Yeats said "things fall apart; the center cannot hold".

Can't I even shop in <u>Greenwich</u> for God's sake?

From Grace Abbott's diary

18

Kirk Abbott came back from Europe that Monday evening. He had not informed his office or his home. He had not told anyone that he had changed his original plans, which called for him to be back Thursday afternoon. It was the quietest day at the airport since the national day of mourning for John F. Kennedy. Kirk moved through Customs easily and grabbed one of the three taxis waiting outside TWA's international terminal. "Where the hell is everybody?" he asked his driver.

"I've been tellin' everybody I talk to for twenty years that this country is going to hell. It's finally happened," the driver said. "You watch morals loosen up. You know what I mean? And you watch everybody taking everything for granted. No work. People cheating on welfare. You take your television news: everybody sees what everybody else has got. The man in the street believes this bullshit about everyone created equal. People are home because they're scared to death to go out for fear of being blown up or shot. No question, it's the end of the world."

Kirk listened without comment. He looked through the Plexiglas at the medallion and a picture of the man. It showed a shriveled-up cynic who needed a shave and whose name was Harry Fluck. Kirk began to laugh softly.

As the cabbie headed for Connecticut, an occasional truck would highball by them and blow his air horn as a salute to those who dared to be on the road when others cowered in their garages.

"Why do you stay in New York if you feel this way?" Kirk asked the driver, who had the dashboard of the car decorated with stickers out of *Mad* magazine. The stickers said things like LUCY HAS PEANUTS ENVY and PLACE GUM HERE.

"Are you kiddin', chief?" the cabbie said. "I stay in New York because there's no other place. You think I want to see the end of the world in Pittsburgh? Boston, for Chrissake? If it's all over, this is the place you gotta be. We live in Queens. If they get Manhattan, I wouldn't mind going over and getting something for the wife from Tiffany's. A little bracelet, you know what I mean?"

Kirk grunted his approval. Kirk always agreed with whatever cabbies said. One of his ambitions was to drag a taxi driver from his hack, dress him at Brooks Brothers, and install him at a board meeting as senior vice president of United Stores. Kirk believed that if you gave a chimpanzee a shave, he could run General Motors for six months before anyone caught on.

He directed the driver once they arrived at Greenwich, and in a short time they pulled up in front of a red brick colonial house with a circular driveway. A white Porsche was parked near the front door.

"The flat rate is thirty-five dollars, chief," said the cabbie. "Want to know the truth, it's a pain in the ass since you can never pick up a fare on the way back."

Kirk stuffed four tens into the Plexiglas pocket separating the driver from the passenger section.

"A lot of good five bucks is going to do me at the end of the world, chief," the driver said.

"In that case," said Kirk, shutting his door quietly, "Fluck you, Harry." The taxi squealed off, flipping loose gravel all over the back of the Porsche.

Outside lights appeared suddenly, the spots that lined the driveway and the lamps above the entrance. Lisa Bronson, relieved to see Kirk through the peephole, opened her front door.

"Kirk," she said. "What are you doing? Teddy didn't expect you until Thursday. He's not home."

"I didn't think he'd be home, Lisa. Are you going to ask me in for a drink, or shall I stand out here until the neighborhood German shepherds rip off my clothes?"

"We don't have any dogs," she said. "Oh, you're kidding. Come in. You look like you just came from the airport, with your suitcase and everything. Either that or you've just left home." She giggled at that, slightly embarrassed to be making light conversation with the president of her husband's company. "Let me make you a drink," she said, retreating in her quilted bathrobe, her streaked hair pulled back with an elastic. She had been about to bathe before the interruption.

Kirk sat in the living room, recently decorated with blue toile walls and antique furniture. Lisa Bronson came back with Scotch and two glasses filled with ice. "You want water, Kirk?"

He signaled no and took a long swallow, coughing softly from the sudden smoky taste. "That's very good."

"I wish you had called first," she said. "Teddy's at a meeting. I thought your driver would get you. Or Grace." She looked puzzled.

Kirk took another long drink from his Scotch. "I think that Teddy and Grace are in the same meeting. I came here to see if you would like to attend."

"That's ridiculous. He's with some merchandisers in New York at the Americana. I'll call him."

Kirk shrugged and she indignantly whirled from the room

to the den where he could hear her punching the Touchtone buttons. He knew what the result would be, and she returned minutes later. "I'm getting dressed," she said. "Make yourself another drink if you like. We'll take the Porsche."

Driving through a deserted and darkened Greenwich, Lisa Bronson said to Kirk bitterly, "You certainly aren't acting much like the betrayed husband."

"And then again I might be," he said. "I might be in shock. I may just shoot Teddy where I find him. And Grace, too. You never know about people under great strain."

Lisa started to cry. "I don't believe it, Kirk. I can't believe it. If you're being cruel on purpose, to hurt Teddy, the way he said you would . . . It makes no sense. We just bought some land on the island. We're going to build."

"I just want you to know the truth about people."

"Oh, Jesus, Kirk. I so pray that you're wrong."

They were driving up Round Hill Road now, past stone walls and stately Episcopal houses where the owners wielded power, played paddle tennis, and rode horses. "Don't go all the way into the driveway," Kirk said. "Park right inside the gates; we'll walk the rest of the distance."

Lisa did as he said, her heart hammering in her chest, her hands clammy with anticipation. She saw her husband's car pulled next to the garage, hidden from the street. The Abbott house was dark.

"I don't want to go in," she whispered to Kirk. "I want to go home. I can't stand it."

"Come on," Kirk said roughly to her. "I want you to see what kind of sneaking bastard violates a man's home." In the darkness, Kirk had his mouth set in a grim smile. Lisa was frantic, feeling a sickness for which she did not know the cure.

Kirk opened the front door quietly and then went inside. Immediately Sandy ran to Kirk, panting and nipping lovingly at his master's shoes. "Shhh. Good boy," Kirk said.

"Shhh. Miss your boss, boy? Stay." Kirk picked up his dog and, with Lisa Bronson, they quietly moved up the stairs and down the long hallway to the master bedroom. Kirk had Lisa by the arm with a firm pressure. She was resisting him, not wanting to see, not wanting to know. They paused outside the bedroom door.

"Oh, Jesus, keep it up," Grace Abbott moaned, straining to hold Teddy Bronson inside her.

"I'm sorry," he whispered. "I keep thinking about your kids coming in."

Grace cared about nothing except having him hard. She completely gave of herself to passion. So controlled in her everyday life, she was never able to control herself when making love. Often she had the shakes, or she would weep for endless moments. "Come on, Teddy," she said aloud. "Don't let me go now."

Kirk opened the door and pushed Lisa in ahead of him. He flicked on the big spot in the ceiling, lighting the room like a stage. "I thought people only had trouble with sex if they were married to each other," he said.

"Kirk," Grace screamed. "Goddam you."

"Lisa, darling," Ted Bronson said, rushing out of the bed, holding a copy of *Forbes* magazine in front of his groin.

Lisa Bronson was biting on her thumb, a nervous habit left over from childhood. She stared at her husband, his face filled with silent pleading. She burst into tears and ran from the room, ran from the house. She raced the Porsche into the street and away in the wrong direction, knowing she would see her husband clutching the magazine in front of himself for the rest of her life. She didn't know where to go and she was afraid.

Kirk walked over and sat on the bed. "Get dressed, Teddy," he said calmly. "You look foolish."

"Kirk," Bronson said, "I'm sorry."

"Sure. Sorry you got caught. I'm sorry, too, Teddy. We're

all sorry. But it's no surprise; I've known for a while. If you can manage to get your pants on, I'll tell you what concerns me the most right now. That's our Christmas season." Kirk began smoothing the bed where he sat. He pulled the blanket up to cover the sheets.

"Christmas is a must for us, and I have the feeling it's going to be a big one. You've been cutting back on inventory at every one of our twenty stores. I think that's a bad mistake. This year, more than ever, people will be home for Christmas. I want to boost all our purchasing and advertise heavily: radio, TV, the works. If I'm right, and I think I am, Christmas could be a big winner. It has to be a winner to bail us out. I want to move that stock up from six and a half."

Grace glared at him from her side of the bed. She had finally put on a nightgown. "You're sick, Kirk," she said. "You planned the whole thing. You knew about us. You deliberately brought Lisa with you to ruin her life."

Kirk ignored her and continued talking to Bronson while he dressed. With his shoes still untied, he looked ridiculous, and felt ridiculous.

"I want to meet with the merchandise managers," Kirk said, "at eleven o'clock. I want to lay out the program, talk it through . . ."

"You must be crazy, Kirk," Bronson said, still making no move to tie his shoes.

"I think you better go make nice-nice with Lisa. She seemed distraught. I wouldn't want any accidents to happen. But remember, I expect those merchandise managers at eleven. On the dot."

Bronson looked at Grace helplessly but she was staring in the opposite direction, puffing hard on a cigarette. For once in her life, she looked disheveled. Bronson left the house suddenly, nearly tripping over Kirk's dog on his way out. He realized that his shoes were still untied, but he couldn't take the time to tie them.

"Welcome home, Kirk," Grace said, sucking smoke deep into her throat and lungs.

"Oh, Jesus, keep it up," he mocked at her in a falsetto voice. "I bet you say that to all the boys." Kirk went to his closet and began to get undressed. Sandy hovered by his feet, whimpering softly.

"Why don't you and your doggy ride into the sunset," Grace screamed at him. "Do you blame me for screwing Teddy? Do you blame me for wanting to hurt you? I've been trying to get a rise out of you for five years, and all I ever hear about is deals, money, United Stores. Just let me get control of United Stores, you said, and everything will be easy. You use this place like a hotel. I don't think I've had an honest conversation with you in months. Teddy doesn't know what you're up to. I don't know what you're up to. The country is falling apart and you're off in Europe or the Far East. I don't even get a goddam postcard. I'd screw the New York Giants if I thought I would get a rise from you. This little scene: I know you set it up." Grace started to sob. "You are the coldest son-of-a-bitch I've ever known," she said. "At least Teddy has some heart."

"He has some heart all right," Kirk said. "You know what he'd do to control United. He'd screw an alligator if he could drain the swamp. Putting some horns on me is supposed to make me slip my cable? I never liked the slippery bastard. And he doesn't know Kirk Abbott."

"He loves me," she cried at Kirk. "He's tender, he tells me his problems."

"Come on, Grace. We're all tired. Let's get some sleep."

She blew her nose into a Kleenex and went into the bathroom. Kirk heard the water running and shut off the bedroom lights.

Grace opened the bathroom door and stood, slender and blond, her face washed. She was in control once more, beautiful as a *Vogue* cover girl, distant, untouchable. "You're going to hurt Teddy and me, aren't you, Kirk?" she said, as if from the bottom of a cistern. "Let me tell you this. You'll never hurt me again." She left the bedroom, shutting the door carefully, and went to the guest bedroom, where she tried to read a book. She couldn't concentrate, and went downstairs to pour herself a brandy. She smoked cigarettes and thought about her life.

Again, Kirk squeezed his eyes shut very hard and tried not to think about anything at all.

UNITED STORES CORPORATION
OFFICE OF THE PRESIDENT

To all employees:

To still any rumors — there will be no manage-ment change at United. We care about you all: your jobs, your families. United is a personal mis-sion for me — and I want you all to feel you can call on me personally *anytime.*

Kirk Abbott

INTERNAL MEMORANDUM UNITED STORES

19

Glory Cohen was living on Carmine Street in the Village. The only change in her appearance from the pictures of her in post offices was that she had let her hair grow quite long and had plucked her eyebrows down to a thin, chic whisper. On the FBI posters she appeared as a little girl with big dark eyes and chopped-off hair. This image had disappeared. She had become a woman in the course of the terror. When it was all over, she wanted the rewards every beautiful woman thinks she deserves: possessions, comforts, freedom. She was drinking black coffee and listening to records of the early Judy Collins, wondering what she was going to do about Enrico Boaz. Glory had almost eight hundred thousand dollars in cash stuffed behind seven loose bricks in her nonworking fireplace. She knew Boaz had hidden almost a million. He continually talked about fleeing with Glory to South America, where money could buy them protection and privacy. She wished he wouldn't talk about it. There was so much more to do.

It was an early Tuesday morning. Glory knew that the City of New York had been given the word the day before. Ten million dollars and there would be peace in the city. Some form of martial law had existed for weeks, soldiers and police systematically searching houses and apartments, block

by block, building by building. The *Times* thundered about
violations of civil rights and human decency. Citizens on
talk shows had complained of police and military brutality.
Several of the networks had editorials calling for payoff
rather than slavery to fascist government. It was just as Alex
had promised them it would be: confusion and disorder —
and deliveries on the button. It had been there all along,
only Alex knew the right places to push, the pressure points.
It was beautiful.

Glory jumped up and grabbed a pistol when she heard the
knock on her door. In the silent building the intrusion
blasted her from her thoughts, where she had no one but a
soulful Judy Collins for company. When she opened the
door, still on its chain lock, and saw Alex smiling at her, she
relaxed.

"I brought bagels and cream cheese," he said, holding up
a paper bag.

Laughing, she let him in, sweeping him, with a deep
ostentatious bow, to a canvas director's chair.

"Breakfast with you," she said. "I never eat breakfast."

"You want to know the truth?" Alex said. "I felt like a
bagel." He seemed very relaxed to Glory. She poured him a
cup of coffee, embarrassed at being caught like any other
woman in the morning, without preparation.

"That's funny," she said, coming over to him and putting
a hand between his legs, "you don't feel like a bagel to me."
Alex reached over and unzipped the fly of her jeans. With
one hand he reached into the opening; with the other he
unsnapped the waistband of her pants. She hugged him
around the shoulders, not stopping him, so he slid the jeans
down her long legs. She kicked free of them, snapping them
across the room where they landed on top of a biography of
Trotsky. Her jeans covered his portrait, the pointed beard,
the piercing closely set eyes. Glory slept on two mattresses
covered during the day with a quilt sewn all over with peace

symbols. They lay down on the quilt. Finally Alex turned her over on her stomach. Glory got up on her knees and fed him into her, still holding onto him, caressing where he entered and making the sounds Alex needed to hear.

He was slow to pull out of her. He rubbed her back and shoulders.

"Hungry?" he finally asked her.

"I'm okay," she said.

Alex brought over the bagels and cream cheese and they lay there feeding each other, covering the peace quilt with crumbs and small bits of cheese. The sun poured through a skylight above them, making it seem as if they were wonderfully innocent with nowhere to go, nothing to do.

"Why did you come here?" Glory asked him, the back of her head resting on his stomach as she looked up to blue sky.

"I wanted to talk to you and Boaz about the next phase. And about Cagnina. I gather he's become the reluctant dragon."

"He puked over some people catching it in that last bus explosion. He can't believe it takes flames before things can be clean."

"He's looking for early retirement. I wanted to see what Boaz thinks."

"We'd better get dressed," Glory said. "Rico went on a hunt for magazines about us in Times Square. I don't want him to see us like this."

"Ah, it's come to this," Alex said. "A lot has happened since I've been away."

"Oh, bullshit. He's never had anyone care for him. He needs to think he's brave and strong and smart. It makes him feel good. And the others pay attention to him when you're not around. Come on, please get dressed, Alex. You know he's vicious. I told him we were finished. It's all he's got over you. He needs that."

When Boaz arrived, Alex was sitting at the table finishing the last of his cold coffee. Glory was changing a record, putting on some Chopin.

"Good morning, Rico," Alex said.

Boaz put down a newspaper and some magazines and looked at Glory. "I am getting the impression," he said, "of something."

Alex raised his eyebrows at the Mexican and was silent.

"Don't you trust me, Rico?" Glory said.

He looked at Alex and Alex smiled a smile as large as he was able. Then he winked at Boaz.

"The place smells," Boaz said. "I know what it smells like."

Alex kept smiling at him. Boaz moved angrily across the room and kicked the record player off its table. The needle screeched over Chopin's *Polonaise* and crashed to a halt. "Fucking faggot music. What did it do, put you in the mood?"

"You're being ridiculous," Glory said to him. "What's the matter with you?"

Alex began thumbing through one of the magazines, paying no attention to Boaz.

The Mexican came after Glory and slapped her hard across the face. In a rage, he picked up a bagel covered with cheese from the bed and pushed it into her nose. She fell back across the bed, landing in a heap on the other side. Boaz leaped over on top of her and began slapping at random, out of control.

Alex sat calmly at the table.

When Boaz ran out of breath and energy, he climbed off Glory, leaving her lying on the floor. Boaz glared at Alex and came toward him.

"I've been thinking," Alex said. "We're about to start mass upheavals. It's getting more and more dangerous to operate. So many eyes. Rewards up to seven figures. I'm cutting you in for two more shares. Out of my action."

Boaz stopped walking. His chest heaved with the beating he had given Glory.

"You deserve it," Alex said. "And I want you to lean some on our attorney friend Cagnina. As a matter of fact, I think I want him leaned on all the way. Do it in front of the others." He handed Boaz an onionskin copy of instructions, which he had typed in England on a rented machine.

Boaz, without a glance backward, slammed the door to the apartment on his way out.

Glory pulled herself up onto the mattresses and lay on her back. One eye was closed and puffy, her bottom lip was bleeding. "You didn't stop him," she said. "You just sat there and let him do it. Why? Why didn't he turn on you?"

"A man never blames the other man. Always the woman. It's her choice whether to say yes or no."

"You hate women, don't you, Alex?" she said. "What are you, some kind of closet queen? Do you put on dresses when you're not with us?"

Alex ran cold water onto a kitchen towel and softly daubed Glory's face with it. She allowed Alex to treat her but she stared at him with loathing.

"I believe I treat everybody the same," Alex said. "Regardless of age, color or sex. I'm a good American. Liberal. I believe in the free enterprise system."

"You're a prick of misery," she said to him, grabbing the towel. It was an expression she hadn't used since Scarsdale High School.

"I'm raising you to two units as of this moment," Alex said to her. "That'll buy a lot of dark glasses."

"Thanks for the bone," Glory said.

"Just keep Boaz tranquilized," Alex said. "You're doing fine. There's nothing I like better than a good love story.

Doggy style. I left you a copy of this week's drill on the table."

Glory got up and began rearranging her record player.

"Thanks for the bagels," she said as he was leaving.

"Thanks for the Chopin," Alex said.

Boaz watched Alex leave from across the street, hunched down in a doorway. After a while, he walked slowly toward Glory's apartment house, scanning his sheet of onionskin.

Kirk Abbott met with the merchandise managers of United Stores promptly at eleven that morning. They came in from the three Manhattan stores and from Hewlett and Brooklyn and Manhasset and Boston and Providence and Hartford and the rest of the chain. They were nervous and skeptical. The manager at Manhasset insisted he be picked up in Kirk's limousine, refusing to come into New York City without escort.

Abbott did not waste time with them. He explained that he wanted a crash buying program for Christmas, with more merchandise than any other metropolitan chain. He wanted to step up radio and TV and newspaper holiday advertising. "We're in this business to make money," he told them. "I'm not operating a ma-and-pa Red and White store. Money is made by being decisive. If you expect to get anywhere in this corporation, you'll jump when I say jump."

"Can I ask a candid question," one of the managers said, "while we're all assembled?"

"Of course," said Kirk.

"Rumors have come to all of us that there'll be a change in ownership at United." The others murmured their assent. "We also hear that you're no longer going to be president. We hear that you're going to be squeezed out by the directors. Sorry to ask that, but some of us have options. We all have families. And we think we have a right to know." The others did not speak. But they all nodded in agreement.

When Kirk was angry his face darkened. His face darkened now and his eyes narrowed. He looked dangerous and cruel. The merchandise managers involuntarily backed up a step.

"Gentlemen," he said, "I own six million shares of United Stores stock at an average of fifteen dollars per share. You know where we're selling now. Approximately six and three-quarters. I did not fight for control in order to take a licking, and I don't give a damn what's going on in the world. Life continues and don't you forget it. I am running United Stores. For now, and for good. Despite anything you may hear to the contrary. You better believe I'm serious about gearing up for Christmas and the first quarter of next year. When this terrorist business has ended — and believe me it will — there's going to be the biggest consumer demand for goods in history. Like a sigh of relief. Now," Kirk paused, his face returning to normal, the lines relaxed, "if there are no more questions, get out there and kick the hell out of the other chains. I will personally be visiting all of your stores in the next week and I want to see your budgets and advertising layouts for the holidays. That's all."

They filed out. Kirk knew they were frightened of him and would respond.

Kirk's intercom buzzed. He flicked on the audio. "Mr. Bronson's here to see you. Mr. Partridge, Mr. Donovan as well." Partridge and Donovan were directors, Partridge representing United's bankers, Donovan the underwriters who were Wall Street's link to the retail chain.

"I won't be free until one-thirty," Kirk said. "Have them wait or come back after lunch." Kirk flicked off his intercom and sat down to work on first half projections. Bronson and the two directors burst into his office over the loud objections of Kirk's secretary.

"It's all right," Kirk calmed her down. "They're part of the team. What is it, Teddy? Gentlemen?" Kirk smiled cheerfully at the intruders. It slowed them. They looked at each other with indecision.

"We've been studying the management chart," Bronson said, "and thought we'd do some tinkering."

Abbott said nothing. He watched them thoughtfully.

"Not that we anticipate anything happening," the banker said. "But we think it would be wise now, with no pressure, no threats pending, to spread corporate responsibility."

The investment director pressed on. "Yes, Kirk," he said. "The board thinks that you should remain as president." He paused. "But not as general manager also."

"What you propose," Kirk said, "is that Bronson would be both vice president–finance and the general manager?"

The others nodded in agreement.

"And I think we should make a policy decision," the first director said, "which I understand is in keeping with your views, that in case of a threat to your life we shall refuse to pay."

"And, in the event I should have an accident," Kirk said, "then Ted would become president. Right?"

"No," said Bronson. "We would leave it open. In case they decided to hit us again. If there's no top man to single out, we'd stand a better chance of being ignored."

"Ted would have full powers anyhow," the second director said. "By virtue of his general managership."

Abbott thought for a minute. He thought so long that Bronson and the directors looked at one another, wondering whether Kirk were ignoring them. Finally he leaned forward and nodded pleasantly.

"You know something," he said. "I agree. It's a very sound policy and Ted is obviously the logical man. General manager? That's fine with me. You may tell the assembled board that I have no objections. It's fine with me and I appreciate your consulting like this. As long as my Christmas plans are not tampered with." Kirk nodded again and went back to the papers on his desk. The directors left, pleased at their easy victory. But Bronson stayed behind for a moment.

"Grace thinks you're up to something," he said. "I don't. I think it's just about over for you, kid. I don't see any way you can stop me now. Have a good morning."

Abbott smiled a handsome full smile at Bronson, which made Bronson wonder if Kirk were really out of his mind. All morning he could not forget Abbott's smile.

20

November 14

It has all fallen apart and I want to live.
There is no way out of madness for any of
them. My mistake was in always feeling apart
—— in feeling that Alex and I were brothers
in a dream of change. The change has meant
horror, perversion. And instead of brothers,
I argue with the animals . . .

Higgins raves at me. "I want a Marlin 336-C
and you get me a piece of shit. I want the
model 425, 4 power scope and a 35 Remington
cartridge. You want me to work with this crap
you get me? You want to make me sloppy?"
They are children. These are games.

I have wanted a minor disturbance at Shea,
a ten foot hole at best, nothing serious. For
this I have Red Cross Extra, 1/2 case should
do it, 40-50 sticks. A lot of noise and lot of
smoke and dust. No lives, if I can get away
with it. Who knows? I know nothing.

Have not eaten solid in four days. Fear
punishment; fear getting caught. I fear the

```
others will turn.  Inevitable now.  Even
Alex, my brother Cain.
    I vomit everything I eat.  And I want to
live.
```

Extract from the journal of Michael Cagnina

Alex leaned over the railing at Rockefeller Center and watched the skaters in their endless circles. His eyes followed one young woman who seemed about nineteen and wore patched jeans with a Levi jacket. Her long hair swept behind her in the wind she created with her motion. She looked just like Grace had looked when they met years before. Beautiful and controlled. Alex lost himself in a vision of the past, as if he had been looking at a picture album.

"Excuse me," a voice came at him. "Excuse me. But are you Jewish?"

Alex wheeled around. A man with luxurious side whiskers dressed in black stood there. A Hasidic Jew. "I'm not Jewish but I'll talk," said Alex accepting a pamphlet. The man smiled and relaxed. Perhaps a convert on a chilly Sunday.

You had to love bread and circuses a great deal to venture out on a raw November Sunday to watch the Jets play at Shea Stadium. But over half a million Americans turned out on their day of rest every week to cheer their heroes and their bums. Violence had always been America's passion. It was her passion now. No one stayed away from Shea Stadium because of terrorists. "Even Communists respect sports," an ironworker said to a network interviewer outside the field. "We got almost seventy thousand people comin' to this thing with the Dolphins. You think any shit bums from Russia or anywhere are gonna mess with our sports? You gonna have seventy thousand people tear those fuckers limb from limb. What kind of creep don't like football?" He was

cheered on by a crowd, all of whom surged forward when
the ironworker was through, each eager to have a chance at
immortality: seeing themselves on the eleven o'clock news.
The broadcaster disappeared from sight.

People tailgated at Shea, greeted strangers and old friends
and bowling league opponents as if the New York Jets were
their own alma mater. They filled themselves full of Kentucky Fried Chicken, ready-mixed Manhattans and whiskey
sours. The beer they would smuggle to their seats, hidden
in the bottom of picnic baskets and Scotch coolers. By the
third quarter of the game, after a halftime ceremony fea-
turing Joe Namath crying into national microphones when
presented with a chauffeur for life from the City of New
York, the fans were screaming for victory, whipped to a
frenzy by the emotion, the November winds, and the al-
cohol. Their joy over a forty-yard completion to the Miami
twenty-yard line almost obscured the destruction on the left-
field wall, which came hurtling down in an explosion only
slightly more resounding than the cheers. Stone, concrete,
mortar, girders, supports came crashing into the outfield,
spilling rubble in every direction. It looked like a slow-motion
treatment of destruction from a De Mille Bible epic. There
were no stands in far left field, but the panic and horror
generated by the blast caused a stampede among the thousands who watched from their seats. The players on the
field saw the destruction, then stared in terror themselves
as they watched the fans fighting and rolling and trampling
each other as they poured over, under, and through each
other for the tunnel exits. The players broke and ran for their
locker rooms, pursued by a horde gone mad with fear and
desperate for survival.

The mayor was at Gracie Mansion, picking with no appe-
tite at the ham, with raisin sauce, on his plate. As a me-
morial to her Connecticut girlhood, his wife insisted upon

the family sharing a big Sunday dinner in the middle of the afternoon.

"Jesus, sweetie," the mayor had told her. "I can't eat a big dinner today. I couldn't even eat a corned beef sandwich. My stomach couldn't hold anything down. I don't know if we're going to have a city tomorrow."

"The ham will settle your stomach," she said. "And there are scalloped potatoes I made especially. I don't want the children to see that you can't cope. If the mayor doesn't stand up in a crisis, who will? You've got to show the media that it's business as usual. That includes Sunday family dinner."

"Could you eat if you'd been blackmailed for ten million dollars? If your people were getting killed?"

"Look, dear," she said patiently. "It's the city's money and you still have to keep up pretenses."

"I'll never be mayor again, I know it," he said. "Which means I'll never be governor, I'll never be senator, I'll never be president. You talked me into this job. I knew it was the kiss of death."

But she prevailed. His Honor picked at the ham and the scalloped potatoes, staring at a telephone on a stand with wheels near his right hand. The telephone was a call director with four lines. The second light suddenly lit, and the mayor snatched it from its cradle.

"Have you heard?" The cry came from one of his associates. Before giving the mayor a chance to answer, he rushed on. "They've blown up Shea Stadium," he said. "There's a riot going on out there. Lord knows how many killed or injured. The car's outside."

"God in heaven," the mayor said, and he pushed his chair over backwards in his haste to get up. Another button lit on the phone. A young man in a double-knit suit came rushing into the room. "Four rings, Your Honor," he said. "We need ten seconds to trace any incoming call. If it's them, stall for as long as you can. There are monitors all over the city to check it out." The mayor stared at his family. They stared back at him. He felt that he was lost. He didn't want to pick up the phone after four rings; he didn't want to pick up the phone after a hundred rings.

"Your Honor." The security man had to call him out of his trance. "The phone."

He picked up the receiver. "Good afternoon, Your Honor." It was Alex. "Hope you're enjoying a day with the family. You have our money?"

"We need time," the mayor said. "The ten million dollars is impossible. We can't pay our electric bill, let alone this. The city is broke. We're prepared to negotiate; we're even prepared to settle something on it. But ten million. I've got to consult further with my people. We're not like a corporation. I can't make the decision by myself."

"Aah, Mr. Mayor. I've always thought you were a foolish man. You've given me no choice. Enjoy your afternoon at Shea."

Alex quickly vacated the phone booth, opposite Sam Goody's Records in Times Square, and walked deliberately down into a subway entrance. He wore gray cotton gloves, a camel's-hair coat and Borsalino hat. He began to hurry as he heard sirens converging at the phone booth above the subway entrance, converging from four directions to see an empty space of glass and aluminum, mocking them with its silence. The Sunday wanderers in Times Square cringed a little at the arrival of police. They thought that this time the squad cars were coming for them.

At that moment the mayor of New York was racing with a motorcycle escort to Shea Stadium to view the destruction, and to try to calm the crowds that remained.

On Monday morning half the commuters to the city carried weapons of some kind in their briefcases, in their lunchboxes, in their pockets. They carried switchblades, scout knives; they carried ice picks and billy clubs; they carried cleavers and brass knuckles and Saturday night specials and .22s and wartime souvenir Lugers and army .45s. They carried nail files and letter openers. They carried Mace and tear gas cartridges. They carried sword canes. Everyone was suspicious of his neighbor. No one tried to stand too close. There was no cameraderie of the sort that exists during wartime, bringing people closer through bonds of common hardship. But people took very seriously the fact that they were truly at war and that some wild bastards were threatening to take bread out of their mouths. Tempers were down to the edge that produces violence. Even in the meek.

"The mayor is messin' around with our bank accounts," Creed Edwards said to Sean Higgins as they had a beer on Second Avenue. They were dressed as hardhats, with coveralls, lunchboxes, dirty sweatshirts, pea jackets.

"He's taking terrible chances with people's lives," Higgins responded. "Terrible chances that no one save the Almighty has a right to do."

"Alex says that all we have to do now is drop a little smoke. Anywhere. And the crowds will take care of the rest."

"Shall we try it? I'll try anything once."

"They'll hang the mayor's ass from the top of City Hall."

"Drink up. Better his ass than ours."

They both knocked on the wooden bar top for luck and left the gin mill on Second Avenue.

At the same time, 4:45 P.M., Boaz, Glory Cohen and Scott Dutton, dressed as businessmen and secretaries, dispersed to different areas of the city. People were breaking from work. Crowds streamed into the streets. Everyone walked faster than usual. They were pushing each other, looking around, paying attention to faces that might explode at them. Boaz, Glory and Dutton were pushing also. Where they pushed into crowds, they also dropped simple tear gas grenades.

The effect was like that of electric prods to the genitals: screams, trampling, panic. The grenades were dropped as the main elevator banks burst open at the J. C. Penney building on the Avenue of the Americas; at Chase Manhattan Plaza in the Wall Street district; in the main terminal of Pennsylvania Station; in the lobby of the General Motors building on Fifth Avenue; down the stairs at the Fifty-ninth Street subway entrance. The city was crippled at rush hour on the busiest day in the week by the five tear gas explosives. Fourteen strokes were reported, twenty-two heart attacks. Crowds marched to Gracie Mansion and chanted into the night.

Alex sat in the Good Times Coffeeshop at Lexington and Fifty-eighth. He drank black coffee with an order of English muffins. Boaz sat on the next stool, stirring sugar into his cup with slow circles.

"Dutton almost got killed tonight," he said softly, looking straight ahead. "We're taking too many risks. You think we can do this much longer, you crazy."

"I'm thinking of moving us to another city. Somewhere fat and happy."

Boaz snorted. "Where's that? Heaven?"

"The mayor has come up to five."

"Let's take it, for Chrissake, and lay off for a while."

"You don't want to be thrown to the wolves, do you, Rico? You don't want Glory given to the FBI?"

Boaz stared straight ahead. He sipped his coffee.

"Be home at nine," Alex said. "I'll call you with instructions for His Honor."

"Cagnina is getting very bad. He didn't like Shea at all,

and I don't like the way he looks at us. Like he's making a decision."

"Tell him I'll be around to soothe his sensibilities. Perhaps we'll take some vacations. Get the people back on the streets; let them do some Christmas shopping."

Alex picked up the check and left Boaz on his stool.

Two hookers were the only people in sight along the block from Fifty-eighth to Fifty-ninth. "End-of-the-world special, baby?" one of them asked, a six-footer with a powdered Afro and white boots.

"Two for one," the other suggested. "Two for the price of one." She was a blond from a bottle and the bottle was cheap.

"You're brave," Alex said. "You're not afraid to be out on the street?"

White Boots laughed. "When you've handled the meat of Shriners on convention and other freaks in this town, you ain't scared of nothing. Want to take a chance?"

"I think I'll go read a book," Alex said, moving on. "But thanks."

"Faggot," the blond yelled after him. "Everybody's a faggot." They moved in the opposite direction, headed downtown on the deserted sidewalk.

Gena Reynolds read the cablegram. She memorized its instructions in the cable office and tore it into halves, quarters, eighths. She sprinkled bits into each ashtray she passed on her way out. Gena was wearing a jersey dress, short and yellow. Her bare legs were tanned as dark as stockings, her auburn hair tied back with a thin yellow ribbon; her shoes were slingback and white. She slid into the open back door of the Rolls-Royce and settled into the cool darkness of the leather. The chauffeur shut the door and walked around to the driver's side.

"Good news, my sweet brainchild?" Antonio Figueroa asked her. The Costa Rican minister of finance had four dark lightweight suits with vests. They all were charcoal black with a very thin white pinstripe. They had no cuffs. With them, he always wore highly polished plain toe black shoes made for him at Baber's Bootery on New Bond Street in London. He had two wool suits in the same style, which he wore in Europe and in North America. He had no moustache and his black hair was thick and parted almost in the middle of his head. A handsome head.

"Good news for the bank," Gena said. "Anastos is upping the initial capitalization from twenty to thirty million. We should be able to negotiate major deals as soon as we open for business."

"And when is that, my pet computer woman?"

"Ah," she said. "That fact I don't know as yet."

"But you will soon?"

"I will soon."

"And what is it again that your Mr. Anastos does? I keep forgetting."

"He is an entrepreneur."

"I remember now. It is a word much beloved by the gringos. It covers, as you say, a multitude of sins." Figueroa leaned forward and slid aside the glass partition to the front seat. "Senorita Reynolds's apartment," he said to the driver, and slid the partition back into place.

"I'm not sure I approve of the term senorita," Gena said to him. "Is there no Spanish equivalent of Ms.?" She was teasing the finance minister, who lacked a sense of humor.

"Bah," he said. "You people up north make it so difficult for yourselves. Life is really very simple. You are a man or you are a woman. You grow up, you love, you work, you die. Along the way you have troubles and sex and children. That's all. The formula is the same for everyone. Why complicate life by upsetting the balance of nature?" He leaned over to kiss the back of Gena's neck. Then he moved his long manicured hand to her breast.

The driver suddenly swerved the Rolls and the blast of a horn from a passing automobile threw them back against the rear seat.

Figueroa pounded on the glass partition. "You stupid peasant," he yelled. "Keep your eyes on the road, not the mirror."

"Do you think the driver is a spy for your wife?" Gena said.

"My wife takes care of the house and brings packages to the orphans' home. What does she know? All the wives of my friends in this country keep their eyes shut."

"Ah, but your wife is the daughter of the president. El Presidente would not like to know that his son-in-law has the eye of the philanderer. You owe your job to El Presidente, I believe?"

"I like to be teased, you bitch," Figueroa smiled at her. "You know the things I like."

"Yes, Antonio. I know the things you like."

The Rolls drove through the city streets. In almost every block there were signs of new construction. Apartment buildings and stores were going up, signs were posted for new development, garden dwellings, condominiums, a sporting club: everywhere the evidence of heavy investment. There were also no policemen. Only an elite National Guard that wore white fatigues with rolled-up sleeves, and sidearms, and carried long, thin billy clubs. The guard directed traffic and knocked heads with equal facility.

Monies sifted into the country from many foreign sources, to be laundered and turned into construction projects, gambling casinos, department stores. Anastos's bank, incorporated under the name Gena S.A., would be the inside bank to develop these foreign monies. Figueroa dispensed all permissions for bank charters and for foreign investment in the country. He had a numbered account in Switzerland that was a secret from everyone he knew. The number had been tattooed onto the sole of his right foot. The man who had done the tattooing had subsequently been knifed in a fight outside a jai alai fronton in Miami and died of loss of blood before the ambulance could get him to a hospital. His Cuban assailants had disappeared into the jai alai crowds and no arrests were ever made.

The Rolls pulled up in front of a new brick ten-story apartment building with palm trees lining its circular driveway. "I would very much like to come up," said Figueroa. "There is not a lot happening at the Ministry this afternoon. Perhaps we can discuss the floor plans of the bank. It is important that it be a showplace. Comfort is essential, the surroundings . . ."

"One thing I learned from my father," Gena said. "Money is more important than surroundings. I don't think it's wise for you to come up this afternoon. I have a great deal of work."

"You'll have no work to do at all," Figueroa said, "if I have no visits. Remember that."

"Antonio," she said. "It's fascinating when you bully me. Aren't you sorry you don't have high boots and a narrow black moustache? I think you could grow a moustache, Antonio. Yes?"

Figueroa grabbed for her, holding her upper arms tightly. "I don't like to be mocked," he said.

Gena broke away from him and laughed. She kissed the palm of her hand and then put her hand on his crotch. "Call me later, Antonio. I'm free for dinner tomorrow night." She got out of the Rolls and walked into the apartment building without looking back. Figueroa rapped on the glass partition.

"The Ministry," he said to his chauffeur. "The Ministry, and watch the road."

Gena rode the elevator to her penthouse, thinking about Anastos's wire. "As the rabbi said," the message read, "it won't be long now."

UNS 200 8 6⅛   PNA 30¼   HM 101

United Stores,
trade of 200 shares

21

*F*ranco Bertelli sat in a Chicago office watching a noon-time news broadcast on a twelve-inch television set. Watching with him was a smooth young man, impeccably dressed. The young man did not smile once through the broadcast. His dark eyes were the hardest eyes Franco had ever seen.

The sign on the office door read GREAT MIDDLE AMERICAN INSURANCE AND CASUALTY COMPANY.

The news commentator was talking in sonorous tones, as if delivering a eulogy. "The reign of terror in New York," he was saying, "seems to have entered a new phase. Last night there were no incidents. However, three more people have died as a result of the Shea Stadium disaster, bringing the total now dead to forty-five. Brave little Bobby Gordon finally succumbed this morning of multiple fractures. The mayor has expressed cautious optimism and confidence that security measures have made continued violence impossible. The rumors of city ransom payments are still entirely un-confirmed and spokesmen for the mayor have continually denied these rumors. In the meantime, New Yorkers are emerging from their homes as the respite from violence enters its second week. People of the city and the suburbs are enjoying their truce. If it is a truce. They are enjoying pre-Christmas shopping and their very shaky peace, in this season of peace and good will to man."

The young man nodded at the set. Franco got up and snapped it off. "Good will for them and a piece for us," Franco said.

"Give Abbott a call," the young man said, without changing his expression. "If he wants any extension, the answer is no. No flexibility. I've had it with this deal. We're going to end up with a department store chain; I can see it already."

"But it's a great business," Franco said. "Think of all the places to lay off money. Department stores are perfect for us. And a New York Stock Exchange listing. I mean, it's legitimate. The biggest chain in the country."

"New York Exchange listing means shit. With these bastards blowing up the East Coast, there's no stock market."

"I still say the business is great," said Franco, "and whoever those people are, they've got to get caught soon. There's no way that someone ain't going to stool."

"Call Abbott," said the young man. He was squeezing a red rubber ball in his right fist.

Franco direct-dialed the New York number and the secretary put him right through. "I just called my broker, Mr. Abbott," said Franco. "He thinks United Stores is a helluva buy. He told me it's on the low of the year, crossing the tape at six."

"I need another month," said Abbott. "I was going to call you. A month is nothing, for all that money."

Franco laughed and winked at the young man. "No way," he said. "Better face it, Abbott. With United Stores down to six, your whole block is worth thirty-six million dollars. You owe us fifty-three million now. That's short by seventeen million. And I know you count pretty good. But you also know that there's no market for six million shares of your stock. There's no market for blocks of any stock. There's practically no stock market at all. You are screwed, Abbott.

Plain and simple. Christmas is coming but no one is going to do any shopping, so earnings are going to be in the shithouse. Face it, Mr. Abbott, you're dead."

"There's the possibility of merger," Abbott said, sounding desperate. "If we do survive Christmas, would you be willing to loan the company five million dollars? Not me. The company?"

"You must be on tilt, Abbott. This ain't the Hearst Foundation. You pay us the fifty-three million, or we buy in your stock. The loan is due in your office at noon on December twenty-third."

"It's impossible. That's my busiest week of the year," Abbott said.

"You bought the original proposal," said Franco, looking wearily at the young man. "You jumped at the deal. This has been no picnic for anybody. My people are angry at me; they're angry at you. I'm not happy when my people are angry. But once United Stores is mine, I think they'll see what a business it really is. It's a great business."

"I don't think I want to talk to you anymore, Franco," said Kirk.

Franco hung up. "He's dead. See?"

"You're talking a lot of money," the young man said, in a tone that wiped the smile off of Franco's face. "Make sure you're on top of it." He switched the red rubber ball to his left hand and squeezed slowly. "Make goddam sure you're on top of it."

Kirk Abbott rubbed his eyes with both hands, trying to ease some of the tiredness from them. In the weeks since Franco had called, he had been working day and night with his stores, gearing up for what he felt would be a banner Christmas. There had been no assaults on business or individuals or city property for what seemed a long time. People in their urban cynicism began to believe it had all been a bad dream. Not much worse, in retrospect, than a newspaper or transit strike. When all was said and done, they were New Yorkers. Hadn't they seen it all?

Taking a break, Kirk walked out onto the mezzanine floor, overlooking the main selling area of Ungerman's, the Fifty-ninth Street store. The budget for Christmas decorations had been set at twenty-five thousand. That was forty-five hundred over Bloomingdale's and represented United Stores's biggest holiday expenditure in history. Nothing had been spared to make the scene festive and inviting to shoppers. Santas and elves and reindeer were strung out in reds and silvers and golds. They tinkled merrily down upon the shoppers who responded with pushes and shoves and crowding at the counters and cash registers.

My people, Kirk thought. Program them in the right direction and they respond as if you pushed the button yourself. He enjoyed watching the action, and he never saw Teddy Bronson come up behind him.

"It's a whole new ball game, Kirk," said Bronson, his voice nervous and filled with indecision. "We just got a letter."

Kirk turned, reluctant to tear himself away. "What the hell is it, Teddy? Do you need your goddam hand held?"

Bronson handed him a letter written on hotel stationery in block letters with a felt-tip pen.

SEASONS GREETINGS. THE PEOPLE'S REVOLUTIONARY ARMY REALIZES THAT AT THIS TIME OF YEAR YOUR CUP RUNNETH OVER. UNLESS THREE MILLION DOLLARS IN CASH IN SMALL BILLS IS ASSEMBLED WITHIN FOUR DAYS (NINETY-SIX HOURS) FROM THIS MOMENT, CUSTOMERS OF UNITED STORES ARE GOING TO HAVE A MISERABLE CHRISTMAS. MAY WE BE FAIRLY SPECIFIC SO YOU WILL REALIZE THIS IS NO JOKE: YOUR PROPERTY WILL BE VISITED WITH SUCH MEASURES AS WE SEE FIT DURING PEAK BUSINESS HOURS. THINK IT OVER QUICKLY. YOU'LL BE CONTACTED BY PHONE ONCE A DAY UNTIL YOU MAKE A DECISION.

"I've already taken the liberty of contacting the insurance company," Bronson said. "Under the policy, they guarantee us against all damages. But they can refuse to pay the ransom. I told them, naturally, that the demand was for three million."

"And?" Kirk said.

"They refuse to pay off now. They think it may be a bluff. Or a crank letter. They can't get in the business of paying off threats, they say. What do we do?"

Abbott looked straight at the man who was trying to force him out of the company and out of his own wife's bed. Kirk's tone was sarcastic, deliberate. "Public companies should not pay extortion." Kirk quoted Bronson's own words of the past. "I learned that lesson from you, Ted. We should not give in to terrorism."

"But this letter threatens our customers, Kirk. It doesn't say what customers, what stores, where. It doesn't say what they propose to do. They could sabotage merchandise, or set fires, or blow up a department. Christ, they're maniacs. They could do anything."

"You're raising your voice, Ted. You've got to stay under control. We have discussed this possibility; I know that you have discussed it with the board. Everyone agreed to pay no money if threatened."

"*If* you were threatened," Bronson said, lowering his eyes. "*If* our president were threatened. But you're not, Kirk. Or any of the officers. It's our customers. We have, God knows, a sense of responsibility to them. Not to mention the thought of liability. I know we can't afford three million dollars. But an attack would put us out of business. No one would come near a United Store. And frankly, it looks like you were dead right. Business has really been picking up. Sales this month are only off seven percent from last year, and we have almost ten days left."

"I look at balance sheets, too. But you haven't answered

the real question. Assuming you contradict yourself and decide to pay," Kirk said, "where the hell do you expect to get the money?"

"We can raise it. We can pledge the retail accounts, we can do a few things. I mean, I want this company to survive."

"Look, Ted, let me make a few phone calls. I want you to stay calm. You're the cool financial man, remember?"

"Yeah," Bronson said. "But this is war. Don't fuck around here, Kirk. I'm calling the board in now to make decisions."

"All right, call them. I'll be in the board room in about an hour. And Teddy . . ."

"Yes," Bronson said. There was no way he could hide his anxiety.

"Relax."

Abbott walked to his office and leaned back in his desk chair. If only I could get a little lucky, he thought. Everyone has returned to basics as they always do. He longed to call Gena, but he knew that was impractical. He sent her a wire instead, mostly to cheer himself up. Then he direct-dialed Franco Bertelli in Chicago. When he got the call through, Kirk outlined the threat.

"Pay off now," urged Kirk. "It would wreck United Stores if anything happened. If there were violence it would cost you more in the long run."

"You are a sorry excuse for a businessman, Abbott," Franco said. "You're whining to me now after being such a snotty son-of-a-bitch when you got our dough. Our insurance company collects premiums. They make investments. We're not in the business to pay claims; we're in business to make money. That's the name of the insurance game, or didn't they teach you that at Harvard. Jesus."

"But the stock would fall even more," Kirk pleaded.

"Bright boy," Franco chuckled. "We're going to buy in your stock on the twenty-third, anyway," he said. "The less

it costs us, the better. You're going to owe us the rest anyway. You're going to owe us everything."

"Your insurance business will be forced to pay all damages.
Without limit, Franco. Without limit. The insurance commission will not stand any screwing around."

"I know that, sucker. But we're willing to bet that nothing
will happen. And if it does, we'll only be paying the money
to ourselves. From one pocket to the other. We've got position, baby. And we got leverage. What you got is borscht.
I'm busy, Abbott. Go sell some electric trains."

Abbott made an elaborate paper airplane out of yellow
lined legal paper and scaled it 'way across his office. It
stayed up until it brushed against the far wall, then nosed
down gently onto a couch. He made airplanes and tossed
them for fifteen minutes. Then he picked up all the smashed
planes, rolled them into balls, and tossed them into his
wastebasket.

Opening the thick briefcase that he kept locked in his
desk, Kirk took out Alex's black stretch wig and, looking into
a portable mirror, carefully pulled it onto his head, combing
it into place. He smiled at himself in the mirror, showing all
his teeth. Then he stuck his tongue out. Then he smiled his
grim smile, showing no teeth at all. Kirk lifted a partition out
of the bottom of the briefcase and removed a handmade
Ruger Super Blackhawk 44 Magnum. He sighted down its
long six-and-a-half-inch barrel, using his free hand to steady
both his pistol and the sight picture of the opposite wall.
Kirk's hand was well up on the gun grip, as he had been
taught by the maker. His position was comfortable and he
was able to squeeze the rough trigger in a line with barrel,
wrist and forearm so that when the pistol recoiled, it would
recoil straight back, not spoiling any shot. He squeezed off
six shots, one after the other, the hammer falling onto empty
cartridge chambers. Looking at his watch, he stripped off the

wig, replacing it and the Ruger in his briefcase. He snapped it shut, twirled the combination, and locked the case in his desk. He combed out his own blond hair, which had become slightly matted. Then he washed his hands and face carefully in his private washroom. Feeling refreshed, he left his office to proceed to meet the directors in the board room.

"Don't be embarrassed, gentlemen," Kirk said. "I'm your president, remember?" His warmth reassured them. Bronson had guaranteed them that Kirk was a dreamer. It had never seemed so obvious.

"It's all right, Kirk," Bronson said. "I've spoken to the banks and arranged the necessary loan. They are preparing the cash now for the payoff." Kirk moved his eyes across the directors' faces. Anonymous men, anxious to vote on one side.

"That's fine, Ted," Abbott said. "If you all want it that way. I'll handle the delivery myself."

Bronson was shocked. "You can't," he said. "You're the president. It's three million dollars."

"I'm aware of the amount."

"I didn't mean it that way, Kirk. It's just that with so much cash, it should take a team — police, private detectives. The FBI will insist on being involved."

"I'm not interested in blowing either the delivery or a chance to get those madmen. I am the president of United; I'm going to do it myself."

Bronson tried to steer Kirk off the subject, but he interrupted and pressed on. "In addition to the arrangements, I want extra detectives in each store immediately. On duty from an hour before opening to an hour after closing. Until Christmas is over."

"Come on Kirk. Do you know what that would cost? We can't go for that. It makes no sense. I want to talk about the payoff, not about nonsense."

"There's no need to talk, Teddy. It's already set in my mind. I'm handling it myself."

"I don't think so, Kirk."

Abbott looked at the Board of Directors. There was not a friendly face among them. They represented the banks, the investment community, the civic-minded senior executives who served on boards for prestige and for the added lines that filled up biographical material in *Who's Who* and obituaries. Kirk felt a sudden flash of anger that crossed his forehead like a razor. He couldn't speak for a moment. Then he motioned to Bronson to follow him outside. Teddy pulled his vest down taut and stood up as stiff as he could. He was determined to resist any demands by Abbott.

"Look," Kirk said, when they got outside, jabbing a stiff finger into Bronson's vest. "I want to let you know that I'm sorry Lisa is being unreasonable. Especially now that you're making it big. So far you're lucky; no one knows about it. She'll take you back if there's no big scandal. *If* is the operative word."

"You son-of-a-bitch," Bronson said. "I think you're threatening me."

"Teddy," Kirk said. "At a time like this? I just want to be perfectly open with you. I'm thinking of suing Grace for a divorce. Adultery with a named correspondent. Theodore L. Bronson. I suppose it will find its way into the papers. A nasty, dirty business, and people love to live vicariously."

"Kirk, I didn't believe that anyone could be that low."

Abbott smiled at the remark, as a drill sergeant would smile at a recruit who asked if he could have time off to call his mother. "Twenty more detectives in each store starting today at noon," Kirk said. "And I don't want to hear anything more about that payoff. The job and the responsibility is mine."

Nancy – guitar, koala bear??

Scott – books, ski boots, magic kit

Kirk – Something in silver w. monogram

Ted – Something in gold.

From Grace Abbott's
Christmas list

22

*I*n his library on Round Hill Road, Kirk had had a wall safe inserted by a local carpenter who specialized in security for Greenwich homeowners. Kirk covered the safe with an 1864 Chapman and Hall London edition of the works of Dickens, twenty-six volumes. On the morning scheduled for the payoff, he removed volumes four through ten, *Nicholas Nickleby* through *Barnaby Rudge,* from the shelf and opened his safe. From it he took his Ruger Blackhawk, for which he had a license. He also removed several piles of United States currency. He separated the papers of his dog from the personal documents and put them into his inside suit jacket pocket. The Ruger he strapped into a leather shoulder holster made for him by Abercrombie & Fitch to fit neatly under his armpit and show no bulge. He went to find his wife.

Grace Abbott was eating half a grapefruit, being very careful not to squirt any juice onto her housecoat. She was sitting in her breakfast room looking out a big window over the broad expanse of their back lawn. A stable and small corral lay at the end of the lawn. No snow had fallen yet in Connecticut, although it had been threatening almost daily for several weeks.

"A pensive pose," Kirk said to her, coming into the breakfast room. "What do you see out there?"

"I see the ghost of Christmas past," she said. "What do you see?"

"I see a woman eating a grapefruit."

"Jesus. And I thought I married a romantic. Did you have coffee?"

"Long ago," Kirk said. He tossed a packet of cash at Grace, wrapped up in a thick elastic band. She caught it and riffled the bills, holding them up to her ear.

He tossed two more packets of bills at her. She made no move to catch them. One sailed past her shoulder and hit the window, then fell to the floor. The other packet bounced off her chest. "Any more?" she asked. "What the hell do you think you're doing?"

"That's your allowance for the next three months," Kirk said. "Anything beyond that is up to the lawyers."

"You do have a flare for the dramatic, darling," Grace said. "You are unbelievable. Those lawyers will be thrilled with the stories I have for them. I assume the gun is for the baddies if you meet them today?"

"Teddy told you about the money? Of course he did. He needs you, Grace. I think it's made in heaven, you two."

"You want a divorce?"

"Whatever you want to call it; it's your decision." Kirk's dog ran into the room, rubbing himself happily against his master's leg.

"You know," Grace said, "I have had a feeling that your precious dog has been spying on me all these months. I'm prepared for anything that may happen to me and the children. You never gave a shit for the horses. But what are you going to do without Sandy?"

Kirk picked up his little dog, scratching the cocker behind his ears, and down his neck. "Don't worry about Sandy," Kirk said. "I have plans for him."

"I'd like to know about your plans for us, Kirk. I'm sure you've got plans for us."

"You should have thought about things a long time ago," Kirk said to her. "The Bronson thing was a stupid move. You didn't understand what would happen."

"You know something, Kirk?" Grace said. "We've never talked very much about this, but you must have had one hell of a childhood."

"I had a classmate in college who came from Santa Fe, New Mexico," Kirk said. "He committed suicide during Christmas vacation freshman year by plugging up the dual exhaust pipes on his chopped and channeled Ford. He left a note in the car that said, 'The line between love and hate is very thin.' That's all he said. It impressed all of us who knew him tremendously."

"Divorce isn't a very philosophical word," Grace said. "You're going to get deep with me with a pistol strapped to your chest?"

"If you want me, Grace," Kirk said, "you can reach me at the office."

She suddenly began yelling at him. "I don't want you," she screamed. "I won't want you. And whatever I do want, I'll get. That's a promise." She heaved one of the packets of bills at him. It missed Kirk and hit a lamp. The elastic holding the bills together snapped and money floated all over the breakfast room. A few of the bills settled slowly in front of Grace. She let them fall and buried her face in her hands.

Kirk had Skelton, his driver, take him to the outskirts of Stamford. Kirk sat in the back seat, patting his dog during the entire ride, trying to scratch some solace out of Sandy's happy silence. Skelton pulled the limousine into Frazier's Dog Ranch, which had a discreet sign and lone driveway that reminded Kirk of the approach to a private girls' school.

Kirk carried Sandy into a stone Tudor mansion where he was greeted by a middle-aged man in gray trousers, English checked houndstooth jacket and the unmistakable smell of rum on his breath. "If rum gets in the way of your handling my cocker spaniel, Frazier," Kirk said, "you'll be sucking on a jug of Thunderbird on the West Side. You'll be lucky to get a job walking a cat."

The kennel owner spoke with an Oxford accent covered by a rasp that he must have inherited from the cold stone walks of his establishment.

"Mr. Abbott," the man said. "Style is as important in handling a dog as in choosing a wardrobe or a shotgun. I have style," he rasped. "My people have style. The dogs we care for leave here in style. We'll exercise Sandy twice a day in open fields. We shall manufacture the special box you requested on the phone. Whenever you are ready, ring us up and tell us where to send him." He held out his hand to Kirk. Frazier's palms were continually damp, his skin dead white, even in summer. No sun could ever make him appear healthy.

"I am paying you a bonus, based on the condition of my dog upon delivery," Kirk said. "You need generous people to help you realize the requirements of your habits."

"I understand you," Frazier said, taking Sandy out of Kirk's arms.

"I'm glad you do," said Abbott. "Because I want my dog healthy and on tap whenever I move. We don't want Greenwich to know what goes on in the men's rooms of Penn Station. Or where you really go on vacations. Do we?"

"I'll await your call, sir."

"You do that," said Kirk, who left the Tudor mansion by its long driveway. Once he looked back to see the kennel owner framed in the doorway and Sandy barking into the cold December air after the car.

"You'd better stop at United Stores to pick up the rest of them," Kirk said to his chauffeur. "It will take a while to set the details. You can have the car until about three. Stay within phone distance; I'm much more comfortable with you than in an unmarked patrol car." Skelton nodded his approval and whipped the limousine, in light traffic, along the familiar boring route to New York City.

Later in the day Skelton was replaced at the wheel by a man from the FBI. The agent's partner rode shotgun, his head turning often to check the sidewalks, his eyeballs almost clicking as they rolled from face to face. Everyone looks suspicious to the man who rides shotgun.

Kirk sat in the middle of the rear seat, between Teddy Bronson and a sergeant of detectives from the New York Police Department. A small suitcase sat cradled in his lap. It held a brown paper package containing three million dollars.

"Now," the sergeant was saying, "we've got people all over Grand Central and outside at every exit, and in cabs positioned at every door. The people you'll see who aren't ours are probably theirs." He indicated the FBI men in the front. "If you're in trouble, just raise your right arm straight up in the air. We'll be all over the place."

Abbott nodded.

"You're positive, Kirk," Bronson said, "that you don't want me going with you? You know, I'm prepared to."

"You're terrific at cops and robbers, Teddy," Abbott said. "But it's very clear now. All they want is the money. They don't want me."

It took no time at all to reach the Forty-second Street entrance to Grand Central opposite the Biltmore. Kirk wondered if college boys still met their dates under the Biltmore clock. Probably not, he decided. Nobody did things like that anymore. Not in New York City.

"Okay, Mr. Abbott," the police sergeant said. "It's time. Remember to shove that arm in the air the first sign of trouble. Let *us* be the heroes."

Kirk slid out of the car with his suitcase. He proceeded to Grand Central's terminal entrance and pushed in, moving quickly down the marble stairs of the grand staircase and across the floor. He passed the ticket windows and the information center, pausing where the magazine stand faced a long series of phone booths.

"Goddammit, why doesn't he slow down?" said a plainclothes detective into a walkie-talkie. "He's going to shake everyone on his tail. Who's the fuck's side he on?"

"Relax," cracked the answering voice. "We are observing."

"Why we let him make the drop, I'll never know," said the first cop. "Everybody wants a pat on the back. Then it's us who get killed."

"Subject moving into phone booth," came the second voice. "Bring your people in closer. Tighten them up. Tighten them up." Policemen and FBI agents swarmed over the terminal, disguised as everything from college students in Yale mufflers to hookers in stacked heels and hiphuggers.

Kirk entered the end booth nearest the train tracks and shut the door behind him. He checked his watch and waited. A few minutes later the phone rang. Kirk answered it immediately and listened. Detectives could see him turn around, look out onto the main terminal floor and nod in agreement. Then he hung up and proceeded across the floor into a men's room. Kirk moved so quickly it was impossible for any of the police or FBI to keep a close tail without being obvious. As it was, the FBI team who had been in the limousine had to run across the floor to get into the men's room at the same time as Kirk. They pushed their way in as Kirk was coming out. He gave no sign of recognition, and the FBI men were forced into the elaborate pretense of

washing already clean hands and drying them equally carefully on paper towels. Only then did they exit hurriedly from
the men's room.

A detective dressed as a commuting businessman picked
Kirk up and stayed with him all the way to the lower level.
"He's carrying a key in his right hand," one of the men on
the walkie-talkie said.

"And the briefcase?" came back a frantic response.

"In his left hand, schmuck. Jesus, he's walking fast. We
can't follow close."

"You lose him, it'll be a cold Christmas."

Grand Central Station was nearing peak traffic. Vacation-
ing children and shoppers taking advantage of the apparent
terrorist truce milled about the enormous spaces.

Kirk scanned the lower level, where the local trains arrived
and departed. He was in turn watched by several pairs of
eyes, including Sean Higgins, who stood by a post smoking
a cigarette. Higgins wore a brown loden coat with a hood. A
big plastic button pinned to the front of his coat proclaimed
to the world, BRING BACK ALLIE SHERMAN.

Kirk stopped in front of a bank of lockers, checked his key
number, and proceeded along the row until he came to the
right one. He inserted the key and opened the locker. He
snapped open his briefcase and placed the brown paper
package inside. Then he slammed shut the locker and twisted
the handle several times to make sure that it was secured. He
stared at the locker as if memorizing the number and the
place. Finally, with briefcase in hand, he walked back to
the stairs.

Higgins noticed the delivery boy first, because he had
been waiting for him. Right on the button, Higgins thought.
If everybody is as stupid as they're supposed to be, we're in
great shape. Move it, he thought to himself. Get the package
and move it out.

"Trade you a *Playboy* for the *Post?*" a rumpled man said to Higgins, making the Irishman jump. It was one of the detectives.

"Huh?" Higgins said.

"You've got the paper under your arm," said the detective. "Thought you might want to trade it for this *Playboy* I'm done with. Waiting for a train?"

"No, pal," Higgins said. "I'm mowing the fuckin' lawn. Buzz off. I haven't read my paper."

"Now wait a minute, friend," the detective said. "I was just making conversation. I seen you waiting here for a long time and I wondered."

"What are you," Higgins said, "some kind of queer? I'm going to Bronxville." He held up a schedule. "The 4:46. You got a problem?"

The detective swung away and stared at the delivery boy in blue denim uniform pants and jacket. The boy was carrying a bouquet of flowers and had just stopped in front of the wall of lockers. He fumbled in his pants pocket and produced a key. Then he moved up and down the bay of steel containers looking for the right one. With a smile of sudden discovery, he placed his key into the locker where Kirk had deposited the brown parcel. Pulling the parcel from its resting place, he put it under his arm as the door slammed shut. He began to double time toward the stairs to the upper level. The detective, having forgotten completely about Higgins, dropped his *Playboy* and took off. Everyone else on the detail, from different areas of the lower level, took off as well. The wraps were off and they elbowed through anyone in their way. Rudely and without apology. They ignored the complaints of those who were late, or in a hurry, or who never did anything in New York except at double time. Sean Higgins spat on the platform and ripped up his Zone B schedule to Bronxville.

Kirk never stopped until he got into the rear seat of his

limousine. The FBI pair were in the front seat, Bronson and the police detective in the rear.

"A flower boy picked up the package," said Bronson in a whisper. "They're after him now."

The detective patted him on the knee. "Fine, Mr. Abbott, the delivery boy is in his truck and off into the streets. We've got four cars strung out all around him and a WOR traffic helicopter above the truck. No screwups this time."

"We're not following him, are we?" asked Kirk.

"No need to."

"In that case, if you don't mind, I think I better get on to business. This should be the biggest day we've had in months," said Kirk.

"We don't mind, Mr. Abbott, but —" The detective hesitated and glanced at Kirk's briefcase. Kirk glanced at Bronson. Bronson shrugged and looked away.

"You want to check the briefcase?" Kirk said. "You think the president of the company's got the three million?"

"I'm sorry, Mr. Abbott," the detective said.

"That's all right. We've got to make sure the bad guys were paid off, right?"

"I'm a little sick of insults, Mr. Abbott," the detective said. "We've all got our breaking points. I've been on this thing day and night for months."

Kirk said nothing. He snapped open the briefcase and emptied it upside down, then peered into the lining in an exaggerated manner. "I guess I'll have to subsist on my salary."

"I'm sorry, Abbott," the detective apologized again. "I guess I'll have to live on my salary too."

"I know all about it, Lieutenant."

The delivery boy drove his truck like a tank. He wheeled the truck up Madison Avenue and east of Forty-fifth Street and downtown on Lexington, pulling up to a hydrant in front of the Graybar Building, Lexington and Forty-second

Street. He jumped down to the sidewalk on the passenger side and ran into the building, carrying his flowers and the brown paper parcel. Squad cars bracketed the truck. Plainclothesmen ran into the Graybar Building on the heels of the delivery boy, who disappeared in the crowds emerging from work, his flowers held high like a beacon. Getting lucky, he caught an elevator in a long row of them in the lobby. Since practically no one was going up and practically everyone was coming down, the starter pushed the doors closed: "Wait!" screamed an oncoming detective, flipping his wallet open to show his badge.

"Too late, officer," said the starter.

"Goddammit," said the officer in charge. His companions looked sheepish. "Okay," he said, "every elevator I want covered. Every exit and entrance. Get the building super for the basement and service entrances. When this kid comes down, pick him up." They waited. And they watched. When at last the delivery boy reappeared, emptyhanded, from an elevator, he was grabbed by several people. They flashed identification at him.

"What's wrong?" he yelped. "You don't roust me for being double parked. I'll move it. I'll move it."

"Where's the drop? Why were you running? Why were you carrying flowers in Grand Central?" He had questions from every side.

"Twenty-seventh floor," the boy said, now terrified. "I left everything on the twenty-seventh floor, office 2712." Four officers stood aside as elevator doors slid open, spilling out more workers, including Silver Wheels Edwards, who wore purple shades, a broad-brimmed leather hat and a large tan trenchcoat with more buckles, straps and pockets than could exist in a pickpocket's wet dream. Edwards moved with the crowds to the Lexington Avenue exit and out onto the darkened streets.

"Want to see a pimp?" one secretary said to another, nudging her friend and pointing at Edwards. They giggled at one another, fascinated at the possibilities.

"Why the hell did you carry flowers in Grand Central if you didn't drop them till now?" a detective said to the boy.

"I had to double park at the station, didn't want to leave them in the truck. No shit. I was late. I'm late now."

"What was in the package?"

"How do I know? I just do what I'm told, man, no shit."

"You know what a drop is, don't you? You didn't question all the fun and games? Go to a locker, pick up a package, deliver it only a block away. Don't shit the shitters, kid. We'll work it out at the station."

All he received back for his protests was a twisted arm. He finally sat back in the squad car and stared out at the people going by who were free.

A secretary was typing a stencil in office number 2712. A dozen roses stood tall in a green glass vase on her desk. "We're closing, gentlemen," she said to the detectives, annoyed to be disturbed when she was trying to finish up and leave.

"Never mind that, we're police," they said. "Who picked up a package here a few minutes ago? A brown paper package?"

"I don't know, officer. I was inside. Mary's the receptionist."

"Where's Mary, honey?"

"Mary gets off a little early. That's when I cover the phones. Mary has a baby."

"What about these flowers?"

"Oh, Mary put them in a vase. We have a service that sends us fresh flowers three times a week. Makes everyone happy, you know?"

The detectives shook their heads. One of them took out his pencil and a pad of paper. "All right," he sighed. "Where do I get hold of Mary . . . ?" The others kept shaking their heads.

Alex wore the off-white coveralls of the Penn Central maintenance crew, as in one hand he dragged an empty canvas trash bag over the main floor of Grand Central Station. In the other hand he carried a long-handled push broom by the Merrill Lynch mini-office, by the off-track betting, by the Union News and the phone centers, to the lower-level stairs. No one had seen him walk into the employees' locker room and pull the coveralls from a peg. He grumbled to himself, pulling the bag down the steep stairs. People passing him thanked their lucky stars that they weren't grumpy old maintenance men. Alex dragged his canvas bag into one of the washrooms and began sweeping the floor, starting near the stalls and working toward the sink area. When he had pushed dirt and cigarette butts and ripped toilet paper and old schedules ahead of him into a corner, he lifted the top off one of the trash baskets near the row of sinks. Opening the canvas bag, he placed it over the top of the trash. Inverting the basket, he poured the contents into his bag, complaining to himself when a lot of it fell around the edges of his bag onto the floor.

"There must be a better way to do that," said a man washing his hands. He looked as if he commuted each day to Cos Cob.

"You wanna try it, mister?" said Alex. "Anytime you wanna try it, the job's yours." The man said nothing more. He wiped his hands with a paper towel and rolled it into a ball.

"Go ahead," Alex said, "toss it on the floor. Everybody else does."

The man shrugged and tossed the paper into the pile Alex had pushed together. "Good luck," he said and left.

Other men came in and made their way to the urinals or to the stalls. They avoided looking at Alex, as people everywhere avoid those who clean up after them. He pushed the rest of the papers and the dirt into his bag, making sure that at its bottom rested the brown paper parcel he had hurriedly shoved in there earlier that afternoon. "Anything worth saving in there?" a man smiled at him. It was the shit-eating smile of people who haunted public places and who wrote their phone numbers on the inside of the stalls.

"Just a lot of junk, mister," Alex said. "Just a lot of crap." And three million in cash, he thought to himself. He dragged the canvas sack out onto the station floor.

Book
3

```
39, 800, 000.00
39, 800, 000.00 T


          .0 0 T
```

From the calculator
of Kirk Abbott

23

"You've got the spareribs," Higgins said to Scott Dutton. "I've got egg rolls and those crisp noodles."

"Look," Glory Cohen said, unwrapping packages of Chinese food on the big round table in her living room. "When you eat Chinese, you all mix everything together. Everybody ordered one thing, and we each take some of it. I've been eating Chinese food since I've been a little girl. I know."

"I don't think it's hot enough," said Michael Cagnina. "Why don't you put it back in the oven for a while. I can't stand take-out food if it's cold. Chicken or pizza or anything."

"You are getting to be one fucking crybaby, you know that, Chico?" Boaz looked at the lawyer. Cagnina avoided an answer. He moved over to help Glory dish the food out onto paper plates. The downstairs buzzer rang. Dutton went into the hall to answer it. "Edwards," he said, when he came back to the room.

The black man came into the apartment, flopping his hat against his knee. "Man, it's a bitch out now. Raining. Windy. Cold. Nothing gets cold like this city gets cold. When I retire, I'm going to be somewhere in the sunshine all the time. California. Going to have one of the all-timers for a house. Pool, steambath, you name it. Silver Wheels gonna have it."

"We're lucky it ain't snow," said Sean Higgins.

"You got it?" Boaz asked him. "You got it and no one followed you?"

Edwards reached into his trenchcoat. He tossed Boaz the brown paper package. "On the first day of Christmas," Edwards sang. "My true love give to me . . . three million fucking dollars." The others laughed, gobbled bites of Chinese food, and gathered around to watch the unwrapping ceremony. Boaz ripped the brown paper away to reveal stacks of flat toilet-paper packs. He looked up slowly at Edwards, his right hand pulling a .45 single-action Colt from his waistband, and pointed it directly at the nose of the black man. Boaz thumbed back the hammer.

"Jesus, man," Edwards said, talking rapidly. "I picked up the package in the office. I stuck it in my raincoat and came out of the building easy as you please. No one tumbled; no one followed me. A couple of chicks looked. But they always look. Come on, put that down. There's no way that I rip us off."

"We'll wait for Alex," said Boaz. "Give him a plate, Glory. Lots of spareribs. You like spareribs?"

"Come on, Boaz," Cagnina said. "Put the pistol away."

"You, you four-eyed cocksucker," said Boaz. "You're always saying don't do this, don't do that. Next thing we know you'll be calling the FBI and telling them where to pick up the naughty people who are killing folks and getting rich. I'm about half sick of your whining. You shut your face, you dig?"

"Always full of the spirit of giving, Boaz?" Alex said from the doorway. "I see you've got a gun in your hand. Didn't anyone ever teach you to eat with a fork?" Alex was feeling good. He had keys to the apartment, insisting on access at all times to every member of his group.

Boaz tossed several flat packs of the toilet paper to Alex.

"Does this look like three million dollars to you?" he said. "Edwards picked it up; Higgins was birddogging the whole way. Somebody pulled a switch."

"Nobody pulled anything," Higgins said. "I was on it from the beginning."

"Wait a minute," Alex said. "You mean this was in the money package?"

Boaz nodded.

"What about the flower boy?"

"Not a chance," Higgins said. "I was on him from the time he got out of his truck at Grand Central. He lost the cops going up the elevator on Lexington. But I was right beside him."

"In the office, then . . ."

"Forget it," said Edwards. "He slapped down the flowers and the package. I made the pickup right then and was out the door."

They all looked at Edwards.

"Now wait a minute," he said, backing up toward the kitchen. "Hold on. You know I wouldn't fuck us up. Alex, you know."

"Yes, I know," Alex said. "Forget it. What about their man? The guy who made the drop in the locker."

"I was with him all the way," Sean Higgins said. "I picked him up coming out of the limousine with the fuzz. I followed him the whole time."

"To the phone booth?" Alex said.

Higgins nodded.

"The men's room?"

"I saw him go in and out. Took less than a minute."

"You didn't follow him into the men's room?"

"How could I? With cops and the Feds all over? If I went in and out with him in thirty seconds, they'd have made me the minute I came out."

"Who knows about people," Alex said. "I'm always surprised at what people do. Maybe he did rip off his own company. Are you sure it was Abbott and not a cop?"

"Light hair," said Higgins. "A business dude. Same height as you. It was Abbott."

"Dutton," Alex said. "Give him another call. Let's see what the reaction is."

Boaz slammed his hands down on the table. Fried rice flew from paper plates onto the floor. "I say no," he said. "No more chances. What are we, going soft? That guy had detectives all over the place. He's the president of the company; he could steal them blind eight ways to Sunday. He's the man. He ain't going to rip off his own bread and butter. It was a fucking trap. They weren't going to pay. Believe it."

No one spoke. Dutton had his hand on the phone and was looking at Alex. The dark-haired leader motioned him to put it down. Boaz began Scotch-taping a large floor plan of a department store to the wall. "This is their biggest store. It'll be packed with Christmas shoppers tonight," Boaz said. "Open till ten to make up for lost business in November. We're going to go in there and give them a lesson. After tonight, all we'll have to do is stand around with money bags and hold them open. There won't be anyone in America who will do anything but pay."

"But Christmastime," Cagnina said. "How about a break for Christmas?"

"Oh, bullshit," Boaz countered. "Christmas never meant anything but an ache in the gut to me. It's a time for giving, right? We'll give it to them."

"I think we've killed enough people, Boaz," Cagnina said.

"Alex," Boaz said. "You hear all this that's going on? You agree with me?"

"We cannot be in the business of letting anyone get away with resistance," Alex said. "We hit the department store tonight. Ungerman's, the biggest one. Grenades and Thompsons, maximum damage and destruction. The street floor only. No exits upstairs."

Boaz nodded in agreement.

Cagnina shook his head. "I don't think I can do it anymore."

"Don't worry about it," Alex said. "I understand. We'll work out a passive role for you. Where you're driving or something. At half your usual share."

"I don't care," Cagnina said. "It was never the money. It was supposed to be the idea. I don't care."

Alex didn't answer the lawyer. He went to the plan of the store and told everyone what he expected. When he was done, he asked Boaz to walk him to the stairs. "You get Cagnina's piece of whatever he would realize in the next three months. I don't want him leaving the apartment on his feet. And I want the others to know about it. I want them to observe what happens to people with a change of heart. See you tonight." Alex walked down the stairs to a landing where he turned. Boaz stared down after him.

"Enrico," Alex said.

"Yes."

"Make it original. Something that sticks in the mind."

Boaz didn't waste any time. He walked back to Glory's apartment, where his companions were finishing the Chinese food. "Okay, Michael," Boaz said to Cagnina. "Alex said for you to drive. You can stay in the car and get us out of there."

"I wish none of you were doing this," Cagnina said. "I got sick the last time. I'll get sick again. It shouldn't be the money."

"Have some more food; you'll feel better," Boaz said. "What do you like, egg fu yong? Shrimps with lobster sauce? Maybe some spareribs? We've got plenty."

"No. I'm full."

"Come on," Boaz insisted. "I want you to enjoy yourself. Eat something."

"I can't."

"Eat," Boaz said, pushing a platter of spareribs at him.

"All right," Michael Cagnina said, snatching a sparerib from the plate. Boaz stood over him, watching Cagnina dip it into a large container of sweet and sour sauce.

"Eat," Boaz commanded him. "It'll put hair on your chest."

"Maybe a little," Cagnina said. He put the sparerib bone, with its light coating of meat cooked in red sauce, into his mouth. Boaz suddenly cracked him across the side of his neck with the hard flat of his hand. Almost at the same moment Boaz jammed the long thin bone of the sparerib down Cagnina's throat, twisting as he did, to lodge it in the man's trachea. Then he grabbed Cagnina's hands and held on, as the lawyer contorted and convulsed and writhed around in dreadful agony, trying to dislocate the bone by the frenzy of his movements. It took two and a half minutes for him to die.

"You know where he kept his stash?" said Sean Higgins to the others.

"Tomorrow we can check his apartment," said Boaz. "Tomorrow, after we take care of United Stores and Mr. Abbott."

"What about Cag?" Glory asked.

"We'll dump him on Mott Street," Boaz said. "Right in front of the biggest Chinese restaurant we can find."

"He ain't going to be hungry in an hour," Edwards said. "Only a stupid son-of-a-bitch doesn't know a good thing. Too bad."

"He kept talking about making people's lives better when this was over," Higgins said. "That was his first mistake. You got to take care of number one."

Cagnina's face was distorted in death. His strangulation had drained all the flush from his face. He was turning gray.

"I can't look at him," Glory said. "Let's get out of here and do what we have to do."

They left in pairs, with Edwards and Scott Dutton supporting Cagnina's body down onto the streets of Greenwich Village. Shortly, Boaz picked them up in a green Oldsmobile with dealer's plates, stolen from Pelham, New York. The rain had stopped in the city and the air was still. Christmas decorations shone overhead in clusters of lights strung across streets by neighborhood associations. It was cold. In the low twenties. But New York looked peaceful and clean.

PND 5000 8 40   EK 80   UN8 5

Price of United Stores
the day before Christmas

24

*T*he music in Ungerman's Department Store boomed out over the holiday shoppers. It was heavy on carols and Christmas bells, heavy on Andy Williams and Bing Crosby. Kirk Abbott had been right about holiday business. It was the best in years. People were buying in great quantities, everything from dolls that wet and cried to waterbeds that could be filled with champagne. People felt that they deserved a treat. Kirk stood near the perfume counter in the middle section of Ungerman's main floor. Teddy Bronson stood next to him, looking distastefully at a uniformed and armed guard who walked by them toward the elevators. "There is absolutely no reason on earth," he said to Kirk, "to retain all these goons. You know what they cost, for God's sake. We paid the ransom. This is madness. I want these troops, and that's what they are — I want them out of here by morning. I mean, one man on each floor to watch for shoplifters is one thing, but you have people all over the place. For no reason."

"Do you see them discouraging business?" Kirk asked. "I think it makes people feel safer."

"Look. You're forcing me to go to the board again and operate over your head. I don't want this to get ugly. We can't afford your whims. And I don't think we'll have to, if I can be candid?"

"By all means."

"You know how much better the market's been in the last few weeks. But United hasn't done a goddam thing. No volume. No upticks."

"I read the *Wall Street Journal*," Kirk said softly. "I know the prices."

"And you know the stock is five. That's a new low for the last seven years. I'm going to do something about that, Kirk. As soon as you're out of the picture. You'll do everyone a favor if you back off. Do it gracefully, for Christ's sake. Do something graceful for a change."

"Speaking of graceful," Kirk said, "how is Grace? Staying busy, I hope."

"You *are* a prick. You know goddam well she won't see me anymore. And you know Lisa has left the house with the children. I'm going to stick it in your ear, Kirk. And you'll feel it. I promise you that."

Kirk smiled at Bronson and picked up an atomizer from the counter. It was full of a new Chanel scent, intended for free customer samples. Kirk squeezed the rubber ball, spraying Bronson's neck and lapels with the heady feminine odor. Bronson retreated, brushing at his lapels, looking as offended as if he had been caught full in the shirtfront by a skunk.

"Just put a carnation in your buttonhole, Teddy," Kirk said. "No one will be able to tell you from a floorwalker."

"By morning," Bronson said to him. "These guards will be gone by morning. You are out of your mind, you know, Kirk? Out of your mind."

Abbott held up the atomizer again and shook it at Bronson. Teddy moved quickly away, losing himself in a crowd of shoppers. Kirk put down the perfume in front of a salesgirl. "Not too many free samples, Susan," he said. "But keep everybody happy."

"We'll do our best, Mr. Abbott," she said, blushing the color of the pink smock that all the ladies in cosmetics wore.

Kirk checked his watch, then walked up the back stairs to the mezzanine balcony that looked over the entire ground floor. He positioned himself in a corner, away from the crowds that wandered the mezzanine. Two guards watched the floor from the opposite corner. They ignored Kirk, their eyes sweeping the counters. Up and back, in fields of concentration. It was the way they had been taught to watch for pop-up targets in basic training.

Moving his eyes in the same direction, Kirk noticed a tall black man fingering lingerie at the women's counter directly below him. The salesgirl was laughing and having a good time listening to the black man's request, as if it were the first time he had ever bought underwear for a lady. Silver Wheels Edwards was carrying several large packages, gaily gift-wrapped with papers from another department store.

Two aisles away, Sean Higgins had his fur-lined winter coat on the floor and was wrapping several leather belts around his waist. A salesman, struggling to keep his patience, reminded Higgins please to remove his packages, which were cluttering up the aisle in front of the belt and accessory counter.

Kirk saw Edwards move from lingerie and make his way, carrying bundles, to the escalator leading to the mezzanine. At the same time Glory Cohen stood by the heavily decorated information counter in the center of the store. She held a Gristede's shopping bag by the handles. Fruit covered the top of the bag: oranges, apples, tangerines. The bag smelled like Christmas, and Glory wore a red coat with a long woolen scarf and a white knitted cap with a jolly pom-pom on top. Boaz came up behind her in a leather, fur-lined flight jacket. He gave her a hug that almost lifted her from the floor. "I see everybody but Alex," he said. "Where the hell is Alex?"

"I thought we were missing Dutton, too," Glory said. "But he's over near the elevators in that awful cowboy hat. That's a stupid thing to wear, so recognizable."

"You're wrong," Boaz said. "All people will remember will be the hat. But I'll tell you. I'm not going to wait for Alex. I'm going to start in a minute. That's all."

"You can't do that, Rico, he's got to be in position. There are so many guards."

"Christ, they can't zip their flies by themselves. Those people will be the first to run for the doors."

"I want to wait."

"Glory," Boaz said. "Face it. Alex is all finished. We don't need him no more. I don't. You don't. He's never going to get out of this store. It's about time we gave the FBI somebody. Maybe we'll even apply for the reward."

"I don't know, Rico."

"Go," he ordered. "Thirty seconds. Move. We've got three aisles to cover. *Get going.*" Boaz handed her one package from the floor. It was her basket of fruit. He gave her a gentle pat on the bottom. Then he scooped several gift-wrapped bundles near his feet up into his arms and moved the other way.

Abbott watched in fascination from the mezzanine as Scott Dutton, in his cowboy hat, rode up one of the two main escalators with his bundles. He waited at the top, letting others come up the mechanical stairs. People rushed by him as he rearranged his boxes. Kirk saw Glory go to the rear of the store. He saw her stand against the wall of elevators where they looked out onto the entire main floor. This view commanded the five major aisles loaded with gift items, hardware, jewelry, gloves, luggage and handbags, perfume, lingerie and accessories, stationery, hats and neckwear. Her back against the wall, Glory stooped suddenly and reached into her shopping bag. She noticed that Boaz and Sean Higgins had taken up positions on either side of her.

They were spread out, each edged into a corner of the same wall. Glory pulled a hard round metal object from her bag. It looked like one of her oranges, and had indeed been sprayed with paint that morning. She pulled a small metal ring out of the orange-colored object and rolled it like a candlepin bowling ball down the gift counter aisle.

"You dropped one of your oranges," an older lady with black orthopedic shoes said to her.

"Thank you," Glory said, pulling rings from two more of her special fruit and rolling them up two different aisles, as hard as she could.

"God rest you merry gentlemen, may nothing you dismay," bellowed out of the public address system as the first of the incendiary grenades exploded, sending bursts of smoke and flame almost as high as the ceiling. The second and third explosions competed with screams of agony and fright. There was the instant panic and blind instinct for survival that has characterized every holocaust in history. People with cooler heads would be trampled before anyone else.

Higgins and Boaz had dropped their packages in front of them and ripped off the Christmas wrapping. Snapping the circular clips of ammunition into their Thompson submachine guns, they faced the hundreds of hysterical shoppers surging toward the exits, and fired long, arching bursts over the heads of the crowds. They severed displays of Santa and his reindeer, strings of lights, bells and angels, which came dropping, crashing, floating down upon the mob. The people turned in a body and moved in the only direction open to them — toward the escalators. It was a frozen, terrible moment for Silver Wheels Edwards, positioned at the top of the electric stairs that went down to the main floor. He couldn't fit the magazine into his Thompson. The more frantic he became, the less able he was to function at all. In seconds, women shoppers came screaming up the down escalator toward him, their legs oblivious to the machinery that insisted on carrying them downward. Edwards had seen fear in his life, and hunger, and grief, and pain. But he had never seen panic like this. He couldn't run, he couldn't move. "Dutton!" he yelled over to his companion at the next escalator, who was calmly firing bursts from his weapon into the crowds. "Commence firing" was all Dutton would say. "Commence firing," he kept repeating to himself, as he picked targets at random and cleared the escalator. He lay prone, offering a small target to the guards who were just beginning to fire their own pistols.

A hundred women were on top of Edwards now, sticking their heels in his eyes, his nose, his groin, stamping his life out. It was almost like being tackled in college, Edwards thought, when everybody hit you after the whistle. "Fifteen yards" were the last words on his mind as the women shoppers tore him apart. The key he wore around his neck on a chain fit his safety deposit box in the Chase Manhattan branch in Harlem on West 128th Street. It was ripped from the warmth next to his body and lost forever down a crack in the escalator stairs. Almost two million dollars lay in the box. Two years later, the box would be drilled open by bank officials and its contents reposessed by the City of New York.

Scott Dutton methodically snapped a new clip into his machine gun. He knew he had to clear a path for his escape and he had to do it in the midst of everyone else's confusion. He tilted his cowboy hat back onto his forehead and drew his arm across his brow to wipe off the sweat. He knew he had killed at least two guards and possibly a third, whom he had hit in the chest and had seen crawl away. What he didn't see was Kirk Abbott walking carefully through the shoving people in the mezzanine. Kirk made his way to a fluted wooden column in back of Dutton. He had his Ruger automatic in his hand, the safety flicked off. He had watched

Glory rolling her incendiary grenades; he had watched the others killing and destroying at random. His first shot caught Scott Dutton just behind his right ear. The southerner's head splintered like a horseshoe crab when a rock is dropped on it. Kirk flushed, excited. He picked up a fresh clip from where it lay beside the cowboy hat and jammed it into the Thompson gun. "It's going to be all right," he said to the people who surrounded him in gratitude, who reached out to touch him, to touch their savior. "It's going to be all right," he said as he crouched low. Then, with the machine gun, he made his way slowly through screaming, agonized people, down the jammed escalator to the main floor.

"Let's blow it," Sean Higgins yelled to Boaz. "Or we're fucked." Small fires erupted in various aisles, burning counters and merchandise.

"The main doors," Boaz yelled back. "Make it to the main doors. Drop the Thompsons there. We hit the streets and we make it."

They began to blast through the crowds, people falling around them, some clawing their way right into the paths of the bullets.

"Mary, Mother of God," Higgins said, as a burst from Kirk Abbott at almost point-blank range went up and down his body. Boaz swung around and caught a glimpse of Abbott, ducking under a counter. The glimpse stunned him and he hesitated, not believing what he thought he had seen. Kirk popped up suddenly in a section full of homemade earthenware crockery designed and produced by an old lady in Barre, Vermont. Kirk peppered the area where Boaz stood, shattering all the glass in the elevator doors behind him, but missing Rico, who rolled on the floor to avoid the fire. He came up on one knee and ripped the crockery off the counters like so many clay pigeons at a country fair; their eyes met suddenly and they stared at one another, a sudden moment of silence in a battle across feet and inches.

Boaz sprinted for the doors. People ran from his path, knowing he carried death. Several guards had rallied to Kirk, flanking him. One of them stood beside the main doors, waiting with the hammer pulled back on his .38 to catch Boaz as he went by. Excited by what he knew he could do, he held his breath and squeezed the trigger, steadying his shooting arm with his left hand. The shot never came, as Glory Cohen eased from the mob and put a .22-caliber bullet in the indentation between the guard's eyes. Boaz smashed a glass door with his weapon and hurled himself into the street, leaving the machine gun behind.

The guards turned on Glory. She kicked her shoes off and ran to a door, the men's room. Kirk jumped up from where he crouched, and yelled to several guards to follow him. Two of them preceded him into the men's room. People lay in shock, whimpering on the floor, in the stalls, under the sinks. Some of them prayed. Glory had climbed onto a sink and was trying to raise a window that had been painted shut long ago. Trapped now, she turned and stared at Kirk. Somewhere in the crush she had lost her pistol. She looked like a frightened little girl, her clothes ripped, her long black hair wild around her shoulders. The guards looked at Kirk, questions in their eyes. "Finish it, goddammit," he said. "Finish it."

"Alex!" Glory screamed, as she stared directly at Kirk; it was a cry for help, a plea for mercy. Three of them shot her at the same time and she fell heavily from the sink, flipping over and falling into one of the large, old-fashioned, heavily tiled urinals. Camphor cakes rested on the bottom of each one. Streams of Glory's blood began to eat away at one of the cakes, beginning to cut a hot, lifeless route through its sanitary surface.

Teddy Bronson burst into the men's room, surrounded by half a dozen police with shotguns.

"It's all over, Teddy," Kirk said. "Can you believe it's all over?"

The store guards crowded around as did the survivors in the men's room. "He did it," they said about Kirk Abbott. "He saved us all."

"He took that machine gun and saved us."

"My God," several of them said, wanting to touch Kirk, wanting to reassure themselves. "Thank God."

A police inspector issued orders. Police, ambulances, fire equipment, converged on the store. Kirk looked down at Glory's body, distorted in its death. He shook his head. "Crazy," he said. "Did they really think they could do this? Crazy." He turned to Bronson. "Better see what you can do about organizing the cleanup. I expect you'll want to work through the night. Only two shopping days left." He walked from the men's room, through his wasted department store, observing the wreckage. Medics with black bags and stretchers ministered to the dying and the dead.

Kirk walked up the fire stairs toward his office. Away from the cries and the shouting, he could hear the public address system clearly. Its automatic cheer went on despite the horror, and it came to him without distortion on the empty back stairway.

"Chestnuts roasting on an open fire, Jack Frost nipping at your nose." It had always been one of Kirk's favorites.

Enrico Boaz thought his heart would burst through his chest. Crowds in the street who gather whenever there is a tragedy thought that he was only a victim, maddened by his experience. People asked if he wanted a doctor, a hospital, some coffee. In shock, he waved them all aside, elbowing through people and disappearing down into a subway entrance, a refuge below the streets. Sobbing and sucking wind at an incredible rate, trying to get a grip on himself, he rode a train downtown. Several times he almost passed out, and when he emerged at Fourteenth Street he vomited with enormous relief. Looking in a restaurant window, he took a long time combing his hair, as if that act of restoration would bring some order to his tortured mind. He stumbled on to Glory's apartment and forced himself to bring out a hammer and chisel, ripping out the fireplace in the small living room to remove the currency that lay in piles beneath the bricks.

Boaz knew he had to move fast now. He loaded as much money as he could into a small suitcase and took two pistols — a .45 Colt, which he packed on top of the money, and a police .38 Special — which he stuck in his belt. He had a kitchen glass full of whiskey, Canadian Club without ice. It burned his throat but it felt warming and good as it went down. He washed his face and hands, wiping them on an old dress of Glory's hanging on a hook from the bathroom door. Then he grabbed the suitcase and ran down the stairs.

Grace Abbott watched the account of the department store slaughter on special news flashes through the night. Teddy Bronson had called her as soon as it was over and all she could ask about was Kirk. He had been wounded slightly in the arm, Bronson told her, and had been treated by a doctor.

Then, free to go, Kirk had talked to reporters for an hour. After that he had disappeared, presumably to a hotel to sleep.

Grace called the Carlisle, where Kirk had maintained a suite. But she was told he had not come in.

She wandered around her house, going from room to room, trying to get a fix on what was real in her life. She made coffee. She drank brandy. She watched her children sleeping, feeling, deep in her womb, the same stirrings of life that she felt when she carried them.

Since Kirk had left the house in Greenwich, at least five of their old best friends had called her, all wanting to console her with their own special brand of consolation. She had let one friend take her to dinner locally, at Boodles on Putnam Avenue. He was her lawyer. It was out in the open, an innocent dinner. Later, he knocked over a chair in her living room coming after her, thinking that wet kisses on the neck and touches on her breast could solve both of their problems. She promised herself that the next time she married, she would be in control and she would live in peace.

Grace lay on her bed, flipping channels with the automatic control. Every channel kept interrupting their programming to show film clips from the disaster. She couldn't stand it anymore, and poured herself more brandy and shut off the TV. Not able to abide the silence, she tried the radio, hoping to find a station playing Bach. She heard the end of the *Messiah* on one station, and its familiarity almost put her to sleep. But even before the final chorus, the program switched abruptly to "Chestnuts roasting on an open fire." A chorus of sugar-plum fairies sang at her, "Jack Frost nipping at your nose." She shut it off quickly and went to the window. The rain in the city was snow in Connecticut, and Grace began to cry softly, knowing she would never get to sleep.

del escritorio de
Antonio Figueroa

A. tells me that
everything is wrapped up –
my present, my future.
How much will it
take to make sure of
everything Can I be
sure ?

From the scratch pad
of Gena Reynolds

25

*K*irk had spent the night looking for Boaz. He ended up in an all-night movie off of Broadway, waiting for the sun. He watched *She Wore a Yellow Ribbon, West Point Story*, with James Cagney, and Kirk Douglas with Tony Curtis in *The Vikings*, until he found himself asleep in the back of the theater. Then he went back to the Carlisle and had steak and eggs in the bar, something the Carlisle would always do for him.

After breakfast he went to his suite, shaved slowly, and took a long shower until the bathroom filled with steam. Feeling better, he read the *Times* and the *Daily News*. The *Times* headline carried the largest type since the dropping of the bomb on Hiroshima at the finish of World War II. AN END TO TERROR, it proclaimed. TERRORISTS SMASHED IN UNGERMAN STORE SHOOTOUT.

There were a dozen messages for him. But he knocked the phone off the hook and lay down on a couch in the living room, placing a cold facecloth over his eyes. At eight A.M., he got dressed in a blue, three-piece suit of whipcord made for him in London by Cooling, Lawrence and Wells of Maddox Street. Then he made one phone call. He talked for half an hour and left the Carlisle, walking the long blocks to his store. The area had been cordoned off by the

police, and hundreds had gathered to stare. It took Kirk
some time to identify himself to be allowed to pass.

The main floor looked as if everything had been put on
a giant sale and the total population of New York City had
been turned loose upon it with hundred-dollar bills. But the
total effect was surprisingly orderly. Any employee who
showed up was to be allowed in and paid time and a half for
the entire day. Commercial cleaners needed all the help
they could get obliterating signs of the carnage and restoring
enough merchandise and Christmas decorations to give some
semblance of order. Teddy Bronson was on the floor super-
vising the cleanup. He looked at Kirk curiously.

"Where did you go last night? Half the city of New York
was looking for you."

"I was gathering up my certificates," Kirk said. "Today's
the moment of truth. I had a lot of thinking to do."

"I want to run a monster sale tomorrow," Bronson said.
"The last day before Christmas. Before anybody has a sale.
Full-page ads in tonight's papers, tomorrow morning's papers.
Have the biggest one-day giveaway in the store's history.
Then we'll have a three-day weekend to get everything in
shape."

"I can see you're getting to be a merchandiser," Kirk said.

"I better be everything after today," Bronson said. "Are
you ready?"

"I'm ready," Kirk said.

"The Big Board should have its strongest day in months
today," Bronson added. "Might help you a bit. There may
be buyers in United Stores."

"But not enough. Right, Teddy?" Kirk said.

"You said it," Teddy nodded. "Not me. Everything you've
dug, you've dug for yourself."

"Let's get it over with," Kirk said. "Anyone here yet?"

"Just the insurance people. They came in from London
early this morning."

"That's what I call service. Did they bring a check?"

The two men were dressed like Englishmen. And they were sipping tea which a secretary had to leave the store to find. But the resemblance to an American's idea of the English ended there. The two men were dark, both with thinning black hair, the sides spread back in waves with gelatinous pomade that made their heads glisten like polished auto upholstery. They sat next to each other along one side of the United Stores Board of Directors table. They had assembled in front of them dozens of papers and forms. They looked as if they had every intention of completing their work in short order and taking the next plane back to London.

Bronson and Kirk came into the board room and exchanged greetings. Then the two officials of United Stores began reading and signing the dozens of insurance forms the Englishmen had provided.

"We were led to believe, Mr. Abbott," one of them said, "that there may be a change of management and that this check may not be necessary." The man held out a green envelope with a plastic window in its side.

"I don't know where you got an idea like that," Kirk said, still busily signing his name, over and over. "But I fully intend to be president of United Stores for some time. I intend leaving it here for my children, don't you know?"

Bronson gave him an irritated look, then went back to his own cosigning.

The Englishmen went on. "Possible new management assures me that these monies may not be necessary; that this particular property may be sold and torn down. Luxury flats put up in its place. You understand that Clause 12D of the policy cancels coverage in that case."

Kirk finished signing and looked up at the dark strangers. "You have been misinformed," he said. And he held out his hand for the envelope. "I know all the provisions of your policies. The damage to life and property has been extensive.

And that's the understatement of the year. You're getting off cheap for ten million, my friend. So don't give me any of that industry doubletalk."

The telephone buzzed softly in front of Kirk. "Mr. Abbott," she said. "There are several men here insisting they have a meeting with you. I have nothing about a meeting on the calendar. A Mr. Franco Bertelli is one of them. Quite insistent. Is it all right?"

"It's all right," said Kirk. "Put him on."

"Abbott?" Franco said.

"Good morning, Franco."

"The place sure looks like hell."

"A busy night," Kirk said.

"I'm afraid the piper is here to be paid. As a matter of fact, we got all the pipers. If you take that insurance check, it's all over. Right now. If you don't, we've agreed to give you another thirty days. Time, Abbott. Something that nobody has enough of. You got it if you refuse the check. You take it and it does you no good anyway; it'll go right into the company, the ten million. We'll foreclose, we'll buy you in this morning. Now. You make us pay the money. Okay, we'll own the business. Right? We're willing to pay ourselves. Out of one pocket into another. You want to be a bright boy? Take the month."

"I thought tough guys went out with Prohibition, Franco," said Kirk, putting down the phone gently onto its cradle.

"He's a strange character," Franco said to the young man in the blue pinstripe suit seated in the corner of Kirk's reception office. He was seated so that he could watch the doors and the entire room before anyone noticed him. He gave no indication of hearing what Franco had said. He slightly narrowed his eyes as if that were the only communication necessary. Seated near the young man were the two bankers Kirk had dealt with in the past, one from Paris, one from Singapore. They sat quietly with closed briefcases: well dressed, relaxed, their knees pressed together and their manner silent. They were used to waiting, not like American bankers at all. Two other men sat in the reception area. One looked enough like Justice Holmes to be his twin, and was fingering his heavy gold watch chain. The other, large and florid-faced, balanced bulky legal-sized envelopes on his fat knees and beamed at the entire room. He smiled and nodded, and dipped his big head covered with red hair in every direction. He looked, in his good spirits, for all the world like the ghost of Christmas present in a bespoke three-piece suit. It was Kirk's Swiss lawyer, Rhinelander, who always enjoyed himself immensely.

In the board room, Kirk took the insurance company check, payable to United Stores in the sum of ten million dollars. He handed it to Bronson. "This will take some of the sting out of last night."

Bronson gave it back. "Hold it for the messenger to deposit."

Kirk put the check into his inside jacket pocket. The English insurance men rose.

"Thank you for your promptness, gentlemen," Kirk said. "I must recommend your efficiency to some of our American casualty companies." They said nothing; they did not shake hands. They left the board room quickly, slippery and silent, anxious to be gone from a place where they had left so much money behind.

Kirk and Teddy Bronson followed them out. "Teddy," Kirk said. "That sale tomorrow is fine. Why don't you get on with it. I have one more meeting."

"I know. What do you intend doing with the rest of your life? I could probably get you into our training program."

Kirk shrugged and walked into his office reception area. "Why don't you gentlemen come into my inner office," he said. He nodded at Rhinelander. "Franco, you've no objections to an observer?"

"It's the season for giving," Franco said, drawing deeply on a cigar. He winked at the hard, thin young man. "Bring along anybody you like."

Kirk shook hands with the bankers, and they retired to his office. Kirk waved them all into chairs and stepped to the window. Below him, a Salvation Army band played Christmas carols. Many people paused by the pot to toss in coins. They were thankful for the offtune noises that reminded them of goodness somewhere back in their lives.

Kirk ran a hand through his fine hair, as if to gain time. Franco noticed the gesture and gave the thumbs up sign to the silent young man.

"May we begin?" the white-haired gentleman spoke. He even sounded like Justice Holmes, his careful accent and his appearance marking him as the prudent man, the mediator, the judge. Kirk nodded and sat down at the conference table. The white-haired Yankee glanced around; then, satisfied, he took a pair of wire spectacles from his breast pocket and proceeded to read from a document in front of him. Just before he began, Kirk pushed at him across the table a neatly stacked pile of stock certificates, duly endorsed. The white-haired gentleman placed his hand on top of the pile.

"I am Foster Marshall," he said. "Senior partner of Marshall, Shaw, Lamont and Armstrong of this city, 76 Wall Street. This is a foreclosure sale on six million shares of United Stores common stock, held of record by Mr. Kirk Abbott. The market value per share based on closing prices on the New York Stock Exchange last night, December twenty-second, is five dollars per share. But, in the opinion of First Appraisal Corporation, whose report I am holding, six million shares could not be sold at that price. The fair market value is, therefore, twenty-four million dollars. Accordingly, I have fixed twenty-four million dollars as the fair and reasonable upset price. I shall entertain any and all bids. Do I hear any bids?"

Immediately Franco said, "Yes. Twenty-four million dollars."

The lawyer noted the bid and paused. "I have twenty-four million. Do I hear twenty-five?" He waited. "Do I hear any other bids? No? Twenty-four once. Twenty-four twice . . ."

Franco took a long, confident puff on his cigar, exhaling in smoke rings, one after the other. Perfect circles.

"One," Rhinelander said from his seat at the corner of the table. "One dollar," he said, beaming. "That is to say, twenty-four million and one dollars."

Franco's perfect circles fell apart. He glared at the stranger.

The white-haired lawyer removed his glasses and looked down the table. "Excuse me," he said. "But we do not know you, sir. May we ask you at this time to identify yourself and to produce some evidence that your bid will be honored. Please?"

Rhinelander, still beaming, opened his briefcase. He handed around the table, with a grand flourish, his business card, his passport, a number of bank checks payable to his order and a crisp United States one-dollar bill. The lawyer raised his bushy white eyebrows at the evidence in front of him, and, gravely, passed back to the Swiss lawyer the card, the passport, the checks, and the dollar bill.

Franco got up and went over to the hard-faced young man. "He's from Geneva. Not one of our men. Rhinelander. Ever hear of him?"

"They've got more lawyers in Switzerland than we got motel rooms," the young man whispered. "You think Abbott brought him in?"

Franco whispered back. "Where would he get twenty million dollars? You don't think that Vegas . . . a double cross?"

The young man looked contemptuously at Franco, who returned to his seat. As he did, he casually said to the lawyer, "Twenty-five million dollars."

Almost instantly, Rhinelander countered. "And one. One

dollar more." He handed another bank check around the table.

Franco didn't hesitate. "Thirty million dollars."

"And one," said Rhinelander. "One more dollar."

"Thirty-one million dollars," Franco snapped.

Rhinelander sighed, happy to accommodate. "And again, one more dollar," he said, in accents more French than English. He peeled off another bank check from the large stack in front of him. The big freckled hands shuffled the stack as if he were feeling for a card to fill a straight.

Franco watched the size of the stack and whispered quickly to the young man, "I don't think he's up to anything. I think he's a pigeon."

"You bid thirty-one million dollars," the young man said. "Can you get it on the market?"

Franco answered nervously. "Prices will be a hell of a lot better from now on. I think I can get thirty-one. I'm not sure. But for that price, this is a steal. I'd rather own the business. Right?"

"Schmuck," the young man said. "We're not in the business to own the business."

"But Abbott's broke," Franco said. "He can't pay the deficiency. If we let the stock go for thirty-one, we're out twenty-two million dollars."

"You're out twenty-two million dollars."

"Come on," Franco said, cocky again. "This guy is loaded. Let's push the bidding. I'll push him."

The white-haired lawyer was waiting patiently.

"Thirty-five million dollars," Franco said. He smiled at Rhinelander, and he glanced around for approval at the bankers from Paris and Singapore, bankers who placed their names on questionable loans, often obtaining funds for these loans from sources like the hard-faced young man and his friends.

The bankers from Paris and Singapore were impassive.

They were used to seeing people squirm and it meant nothing to them at all. As long as they got their money, they didn't care.

"Thirty-five million. And one," said Rhinelander.

"Forty million dollars," Franco almost yelled.

Rhinelander hesitated, shuffling his bank notes. Franco looked at him, fearful for a moment. Then he relaxed as the Swiss lawyer smiled more softly, more controlled than before. "And one," he said. "Forty million and one dollars."

"Forty-five million," Franco said instantly. He was happy now, on the offensive.

Kirk took it all in with the impassive stare he used when he was in a casino, when a fine film of concentration seemed sprayed all over him and he heard nothing. He saw nothing but the wheel, the hands and the dice, the fingers of the dealer as he flicked cards at the players. The game was always more important to him than the people who played it. As long as he could remember that.

"And one," Rhinelander was saying. He was being pushed and showed it. "Forty-five million and one dollars." Reluctantly he passed around more bank notes, again shuffling the still large stack in front of him. The hard-faced young man tapped Franco on his elbow. He leaned his face down and stared at Bertelli.

Franco was pleased. "He'll go higher," Franco whispered. "Look at that stack of checks. And all we're bidding is Abbott's marker for fifty-three million." He waved the young man off and said loudly, "Forty-six million."

"And one," said Rhinelander, handing over another bank note.

"Forty-seven million," said Franco.

"And one dollar."

"Forty-eight million," said Franco, feeling triumphant.

"And one dollar," said Rhinelander. The room was as silent as an empty theater.

Franco felt marvelous. He grinned, deciding to be playful. "Forty-nine million and one dollar," he said.

"Fifty million," countered the Swiss lawyer.

Franco looked at his opponent. "And one dollar," he hissed, in a sound that cut the room like a razor.

Rhinelander stared down at the remaining stack of notes in front of him. He shuffled them silently and his heavy breath was audible, the breathing of a fat man who indulged himself.

He looked over at Franco with a strangely empty expression. Everyone else looked at Franco. Franco blinked his eyes and turned to the white-haired lawyer. Then he turned to Rhinelander, who had lowered his eyes and sat silently.

"Do I hear any further bids?" said the lawyer. Franco was blinking. "Then going once, going twice . . ."

"Wait," said Franco desperately to Rhinelander. "You've got more money. Millions more. One more dollar," he cried. "That's all you need. I'm through bidding. It's all yours. One dollar. One more, you can have it."

Rhinelander merely stared at him.

"Do I hear further bids?" the white-haired gentleman asked softly.

Franco was blinking more frequently. "I-I," he stammered. "I'd like — can I withdraw?"

Kirk Abbott laughed. The hard-faced young man walked over and put a hand on Franco's shoulder. He squeezed. "You can't withdraw. You hold the loan." He continued to squeeze.

The mediator nodded. "Sold to Mr. Franco Bertelli for fifty million and one dollars." He rapped a small wooden gavel on the table.

Instantly Franco lunged for Rhinelander's remaining checks, sprawling across the table in his frenzy. He turned them over. Everything that remained in front of the Swiss lawyer were strips of blank green paper, cut into bank-note size.

Rhinelander's face was impassive. He looked over at Kirk Abbott and suddenly smiled at him as if he were his oldest friend. Everyone in the room began gathering up their papers and notes. The mediator began returning the bank checks to Rhinelander.

Franco shredded the blank green paper and scattered the bits across the table, like confetti. Tiny flecks of spittle formed in the corners of his mouth and he shook a finger at Kirk. "You still owe us three million dollars, my friend," he said, in a voice that threatened to crack. "Three million. We can buy a lot of pressure for three million dollars. We can..."

"Sure you can buy a lot of things," Kirk said, interrupting him. "You can buy broken arms, legs. A hit, for three million dollars. So can I. I'll show you." Kirk was totally under control. "Give him bank checks, Rhinelander," he said to the Swiss lawyer. "For three million dollars."

The lawyer produced the checks and handed them to the hard-faced young man, who stood over Franco like a conscience.

"Where did you get it?" Bertelli was pleading now. "How did you get it?"

Kirk shrugged. "In my cookie jar," he said. "It's only three million dollars."

The hard-faced young man laughed without mirth. "Congratulations," he said softly. "I don't know how you pulled it off. Perhaps the company's books will show. Perhaps not. If you ever . . ." He looked thoughtful, then decided against it. "No, you won't ever." He looked down at Franco, who still blinked his eyes and stared at his fresh manicure. "Looks like you just spent our sixty million dollars," the young man said. "Fifty million dollars you bid, and ten million in insurance that we paid." Franco chewed on a freshly polished nail.

"And what have we got to show for it?" the young man went on. "Stock worth twenty-four million dollars. We're thirty-six million in the hole. Right? Thirty-six million dollars." He looked at his fingernails. Involuntarily, Franco shivered. "All done now?" the young man asked the mediating lawyer.

The white-haired man nodded.

"Not quite done," Kirk interrupted. "You still owe me one dollar." The old man shook his head gravely and handed Kirk the one-dollar bill. Kirk folded it quickly into a paper plane and sailed it across the table to Franco. Bertelli lifted his head and looked at the dollar.

"I'll never forget," he said. "So help me." He made the sign of the cross. "We'll remember. We'll . . ."

"We?" the young man said, raising his voice for the first time. "You don't mean we. You mean you. You no longer work for us, Franco." He dropped his voice. "I don't know who you are."

The bankers left together, satisfied that they would be satisfied.

Kirk and Rhinelander were leaving when Teddy Bronson came in the door. His smile seemed jammed onto his face.

"Congratulations, Kirk," he said. "I heard what happened. I know retirement will look good. It should look good."

"Yes, Teddy," Kirk said. "Everybody looks forward to retirement." He took Rhinelander's arm and walked out of the office, onto the ruined mezzanine. Kirk shut the door behind him.

Bronson did not hesitate. He went up to the hard-faced young man, who stood with his hands on Franco's shoulders. Bronson held out a hand of his own. "I'm Ted Bronson," he said. "Vice president — finance of United Stores. I understand you now control the corporation. I'm the boy with all the figures when you need them." He still had his hand extended. But the young man made no move to take it.

"Would you like a report on the business?" Teddy continued, putting his hand in his pocket. "That terrorist insurance was my idea. You heard about it, I assume? The ten million dollars?"

The young man looked Bronson up and down. "I heard about it," he said. "You think you can run this business at a profit?"

"I think it can be the most profitable retail business in America, sir."

"That's what I like to hear," said the young man. "You have a contract?"

Bronson nodded. "I foresaw the need for one."

"Good thinking. I like that. Got it with you?"

"I pride myself on spotting trends," Bronson said, making sure to stand very straight. "I do have it with me." He took the two-page original contract from his inner jacket pocket. "Four years more to go at one hundred thousand a year. Bonuses keyed to profit performance."

"Tear it up," said the hard-faced young man, who softened momentarily, looking sympathetic.

"Sir?" questioned Bronson.

"Tear it up. No one who works for me has a contract. I take care of my people."

Bronson hesitated. The young man quietly waited. Making up his mind, Bronson tore the contract in half. Then again into quarters. He let the pieces fall to the floor. A gesture of confidence.

The young man headed for the door. "No," he said. "Forget it. I've changed my mind. You're not smart enough to work for us."

Bronson and Franco were left alone in Kirk's office. They each looked in different directions, grappling with the emptiness that filled their minds.

Outside on Madison Avenue, the Salvation Army band nodded at people who left them quarters, dimes and nickels. The coins disappeared with dull clunks into the holiday pot.

.0 0 T

5 0, 0 0 0, 0 0 0.0 0
5 0, 0 0 0, 0 0 0.0 0 T

From the calculator
of Kirk Abbott

26

*K*irk Abbott's suite at the El Conquistador looked like the inside of a naugahyde Alhambra. Its saving graces were its cleanliness and the fact that the country's biggest casino was just off the lobby. Kirk had been listening to Gena Reynolds talk steadily for almost an hour about the country, its potential as a profit-making center for their bank, its people, its government, and the advantages of an equatorial climate on one's mental health. Kirk sat on a couch and sipped rum while he listened. At last he interrupted. "But in the long run," he said, "what if it's just a bore? What if this place is a mistake? You can get awfully tired of perfect weather." His tone was teasing, but she took him seriously.

"Are you out of your mind?" she said in an instant rage. "After all the time and effort I've put into this project? Do you know what I've been through putting this together? Aside from playing whore to these pigs, who think that women are nothing but one big hole?"

"Would you change your mind for a million dollars?" teased Kirk.

"Bullshit," Gena said. "I wouldn't change my mind for three million dollars."

"Ahh. But the experience. The fringe benefits."

"Look, Mr. Anastos, whose real last name I don't even

know. This can be the most successful bank in Latin America. And don't kid yourself; I would love to be an important woman down here. Europe is dead; Asia is too crowded and impossible. This is the New World."

"You don't want to lie on a yacht all day?"

"Kirk," she said. "I want to make waves."

"What I love is your honesty."

"Tell me why you wear sunglasses indoors."

"In the first place," he said, "you always see Latin American dictators wearing shades. Inside. Outside. Swimming. In the second place, it allows me to watch people when they can't know that I'm staring. In the third place, how can you tell that the sun doesn't bother my eyes?"

Gena walked over to the couch and sat down next to Kirk. She reached over and plucked his glasses from his eyes. She lay them down on the carved wooden coffee table in front of them.

"They seem like ordinary glass to me," she said. "What are you, nearsighted or farsighted?" She licked her lips.

"I can't see anything farther away than two years."

They kissed several times, the kinds of kisses that people give when they hope they understand one another. "Sometimes I get the feeling," Gena said, "that you're not serious. That your games have no point. No finish."

"I promise you," Kirk said, nuzzling her neck and her ear. "I promise you that I've never been more serious in my life."

"You really can raise fifty million? We need it before the bank can open. That's a law, Kirk. The money has to be here."

"If the cash reserve necessary to open is fifty million dollars, it'll be here. I'll bring it myself from Geneva. Are you positive there will be no taxes?"

She smiled. "That's part of our agreement. Figueroa has given me that in writing. No taxes. He wants the business."

"A shame that he'll miss you."

"My father used to tell me that you can't expect every-thing in life." They kissed. "Your plane," Gena said.

"My plane doesn't leave for an hour. There are ways to save time. You went to business school."

"But my specialty was marketing."

Gena was wearing a navy cotton knit T-shirt and a brown-beige, navy and white plaid seersucker long skirt. She unbuttoned the skirt and brushed it off the couch. She opened Kirk's pants while she let him slide her bikini bottoms over her hips and down her legs. She snapped the pants across the room like an elastic band. They played until neither of them could wait. Then Kirk sat back on the couch and took Gena onto his lap. Too soon, she broke their kiss to murmur something and hugged him, scratching lines across his back. They only stayed for minutes. Yet it had seemed so removed from everything else, like an afternoon nap on holiday. A void.

"I do love you," Kirk said, as Gena lay softly in his arms.

"I do love you," she said back to him, in a very small voice. They kissed each other quietly and slowly, on the cheeks, the eyes, the forehead. "I really don't want you to leave," she said. "I can't imagine myself saying that. I didn't want to say that."

"When I come back," he said, "I won't have to leave."

"I don't believe that," she said. "But I'll remember it anyway." She dismounted and stood in front of a bureau and combed her hair. Kirk watched her naked bottom, perfectly rounded. It seemed flawless, the bottom of a teenager. Reluctantly, he got dressed. "They don't allow half-naked women to go to airports in this country," he said when he was ready. She nodded at him, and hurriedly put on her pants and skirt.

Kirk rang for a porter and walked with Gena to the elevator. They did not walk arm in arm; they did not hold hands. Outside the bedroom, they kept a businesslike distance. But they looked at each other many times, quick glances to see if the other one were noticing. After Kirk checked out at the desk and his bag was loaded into the cab, he looked at his watch. The heat outside the air-conditioned hotel lobby came at them like a damp, sour facecloth. "I want one spin of the wheel before I go," Kirk said.

"*Les jeux sont faits,*" Gena said.

"I wouldn't be that final about it," Kirk said.

Two men were vacuuming the carpets in the casino. All of the games were shut down in the afternoon siesta hour except for one roulette wheel, one blackjack table, and a lonely croupier watching an American shoe manufacturer and his bored wife betting twenty-five-dollar chips on the come. Kirk put five hundred dollars down on the green felt cloth in front of the man who ran the wheel. "All on the red," he said. "The color of her hair." he indicated Gena. The croupier's stare was blank. For years he had seen men trying to impress all kinds of ladies. He spun the wheel and, with a flick of his fingers, sent the little wooden ball in the opposite direction. It whirled at desperate speed around the outside edge.

"What are you going to say when it stops on the black?" Gena asked him.

"I'll say that you'll have to do something about your hair."

The ball, blind and indifferent, finally rested for a long moment in a black nest. Then, with a sudden jerk, it popped into a red hole and stayed there.

"Let it ride?" said the stick man.

"Cash me in," said Kirk. A pit boss in a black dinner jacket gave Kirk one thousand dollars in crisp new colones. "You do not mind being paid in Costa Rican currency?" he said.

"I expect to be here for some time," said Kirk, taking the new bills.

The pit boss nodded.

Kirk and Gena left the casino and got into the cab together. On the ride to the airport he gave her five hundred of the thousand. "Not the whole thing?" she asked. "You were ready to lose it anyway."

"I'm never ready to lose anything," Kirk answered. "Besides, you're my partner, right? There's a difference between being my partner and being my woman."

Gena put the five hundred in her purse and took Kirk's hand. "When will you be back?"

"Less than a week, I hope."

"I hope," she said.

They held hands in silence the rest of the ride. Then they walked without touching, through the small terminal to where the airline was announcing his flight to Miami. It was awkward to stand waiting after good-byes, so they embraced and kissed long enough for a National Guardsman to watch them. When they stopped Gena said to Kirk, "You're wrong about something."

"What's that?"

She spoke very softly. "I *am* your woman."

He nodded and walked through the gate to his plane, not looking back. She watched him climb the gangway and disappear through the first class door. Then she turned and walked, with great deliberation, out into the shock of the sunshine.

The glare bouncing off the windshield of the Cadillac made Gena squint. The car moved slowly toward her, stopping when it got alongside. The rear door opened and she slid in, grateful for the blast of the air-conditioning that was kept on High. The Cadillac slid out of the airport and onto the road back to the city.

"Fifty million dollars?" Antonio Figueroa asked Gena. "It is true?"

Gena did not look at him, even though he sat very close to her. She could feel his breath.

"Less my ten percent. Five million dollars," she said.

"Yes. Net forty-five for me. Very nice and neat. Does he believe?"

"Mr. Anastos believes," she said. "Mr. Anastos is a romantic. He thinks he will fit in very well down here. Oh, he believes."

"Not having money makes you dream," the minister of finance said. "Having money makes you a believer." Figueroa patted Gena's knee. Then he stopped patting and kept his hand on her thigh. Gena tensed slightly. But she did not remove his hand.

Stone Crab Cocktail

Filet Mignon with Mushroom Caps
Stuffed with Fois Gras

Asparagus with Hollandaise Sauce

Salade Niçoise

Cherry Cheesecake

Espresso

Fruit and Cheese

Menu for first class,
Pan American to Geneva

27

*B*oaz caught Frazier, the dog handler, in the midst of the feeding hour, when he was surrounded by dozens of animals.

"You'll have to wait, sir. It'll be about ten minutes. We have magazines inside."

Boaz waited in the main house, and when Frazier finally entered, brushing himself off, the Mexican said to him, "What do you give the mutts for breakfast?"

"Generally they just have water, sir. No food in the mornings. Why?"

"Because if you don't tell me what I want to know, I'm going to feed *you* to your fucking mutts for breakfast."

Frightened, but secretly thrilled, Frazier immediately told Boaz where he had shipped Kirk's dog. Boaz had seemed so pleased that Frazier relaxed, half expecting some money for his information. His gratuity was death.

Boaz left him seated in a comfortable living room chair. Frazier's sightless eyes pointed up the long driveway, no more to anticipate the station wagons from Westchester and Fairfield counties carrying masters and their pets.

The first class lounge at the Miami Airport was not crowded and Kirk could drink his complimentary orange juice and read his paper in peace. He felt an incredible calm envelop him, as if he had been pampered with brownies and milk and covered with grandmother's puff. He looked forward to flying to Geneva, which was always at its best during the winter. Any other year and he would stay to ski. But he was determined to get back to the Caribbean as quickly as possible. Kirk had left his lightweight clothing in a suitcase locked up in the main Miami terminal. He took his London Harness bag containing heavyweight travel clothes and changed in the men's room off the first class lounge. He wore a navy wool suit with wide cuffs and a thin chalkstripe. Rhinelander would meet him at the airport in Geneva and they would go off together to make withdrawals. The impersonal, amplified voice crackled into the lounge, "Pan American Airways announces boarding for Flight 432 for Geneva. First call, gate 30. Departure will be in twenty minutes. All aboard, please, Flight 432 for Geneva."

Kirk put on his horn-rimmed sunglasses and, like any other anxious traveler, checked his passport. Costas Anastos, it read, citizen of Costa Rica. Citizen of the world, Kirk thought, and carried his bag down the narrow stairs to the terminal floor. He walked quickly to Gate 30 and was moved with no delay through a first class line and out the covered gangway to the plane. Kirk paused before entering the passageway, looking down below the belly of the 727 where the last-minute baggage was being loaded. The baggage people were being very careful with an elaborately constructed carrying case that had mesh openings in the edges. Through the openings could be seen a cocker spaniel lying quietly on his side like a good dog. "Good dog, Sandy," Kirk said softly. "Good dog."

Kirk went on into first class where he had taken a seat on the aisle, far forward near service and the cockpit.

"I think we can sneak in a cocktail before takeoff," the stewardess said. She was dark and had long legs. The standards for international hostesses, who needed additional languages and skills, still had not been diluted by the popularity of travel. She'll make a good marriage for herself, Kirk thought. He ordered a vodka martini and put his head back on his seat, closing his eyes.

When his turn came to lift his bag onto the security check counter, Enrico Boaz began to smile and chat with the Pinkerton guard. "Catch anything special lately?" he said.

The Pinkerton guard, a pimply faced kid in a uniform two sizes too big, just grunted his response. "Put your bag on the table, please," he said. He and a woman in a man's uniform riffled through Boaz's large canvas carryon. They haphazardly shuffled through toilet kit, underwear and several shirts. Then they shoved the bag along the table. A boring bag, they thought, going on to some heavy Vuitton luggage owned by Beautiful People.

Boaz stepped up to the metal detection screen, watched by an older guard who looked as if he had been a policeman, put out to pasture and bored with retirement and three six-packs a day. He waved Boaz through the detection doorway. Rico quickly moved across the electric eyes, but not quickly enough. The system set off a shrill tone. "Any metal objects?" the guard asked Boaz. "Keys, penknife, that type of thing?"

Boaz handed him a key ring full of useless keys, locks he had left behind him.

"Okay," the guard said. "Go through again."

Boaz did and again the alarm sounded. "There seems to be something the matter with you, buddy. What else you got in your pockets?" Boaz was wearing a trenchcoat over leather pants and a suede jacket. He fumbled through every pocket nervously, finally producing a nail clipper and a Zippo lighter. Without being told, he walked through the metal detector again, leaving his possessions with the guard. No alarm was triggered. "Again," said the old guard. "Nice and slow." Boaz held his arms away from his body and repeated the procedure. Nothing. "Okay," the guard said, handing Boaz back his things. "If you wanna know the truth, the machine's too fucking sensitive. Have a good flight."

Boaz smiled and picked up his carryon, walking quickly to board the plane. The first thing he noticed as he entered were the stewardesses. The second thing he noticed when he walked through the first class section was Kirk Abbott, his head back on the seat, obviously asleep, even though dark glasses hid his eyes. Boaz had a feeling of frenzy, a flash of triumph. People nudged behind him, urging him to move on along the narrow aisle back to the tourist section. He moved on, clutching his canvas satchel tightly in both hands, holding it in front of him almost as a shield. When he took his seat far aft in the plane near the washrooms, all he was sure of was the passenger with the fair hair and the sunglasses.

The attendants swung shut the doors to the 727 and the pilot began backing away from the portable loading gate. "Mr. Anastos," the stewardess said to Kirk. He opened his eyes behind the shades and acknowledged that he was back from limbo. "I'll have to take your drink," she apologized. "We're taxiing for takeoff."

He finished in a quick gulp before she took the plastic glass.

The plane was full. Even first class had no empty seats, and the passenger cabin crew, one steward and four women, complained to themselves about what promised to be an overly busy flight. The plane was cleared with no delay, and it took off into the Florida sky as easily as a football is tossed on a beach. The plane banked, and the strip of hotels looked from above like a real estate developer's gameboard. Then it gained altitude, swinging out over the Atlantic, heading east. Moving still higher, it plunged into spongy white clouds that made the ocean disappear and the passengers loosen their seat belts.

Boaz sat in the middle of three seats with a woman from Revlon on one side and an oral surgeon on his way to deliver a paper in Zurich on the other. Boaz held his canvas bag on his lap.

"Sir," a stewardess said to him. "You're going to have to put the bag under the seats."

"It won't fit," Boaz smiled at her. "I tried it, but it won't fit."

"I'm sorry, sir. It's regulations. Perhaps I could bring it forward." She was being accommodating.

Boaz got up, scraping by the heavy knees of the oral surgeon. "I'll take it to the men's room," he said. "My toilet kit is in here. Then I'll let you have it."

"Fine, sir," she said, wondering if he were an actor. He looks like someone I've seen, she thought. Probably in spaghetti westerns. She waited by his seat as Boaz disappeared into the restroom. The plane entered some turbulence and bumped along with increasing violence.

Boaz held onto the plastic support bar, and even though he tried to be careful, he peed all over the floor and himself. Cursing, he wiped his pants with a paper towel, then carefully washed his hands and face. Then he combed his hair and looked at himself in the mirror. The plane took some more bad bumps and the intercom requested everyone to return to their seats. Boaz unzipped his carryon. Delving beneath his clothes, he pulled out the false cardboard bottom that lay between his shirts and underwear. It took him two minutes to assemble his machine pistol and snap in a fully loaded clip of ammunition. The stewardess knocked on the door. "Sir, are you all right? The captain wants everyone in his seat. We're experiencing some turbulence."

Boaz slid back the lock and lurched into the aisle, shoving the barrel of the machine pistol into the girl's belly. "Let's go, baby," he said roughly. "We can bring my bag up to first class now." He pushed her along the aisle as people slid down in their seats to make themselves inconspicuous, their hearts pounding the minuet of fear. Several passengers began to cry; others saw faces in their minds they believed they would never see again. In a matter of seconds Boaz was pounding on the locked door of the cockpit, his face turned toward the main cabin. Anastos was staring at him, his glasses tucked into his pocket. Boaz stared back into his eyes, the shock of recognition as brilliant as an alarm. Boaz fired a burst from his pistol into the door lock and wrenched open the flimsy barrier. The flight engineer dropped a small pistol onto the floor when Boaz stuck the muzzle of his weapon into the captain's ear.

"All right," he said. "You get this plane headed southeast. Algeria. Dar-el-Beida Airport. And no games. Life is cheap to me. I want to prove this. I am going to burn up one of your passengers in about a minute and a half." Picking up the flight engineer's pistol, Boaz backed out of the cockpit and down the main aisle, pausing as he reached Anastos. He motioned him with the pistol to stand.

Kirk felt that everything he was doing was in slow motion and fought to clear his head of confusion. He carefully got to his feet, grabbing for an idea. Boaz moved the machine pistol to Kirk's face and was about to ask him to beg for his life when his smile turned into a contorted grimace, as if he were wearing a rubber mask of tragedy. Passengers screamed and vomited around him, clutching their ears. Oxygen masks dropped from their compartments. A hostess yelled, "Pressure."

Boaz lunged for the cockpit, his brain pounding, as the aircraft took a sudden dive, causing him to grab for an upright seat. Kirk left his feet, diving into Boaz, ignoring the pain as he tried to get his thumbs into the veins in the man's neck. They fell to the floor and Boaz fired both pistols wildly, hitting the steward and two passengers. The copilot and flight engineer jumped on top of the struggling pair, kicking the machine pistol out of Boaz's hand. Several men and a woman with a short mink jacket all began pulling and kicking at Boaz. He fired two shots in rapid succession into Kirk's chest almost at the same moment that the pilot leveled the plane off and the flight engineer emptied the machine pistol into Boaz's brain, splattering the others in the struggling pile with skin and blood and bone and cerebellum. The plane's pressure returned to normal. Passengers and crew huddled together as close as was humanly possible, hugging and kissing each other. Some people sobbed. Others, their juices pumping, exulted in the victory. A man in a double-knit suit, suddenly brave, looked around for more hijackers to kill. People congratulated Kirk, putting pillows to his head, whiskey to his lips. The woman in the mink jacket held a linen napkin to his chest, as if covering the holes would make them go away. "You were fantastic," she said. "You saved us."

The captain came on over the intercom, telling them they were on their way back to Miami.

"For once, someone had the guts," a man said to Kirk. "It's the only way to stop it."

The woman nodded. "My husband just sat in his chair," she said.

The ride back was a party, but Kirk could feel his eyes glazing over. People kept patting his cheek, kissing him, calling him hero, calling him Anastos. After a while, he didn't even want to complain that he really wasn't Anastos. He didn't want the party to be over so soon. Whiskey was dribbling down his chin when all of a sudden he couldn't swallow anymore. There was a bubbling in his chest that reminded him of indigestion, which reminded him of eating too much apple pie, which reminded him of childhood, and he died. The woman in mink kept the napkin pressed to Kirk's chest. The man in the double-knit suit asked if dinner would still be served.

Bendel's - Something	.0 0
Simple	.0 0
	.0 0 T
Gordon's Gin	.0 0 T
Clamato Juice	
Whole Wheat bread	.0 0 T

From the kitchen bulletin board
of Grace Abbott

	.0 0
	.0 0 T
	.0 0 T
	.0 0 T
	.0 0 T
	.0 0 T
	.0 0 T

28

A half-hour CBS special, built around film clips of a military funeral in Miami, was devoted to plane hijacking. The special signaled a turnaround for the networks, a plea for individual acts of courage in skyjackings, muggings, robberies. The acts would presumably lead to collective action by aroused citizens. The White House encouraged it; governors and mayors of the large cities endorsed it. The program was repeated in spots for several days. Part of the coverage of the funeral involved a company of marines marching slow step and a horse with a riderless saddle.

"It is a half-holiday in Florida," the announcer was saying. "The shopping malls and the liquor stores and the racetracks all open at one. A bill has been introduced in Tallahassee in the state legislature, awarding a special distinguished service medal to Mr. Costas Anastos, a citizen of Costa Rica. This is only the second time in Florida's history that this has been done, the first medal having gone to Roger Bennett, who pioneered the citrus industry.

"In Washington, D.C., this morning, a similar bill has been introduced in Congress by Whelan Dudley Cooke of Hawaii, chairman of the House Banking Committee. Mr. Anastos, a banker himself, took chances all his life. Consumed with his business enterprises, he left no widow, no children, no known relatives. So now people who care about humanity have become his family. Airline officials from all over the world have gathered here this afternoon to pay their last respects to this heroic gentleman."

The drums were muffled, the flags at half-mast, and the marine sergeant with campaign ribbons from Iwo Jima, Korea and Vietnam led a small cocker spaniel on a leash in back of the caisson. The President agreed that it was great public relations and cabled the networks. "Well, sweet goddam," he said to his aides in the backwoods drawl he liked to affect. "That's what we like to see."

Teddy Bronson had been playing squash. He had played a lot of squash lately, dogging his club's locker room and steam rooms for members who might know of job opportunities. He had had two offers since leaving United Stores, one at twenty-five thousand, one at thirty-two, five, if he would move to St. Louis. His alimony and support payments to Lisa were scheduled to be over twenty-seven thousand, based upon his former salary and benefits.

"I'll check around for you, Bronson," several people told him, "but what you're asking is a little out of line. If I were you, I'd move to St. Louis." Depressed and bitter, he drank in his club's locker room with anyone who would hear his story. He drank gin and tonics and Knickerbocker beer, buying for anyone whose ear he could bend. And he watched television in the locker room, drinking alone and watching, when there was no one else around but the attendant and the squash pro. They all watched the news coverage of the funeral in Miami. "Making a pretty big deal out of it," the attendant said.

"Must have been a big shot," said the pro.

"Wait a minute," said Bronson. "I want to hear this, be quiet." He sat up straight in his chair when a flash of the body was shown being carried off the Pan Am plane. Then the face of Kirk Abbott filled the screen, taken from the passport photo of Costas Anastos. "I don't believe it," said Bronson. "I don't believe it." He began to laugh, slowly at first. Then, as the funeral procession moved into view and the muffled drum beat a chorus of tribute, Bronson's laughter became almost hysterical. He drank his beer, choking it down. The attendant and the pro looked at him carefully. They looked at each other.

"What don't you believe, Mr. Bronson?" they asked. "Tell us the joke."

Teddy Bronson wouldn't answer them. He kept chuckling and staring at the television set and drinking his Knickerbocker beer.

Grace Abbott was lying on her stomach while lotions were being worked into her back. Her hair had been washed, she had had her facial. A manicurist was seated beside her, working on her nails. Grace had insisted on a portable TV being in the room, because she could not stand people talking to her when she was supposed to be luxuriating. The fingers of the masseur, Von Cedarstrick, dug deeply into her naked lumbar region, making her say "ohhh" with the pressure. Von Cedarstrick worked only for the Tiger Salon, which had replaced Elizabeth Arden as the place wealthy women in New York went to make themselves feel beautiful. Von Cedarstrick was a young giant of a Finn who, from time to time, had made house calls in Connecticut for Grace.

"There's nothing like a massage in your own bed," she had told the masseur when he visited. "And to know nothing else will happen and it's all respectable." Nothing else ever did happen. Von Cedarstrick put his bottles back in his black bag, returning to New York with nothing but well-exercised fingers and a ten-dollar tip.

"Mr. Costas Anastos," the television voice was saying, "seems almost as elusive in death as is Mr. Howard Hughes in life. All that seems to be left behind is his suitcase, his passport, and his cocker spaniel, who was found as baggage on the plane in a special carrying case built in Connecticut."

The words came to Grace out of the haze. She raised her head slightly and lifted her eyes to the television screen. Seeing a flash of the passport picture, she pushed herself up onto her elbows. The sheet that covered her lower back and legs fell to the floor. She paid no attention, watching in horror while the filmed funeral procession paraded by her eyes. It surprised her that Sandy acted so restrained. Kirk's dog had always been so active. He had always been so frisky, she thought, watching him being led patiently by the marine sergeant in dress whites.

"You want another channel, Mrs. Abbott?" the manicurist said.

"Yes," she said. "Another channel would be perfect." She let herself collapse on the massage table and allowed the young, strong fingers of Von Cedarstrick to give her the only reality she cared about. She hoped it could go on for a long time. The Finnish masseur tapped her on her thigh. Grace knew it was the signal to roll over. She did so almost automatically.

"I don't think of myself as dull," said Rhinelander into his telephone. He looked out onto Lake Leman in Geneva, a comforting view. "I think of myself," he continued, "as a universal man. Leonardo da Vinci without the talent," he said. "Of course, there are certain things I admit I am good at." He paused. "A New Year's lunch? Absolutely. At Le Mazot? Fine. My young lady will ring you next week." Pause. "And the same to you, I'm sure." Rhinelander sat back in his chair and patted his stomach. He looked out on his city and thought about how lucky it was that people believed the Swiss were only good at making chocolate and cuckoo clocks. His assistant burst in upon his thoughts. "Monsieur Rhinelander, I can't believe it," he said, as excited as if it were a birthday or Whit Monday.

"Now slow down, Charles," Rhinelander said. "No one ever made a franc by rushing."

"Look at this," the young man almost shouted, slapping down the evening paper. The news service photo of Costas Anastos covered the bottom right side of the front page. Rhinelander scanned the story, then read it again slowly. "You know what that means?" The young man was jubilant. "One hundred seventy million Swiss francs. Fifty million dollars. There is no surviving family, the paper says. No wife, no children, no parents. No aunts, uncles, cousins. That money is *ours*. And the government can say nothing. No one can say anything."

"My, my," said Rhinelander, beaming. "My, my." He stared at the picture of Anastos. "Why don't you and I have an early luncheon and stroll perhaps along the Quai du Mont Blanc, down to the Crédit Suisse."

His assistant nodded, grinning like a child. He left Rhinelander's office with a song on his lips.

The fat lawyer looked out upon Geneva and felt very warm. He began counting upon his fingers the clients that it would be his pleasure to dismiss. He cut the tip off a cigar and sniffed its aroma, not being able to remember when he had ever smelled anything quite like it.

Gena Reynolds looked at her face in a small pocket mirror. She was pleased that no freckles had burst into life over her nose. I've outgrown freckles, she thought to herself, as the cab let her off in front of the sun-bleached Costa Rican government building. She wore a blue Donald Brooks suit over a white blouse and carried a black leather shoulder bag, hugging it closely to her side. Once in the building, she walked swiftly up two flights of marble stairs and didn't pause to announce herself to the receptionist at the Ministry of Finance. She burst into Antonio Figueroa's private office, hung with French Impressionist paintings and an enormous Dali. The Dali dominated the room. It was an oil of the Battle of Waterloo pouring out from between the spread legs of a woman. Two girls were with the minister.

"A nice way to keep the wheels of commerce oiled," said Gena. Both girls faced Gena, with wonder that anyone would speak that way to a man of power. Gena took a newspaper out of her shoulder bag and put it down in front of Figueroa.

He nodded.

"You heard?" she said.

The minister looked at her almost without interest. "Your visa has been revoked, my dear," he said. "Are you all packed? It was good of you to come and say good-bye. Good of you, but unnecessary."

Gena continued to stand in front of the desk. She smiled at the minister and waited.

"All right," he said finally, impatiently. "Go, go," he said to the two girls. "I'll have you called."

They glided out of the office together, like a sister act that had just flunked an audition. They shut the door quietly behind them. Figueroa waited for Gena to speak.

Still smiling, she said, "Technically, Antonio, I am the sole owner of the bank. I was thinking that, perhaps, on a small scale, you could raise the necessary deposits. And decrease the requirements for the opening cash reserve. I'm sure something could be arranged."

Figueroa laughed as if the proposition were absurd. "I find it difficult to believe," he said, "that you're saying this. I am being kind allowing you to leave freely. Do you appreciate that? Perhaps you came here to show your appreciation?" He leaned back in his chair.

Gena opened her bag again and slid a picture across the desk at him. She slid several more pictures across the desk, as if she were dealing him a hand of poker. "Duplicates of these," Gena said, "are in the possession of a good friend who has instructions to mail them to your discreet president. And to his daughter, your discreet wife. Also to select newspapers here. And in Rome, Paris, the United States." She laughed at him. Indeed, he seem fascinated at the pornographic snapshots of Gena and himself. "You can raise the bank deposits," she said. "You are a man of power."

Figueroa thumbed continuously through the pictures. He finally looked up at Gena. "I believe we can work out a satisfactory arrangement," he said.

"For the good of your country," Gena said.

"For the good of my country."

Gena left Figueroa staring at the photographs, the huge Dali leering down at him, the office dark in the midst of the Costa Rican day.

Gena walked in the sunlight the several blocks to the market district and sat down in a sidewalk café. The headwaiter, waving off his little men, came to her himself. "Senorita?" he smiled at her. She smiled back.

"Champagne."

"Excellent," he said. "A glass? A champagne cocktail?"

"A bottle," she said.

Waiting for it to arrive, she watched the crowds move by the café, warming themselves in the busy markets. She noticed a tall man with blond hair walking away into the crowds, the tips of his horn-rimmed glasses showing behind his ears. Gena jumped up with a start and followed him. He quickened his pace and she began to run, knowing the hair, knowing the back with its strong, straight shoulders. She elbowed her way through the crowd, desperate as she almost lost sight of him. People muttered at her and said rude words, but she ran on, catching up to him as he began to cross a street. She grabbed his sleeve, tears beginning to swell into her eyes. "*Perdóneme*," she said.

The stranger turned and she looked into a face she had

never seen before. The man was interested, questioning. But Gena shook her head and turned suddenly away. She shook her head again, but couldn't stop the tears.

As through a veil, she could see the headwaiter back at the café. Proudly, he was holding up her bottle of champagne.